REVIEWS:

Brilliant whodunit that v
end, with some romance
kind of book.

A really great read, kept me guessing right up to the
end, and I enjoyed the setting of the book too.

At 80% read I thought I'd worked it out. I hadn't. A
typical whodunit that is perfect for the holiday.

A very enjoyable read, with a fascinating heroine,
surprising plot and interesting settings. Great follow-
up to Snowflakes and Apple Blossom, which was
also very enjoyable.

I had been looking forward to reading this book for a
while and I wasn't disappointed. I was hooked from
the start, I loved all the twists and turns and Aprils
imagination running away with her on occasions. I
loved that I thought I knew who did it all the way
through, but I was wrong and wouldn't have guessed.
I would recommend it. After reading Snowflakes and
Apple Blossom also by Alexandra, I knew I was in
for a good read.

An April Stanislavski Murder Mystery

ONE TINY

MISTAKE

Alexandra Jordan

(Previously entitled High Heels in the Sand)

PLEASE NOTE:

This novel is an updated edition of *High Heels in the Sand* by the same author.

For Graham, Benji and Daniel. Just because …

Happy Birthday, Wendy!

Best wishes,

Alexandra Jordan

xx

Chapter 1

Millerstone, Derbyshire

GOOD Luck cards littered the dressing room wall. The acrid scent of hairspray hung in the air like the remnants of a bad dream. But I was so happy I almost danced through the door.

I was absolutely buzzing. We all were.

Still in costume, a navy pencil skirt and white blouse, the adrenaline soaring through my veins, I threw a smile to Laura, our wonderful and very talented wardrobe mistress, having in an earlier career made two wedding dresses for *Emmerdale*.

'Phew,' I murmured, relief echoing around the room.

She grinned, her needle and thread never stopping for breath.

'Well done, April. Great performance.'

'Thank you.'

As a general rule, summer evenings in the Hope Valley are beautiful. The skies set like orange marmalade, bright and glorious and proud.

This particular evening, however, had seen a torrential thunderstorm, warm rain bouncing off the pavements like pearls. It was the second Tuesday of June, the tabloids were full of the Middle East and Miley Cyrus, and the sky shielding the hills was jet black.

St George's Memorial Hall had been muggy, humid, for hours. An eclectic place used for jumble sales, Mums and Toddlers, and yoga, it was all set to be our theatre for the week.

We'd put out chairs and cushions for the punters, brought in milk, tea, coffee, sugar and shortbread. The stage was set, the lighting checked, the costumes pressed. Other than the millions of butterflies fluttering inside, we were ready to go. We, the Village Players, were ready to perform The Happiest Days of Your Life, a brilliant 1940's farce. I was to play Miss Gossage, a teacher at St Swithin's.

And tonight we were ecstatic, having utterly nailed the dress rehearsal. It was, however, the befitting result of three arduous months of learning lines, increasing pace, and gathering props, costumes and furniture.

We were ready for a drink at the Flying Toad.

Well, nearly.

You see, not only was it our dress rehearsal, it was also the very evening my handbag was stolen.

I was unbuttoning my blouse, starched by Laura to within an inch of its life. Gemma Jameson, Miss Harper in the play, had already changed and was sitting before the mirror. Her lovely face was a calm and welcoming reflection as she pulled hairgrips from her dark hair and it tumbled into a waterfall of curls.

'Went well, didn't it?' Laura continued, hanging up my blouse.

'I do hope Percy remembers his lines, though,' I said. 'Completely threw me.'

'No, you did well to recover. No-one could tell. I shouldn't worry.'

I grinned ruefully. 'I'd rather not have to recover. I know he's got a lot on, what with the shop and his wife and kids, but still.'

'It'll be alright on the night.'

The makeup mirror runs the whole length of one wall, flanked by a row of sixty watt light-bulbs that simmer with heat, dazzle if you look directly at them. Beneath the mirror sits a deep mahogany shelf, its edges scratched white from years of use. Tonight it was littered with an unruly selection of makeup, handbags, tissue boxes and scripts, pressed open and marked carefully with yellow highlighter.

I pulled on my blue tee-shirt, turning to collect my Levi's from the back of the chair. It was only then that I noticed a gap where my handbag should have been. In between my makeup bag and straighteners.

I tried not to panic. It couldn't have gone far. 'Gemma?' I said.

'Mm?' She was expertly filling in with red lipstick.

'Have you seen my bag? It was just here – on top.'

I patted the empty space, the wooden surface suddenly dark and sinister.

Lipstick poised, she shook her head. 'No. Sorry. What's it look like?'

'Kind of brown. Tan coloured.'

'Sorry – no.'

'Laura?' I said.

She looked up, frowning. 'Toni didn't move it, did she? She was clearing round a bit earlier.'

'I don't know. I'll look.'

Toni is the village hairdresser. My closest friend, she does hair and makeup for the Players – that's how we met. She's brilliant at taming my long, wavy hair. But she usually left once it was Curtain-up to go home and look after the kids.

I searched the entire room before reality hit and I panicked, my heart thudding violently. As I wriggled frantically into my socks and trainers, I scanned the room. Nothing. There was nothing. I scrambled to the door.

'Just checking the others.'

'I'll come,' called Gemma.

'Thanks - it's okay - you get ready. I need that drink.'

I rushed to the men's dressing room, a very small affair next to the toilets. But even as I did, I realised I was being quite ridiculous. There was no way my bag would be there. In fact, no-one from the Village Players would have taken it. They were all lovely people, even young Steve Yates, the loner who helped with the lighting. And no-one else would have had access to our dressing room. Although someone could always have moved it by mistake, I realised. So I knocked on the door.

Alfie Brighouse, our director, was an absolute angel.

'Now calm down, April - come on, darling. You just sit down and let me take over.'

And he did. He took charge completely, unlocking cupboards, clearing corners, and searching the hall from top to toe, even the space beneath the stage where we keep the scenery. All the while apologising profusely to everyone.

'Laura darling, just look behind the ironing board, would you - it could have ended up anywhere.

Sorry, Robert darling - just checking. So sorry about this, everyone, but you were all wonderful, and you all looked *absolutely* fabulous. But poor April ...'

As you may have guessed, Alfie is as gay as you could wish for. A talented member of Birmingham Rep for many years, he went on to teach drama at our local comprehensive. Now retired, a tall, slightly balding man with a paunch, he devotes himself to the Village Players. There is nothing he wouldn't do for any of us.

And we love him for it.

But Alfie didn't find my bag. Nor did anyone else. We realised someone must have sneaked in somehow, through the back door.

I was angry and upset, of course, but the bag was easily replaced. It was the loss of my beautiful sapphire ring and eighteen-carat-gold bangle, twenty-first birthday presents from my parents, and my lovely Raymond Weil watch, a present from my ex when we'd just married and were still in love, that upset me more than anything. Irreplaceable. I'd had to remove them for the dress rehearsal, of course. Miss Gossage would never have worn such adornments. I really should have left my jewellery at home when I was in a play, but I never thought, merely pushed it inside my bag as I changed into costume. We all did it. Stupid. Utterly stupid.

The loss of numbers on my phone and the few receipts in my purse that would have been claimable against tax were also a damned nuisance. But well - I reported the theft to the police, they took a few statements, I claimed under the insurance, and that, I thought, was that. These things happen.

Or so I thought.

But when Sean rang the following Monday, I discovered my theft was only one of many. Millerstone, a beautiful Peak District village; the inspiration behind Charlotte Bronte's *Jane Eyre*. But statistically, suddenly, the village with the highest burglary rate per capita in all of England.

*

Sean McGavin is an old friend from school. We were in the same class all the way through, both top in English every year. We had a brief romance in the sixth form, but it was all very innocent – you didn't sleep around at sixteen in those days. We did spend hours kissing beneath the sycamore trees in the park, turning each other on to the point of internal combustion, but it never went any further.

He became engaged about the same time as I did, and married the same year, both our weddings at St Mary's, the local Parish church, both with photos in the local paper. But there the similarity ended. He and his wife were very happy, becoming blessed with a little girl, Ruby. Whereas Jeremy and I divorced. I remember going to Ruby's christening on my own, deeply miserable, thin as a rake and skin like orange peel from not eating, envious of all the happy, smiling faces.

But that's by the by, in the past, a dusty cobweb that should never have gathered in the first place. I knew Sean had been working for the Sheffield Star, although I'd not heard from him in ages, and it was really good to hear from him now.

Although, I did wonder – we were now in our forties, so why the ever-so-sudden interest?

'To what do I owe this honour, kind sir?'

His voice was warm and deep; dark cocoa in a tall mug.

'I just wondered if you fancied meeting for coffee some time.'

I grinned. Years pass without a word, then he wants to meet for coffee.

'Well, that's really nice of you, Sean. But what about Heather?' I joked. 'Won't she mind you taking me for coffee? All alone, with an ex-girlfriend?'

His wife was beautiful. And their daughter, I remembered, very cute.

'We split up three years ago.'

'Oh ...'

Ouch. That was a shock, a punch in the stomach. They'd seemed like the perfect couple.

'Sorry,' I replied. 'I'm really sorry to hear that, Sean. I didn't know.'

He sounded suddenly hollow, empty. 'It's okay, don't worry about it. Anyway, this is purely professional. I'm in need of some help – information.'

I was bemused. 'From me? Why?'

'All will become clear. But not over the phone.'

That did it. I was in.

'Okay. Coffee would be lovely. When?'

'Whenever, really. How about we meet in the Library Café in Sheffield? That okay with you?'

Sheffield is Millerstone's nearest city. It was once a place of steel mills, described by George Orwell as *a hideous, frightful, ugly, stinking industrial hell hole – if at rare moments you stop smelling sulphur it is because you have begun smelling gas.* But now the industry has gone, replaced by beautiful people, uni students, and ladies who lunch. Okay, so that's the posh bit …

'Fine,' I replied. 'I just need to finish an assignment, but it shouldn't take long - a week at most. Can I get back to you?'

*

I'm self-employed, a writer of romantic novels, typical Mills and Boon stuff. Well, it earns a living and I don't do badly out of it. I'd had a deadline to meet, a trio of short stories for a woman's magazine, good for keeping the old *nom de plume* in the public eye, so had been pretty busy. Also, I'd had Ed staying for a long weekend, and been out a couple of times with Colin, so I needed to catch up. Yes, I know. Two guys. But not at the same time. Officially, I was seeing Ed. Colin was just a friend who took me out to dinner whenever Ed worked away.

Ed was Welsh, tall, dark and handsome, with a voice like Otis Redding. A buyer for M&S, he lived life on the edge, skied, surfed, climbed, and lived in the most delicious chocolate-box cottage (not just *any* chocolate-box cottage) at the centre of a small Staffordshire village. There were no pubs or post offices left to keep the place going, so the majority of households consisted of weekend trippers from the city. Still, it was nice enough.

Ed and I had met at a party in Kent – mutual friends celebrating their engagement, finally, after dating for ten years. I'd actually gone to the party with another guy; Hugh Jacobs, if I remember correctly. But I'd finished with him the following week. He wasn't really my type, anyway. No - Ed was older than him, more mature, more on my wavelength, so to speak.

And then there was Colin, the warmest, gentlest man you could ever wish to meet. Mousey hair, big green eyes and the most gorgeous long lashes; any woman would be envious. He was so laidback you could have poked him with a machete and he wouldn't have budged. There was just something about him that made women ooze affection. He worked as a freelance IT consultant, and this paid for both his apartments, one in Sheffield on the edge of the Peak District, and one in St Raphael on the Cote d'Azur.

They both worked away a lot - Ed to source products for M&S, Colin to work for any company that would employ him. Which, as you can imagine, made it easy for me. I didn't at that time feel the need to choose between them, so maintained the status quo, seeing them at different times. Ed was affectionate, confident, very sexy and fun to be with. And Colin - well, Colin was just Colin, the perfect gentleman. I met him on a night out with Toni. Her mother Florence - Flo to her friends - a jolly, buxom lady, had come over from Manchester to babysit. So we made the most of it, got all dressed up, and went out.

Toni, mum to Abigail and Jack, with bright red curly hair and a ready smile, is always fun to be with, even though she's on a constant diet, scared of ending up like her mother.

We met Colin in *La Romantica*, a small Italian restaurant not far from his apartment in Sheffield. He was on his own, waiting for his main course, a red candle furbishing the old, knobbly table, and we just seemed to get talking. He flirted with me more than Toni, and that upset me a bit, I must confess. After all, she was the single one. So I felt a little uneasy when, after she went to the loo, he asked for my number. Looking back, I could see that was actually very kind of him.

He rang later that week, offering to take me out. I did tell him I was seeing someone else, but he insisted, saying we could just be friends.

'Besides, he can't be that caring or he wouldn't let you out on your own, now would he?'

'He's working away. Actually.'

'Well then, he won't mind if I take you out sometimes. He can't expect you to stay home all alone.'

I could just picture his lovely green eyes at the end of the phone, smiling at me, melting me. 'He might.'

'A delicious meal and a bottle of red wouldn't hurt, would it? I promise to be well-behaved.'

And he was. Always. Amazing.

Can you believe that? Years of hanging around on my own, hopping from one boring man to another, life passing me by, then two absolutely drop-dead gorgeous guys come along at the same time. And no kids, either of them, just ex-wives no longer interested. So - no baggage. Which can be a real problem when you get to my age.

Anyway, I digress. As usual.

I rang Sean back the following week.

Parking my sky-blue Mini Convertible, my pride and joy, in the carpark, I checked my makeup in the rear-view mirror (heart-shaped face, kind mouth, blue eyes a little too creased for my liking), then raced to the entrance before the rain could spoil my hair. Only a slight drizzle, but a girl has to think about these things.

The Library Café is smart, intellectual, air-conditioned, with clean lines, modern in orange and black, with good food. I stood up as Sean entered, recognising him immediately, not having seen him since Ruby's christening ten years earlier. He was still very good-looking, kind of Irish, with deep blue eyes and thick, dark hair. In fact, I used him in the novel I was writing at the time. Changed his name, of course, and made a few other alterations, but it's definitely him.

We hugged. 'Sean, you look fabulous - lovely to see you.'

'You too, April. Thanks for coming.'

His voice was warm and soothing. I remembered it breaking in the fourth year, seemingly overnight, and how his hair became very thick and coarse at the same time, hanging in untidy spirals around his spotty face.

Pecking me on the cheek, he took a step back. 'But look at you. You're obviously doing well for yourself.'

I tried to blush coyly, which I admit doesn't come easy these days. I'm too blasé about the whole thing, my success and everything. I spread out my hands, emulating *The Fonz.*

'Hey …' I tugged the lapels of my Chanel jacket - dove grey and gorgeous. 'Just a little thing I threw on.'

I did feel good, having had my hair highlighted again after the play. I'd had to dye it brown. I can't stand wigs, and Miss Gossage would never have worn ash-blonde highlights.

'Very nice, too.'

I shook the compliment away. 'Come on, let's get comfy. Latté? Cappuccino?'

'It's okay - I'll get them.'

'No, no, it's fine. You get them next time.'

He grinned. 'Okay, you win. Cappuccino, please - thanks.'

The coffee was delicious, Italian and strong. Breathing in its rich scent, I allowed Sean the usual courtesy of catching up with the events in my life, and of talking about his own. And then I asked the question.

'Come on, Sean, I'm intrigued. It's great to see you again, but what is all this about?'

Mysteriously, he turned to check the - empty - tables around us before speaking.

'I'm investigating the burglaries, the thefts.'

An awful embarrassment crept over me, and I giggled.

'Sean, stop being such a drama queen. What is it, really?'

'Your village is rife with crime.'

He looked me straight in the eye, and I shivered.

'What?' Cossetted in my little study, surrounded by my stories, my characters, I'd not heard anything about anything. 'Exactly what do you mean?'

'You mean you don't know? Seriously?'

Still unconvinced, I shook my head. 'Seriously.'

'You've had your handbag stolen?'

How did he know that? 'Yes?' I replied.

'And the police didn't say anything?'

'No?'

'Well, I am surprised.'

He studied his coffee carefully, scraping off the chocolate sprinkles with his spoon and eating them.

'Well, I suppose we were busy,' I explained. 'It was the night of our dress rehearsal. The chap just took a few details and went. Come on Sean, what's going on?'

Placing his spoon back onto the saucer, he took a deep breath.

'They're really at the end of their tether with this one. Millerstone has achieved the highest number of burglaries, per capita, for an English village, over the past twelve months. So far, there have been thirty-two simple thefts - stuff left lying around and acquired - and fifteen actual break-ins. That's how I know about your bag.'

So much going on in such a small village. And I'd not heard one word.

'Wow.'

'My editor's asked me to investigate, and the police have been kind enough to give me names and addresses, including your details and a Mister Abercrombie Jones, burgled in May.' He grinned proudly. 'I'm Senior Crime Reporter now.'

I smiled, not at all surprised. 'Still with the Sheffield Star?'

He nodded.

'Well done, Sean. Congratulations.'

'Thanks.'

I shook my head in bewilderment. 'But I still can't believe it. Surely I'd have heard something about all this? Why haven't I?'

'April, you're obviously a very busy lady, all these books you churn out. And no, I'm not envious.' He smiled, sat back and folded his arms in delight.

I blushed for real this time. 'Okay. Point taken. So what happens now? Why do you need to talk to me?

I can't tell you much about what happened, I'm afraid. All I know is that someone stole my handbag.'

'It's not that. I just wondered if you could glean some inside information. You'll know people in the village, won't you? Even if it's just the postman or the woman at the petrol station. If you could just get talking - someone must know something. You could be an Inspector Morse ...'

I wasn't quite so sure about that. Inspector Morse? More like Inspector Clouseau. I nodded anyway.

'I suppose so. But let's face it, Sean, I've only just found out about it myself. If no-one's said anything to me before, they're not likely to do so now.'

'Well then, don't you think that a bit strange?'

I laughed. 'Not really. I'm a writer. I sometimes don't see anyone from one month to the next. I do a bit of amateur dramatics and have a few close friends around the village, but that's about it.'

'Then you'd better start digging. Please?'

2

MILLERSTONE is a stone-built village at the edge of the Peak District, slightly to the north of the River Derwent and ten miles west of Sheffield. Named after the ancient millstones strewn across the moorland above, it's said that our millstones used to turn the flour grey, so when white bread suddenly became fashionable in the mid-eighteenth century, we had to import French millstones to make white flour. The dozens of millstones already produced here couldn't be sold, so they were left, just as they were. They're still out there, and the sight of those huge grey millstones, set amongst the bracken and heather, is a sight to behold, a true symbol of the beautiful Peak District.

Abercrombie Jones and his wife Lorna lived just off the main road. Tall wooden gates provided access to the property, set within a stone wall that stretched quite a way along. Pushing one gate open, Sean and I found a modest country house that I'd guess was built around the early eighteenth century, its stone mullion windows peering down upon a square and lovingly-mowed lawn. It was a beautiful place, with rambling roses climbing the walls and the scent of honeysuckle in the air.

*

Originally from Caernarvon, the Jones's were gregarious types, with money, influence, horses and sheep roaming the land, and three daughters at uni, all with private educations under their belts. As a result, they positively welcomed our intrusion into their beautifully ordered lives.

Abercrombie opened the door, his smile white and sparkling, his flagged hallway rife with dog hair and muddy boots.

'Come on in, come on in,' he cried.

'Hello,' I volunteered, taking his outstretched hand. 'I'm April.'

'April - lovely to meet you. You're the author, aren't you?'

I smiled. 'Yes, I am.'

'How interesting. I must admit, we've not read any of your books, but it's always good to meet a local who's doing well.'

'Thank you,' I replied.

He turned to Sean. 'Sean McGavin, isn't it?'

Sean shook hands. 'Nice to meet you, Mr Jones. Thank you for taking the time to see us.'

'Call me Abercrombie, please. And it's not a problem, not at all. You are quite welcome. Come on through. Lorna's just in the kitchen. The dogs are out the back, so no need to worry on that account.'

Tall, with arms that seemed to go on for ever, Abercrombie reminded me of Bruce Forsyth, with his white moustache, and that way he had of waving his hands around. Well-spoken with no trace of an accent, he made me feel immediately at home.

The kitchen was huge, cluttered and worn, yet cosy, with the lingering scent of warm toast. Lorna greeted us with a smile, hastily removing her reading glasses. Petite, well-cared for, her silver hair arranged just so, her clothes expensive, casual and unfussy, she must have been in her early sixties.

'Hullo there - come on in,' she called. Her Welsh accent, soft and mellow, was like the sound of a waterfall blown by the wind. 'Lovely to meet you. Would you like some tea, or coffee?'

I felt her steely blue eyes appraising me.

'Coffee, please,' Sean and I murmured at the same time.

She waved at the huge table. 'Sit down, both of you. Make yourselves at home.'

Sitting beside Sean, I smiled. 'Thank you.'

She peered more closely at me. 'I've seen you around, haven't I? You're in the Village Players, aren't you?'

I grinned. 'Yes. For my sins.'

'Oh no, you were very good in the last one. What was it now - I can't remember?'

'The Happiest Days.'

'That's it. You played a very good part. We really enjoyed it.'

'Thank you. Me, too. But none of it would be possible without Alfie, our director. He is just so brilliant.'

Pulling cups from the drawer of a large blue cabinet, she placed them onto the table, allowing Abercrombie to fill the kettle.

'Of course. We have met Alfie a few times. We're patrons, you know. We come to see everything. Abercrombie did drama and politics at university, so he has a keen interest. But when his parents died – in tragic circumstances - he had to give it all up and look after the business.' They exchanged sad glances. 'Although Alfie does say he might not be doing the next production. Emilisa Meadows-Whitworth is coming back – have you heard?'

I groaned inwardly. 'Is she? No, I haven't.'

Emilisa and I hadn't got on that well in the last play she'd produced, a Restoration comedy, two years earlier. Tall, very slim and glamorous with long, dark wavy hair, everything always just so, she was the eldest daughter of an Italian doctor and his wife. Married to Neil Meadows-Whitworth, Professor of Biochemistry at Sheffield University and lecturer for the Open University, she was always too full of herself, wouldn't listen to anyone else's opinions. I was glad when she'd decided to leave, once her youngest had gone off to uni.

'Why has she decided to come back - do you know?' I asked.

Spooning coffee into a solid silver cafetière, Lorna lifted her eyebrows thoughtfully.

'I've no idea. But she is very talented. As you are.' She looked up at me. 'A writer. Interesting. Have you ever thought about writing a play for the Players?'

I had to admit, the thought had never occurred to me.

'I don't know whether I'd be any good as a playwright, to be honest.'

'Oh, I'm sure you would be. You have the best of both worlds – writing and acting. It would be a doddle.'

I smiled at the compliment. 'Well, I do enjoy reading plays, working through the characters and so on. And I suppose it wouldn't be that different to writing a novel. I'll think about it.'

Abercrombie, who was now emptying the dishwasher at the far end of the kitchen, turned, waving his big hands around.

'I'm sorry, my dear. Just ignore my wife. Put you on the spot a little, hasn't she? Are you here to write about the burglaries, then? Is that it?'

I shook my head. 'No. I - we just thought we'd do a bit of detective work, try and catch the idiot who stole my handbag. If we can.'

'You've had your handbag stolen?'

Sean took up the story. 'Actually, it was me who asked April to help out. I work for the Sheffield Star. My editor's asked me to dig a bit deeper into all these burglaries, thefts – the crime around here. Apparently, the police are at a loose end.'

'Oh, dear,' Lorna murmured. 'You do wonder why you pay your taxes, don't you?'

'It's someone who knows what they're doing, that's for sure,' I said. 'They're managing to fool everyone, by the sound of it.'

She folded up the newspaper she'd been reading and put it to one side, her tiny hands pressing hard. She was a paradox, small and delicate like a flower, but with an edge. A Venus flytrap of a woman.

'It's all very sad,' she said, pouring hot, fragrant coffee into white china cups. 'Millerstone used to be such a peaceful village. There was never any trouble.'

23

They sat down together, her husband patting her hand protectively. His was like a mountain beside hers.

'Now then, don't go upsetting yourself again, my dear. Things are different these days and we just have to get used to it. Unfortunately.' He looked across to Sean. 'Just what is it you're wanting to know? Because the sooner we catch these people, the better.'

Getting down to business, Sean pulled out his notepad and pen, checking quickly through the notes he'd already made.

'Right, then. I understand you were burgled on May nineteenth?'

Abercrombie nodded. 'That's right. We'd been out for the evening – to Sheffield, to the Cutler's Hall. Got back to find the French windows damaged, and the bloody safe gone. We called the police straightaway, but they couldn't find a thing. No fingerprints. Nothing. Not a stitch. Just a few footprints and some tyre-tracks in the mud.'

Lorna looked anxious, her tiny fingers twisting themselves around each other in a game of *Here's the church, here's the steeple ...*

'We've had an alarm fitted now, of course,' she revealed. 'But I still get worried. You don't know if they're out there watching, do you? I mean, we allow people to walk on our land all the time, but you don't know if they're still out there at night-time, do you?'

Abercrombie had obviously had this conversation before.

'I still think it was the workmen, Lorna, and we've never been burgled before, have we? Not in all these years.' He turned to Sean, busy scribbling. 'We had workmen all over the place last year. New bathrooms, new plumbing, new roofing on the stables. It could have been any one of them, or even someone they knew. And they knew exactly where they were going. Walked straight in - through the French doors, up to the safe, and lifted it. It must have taken at least three of them - it was such a big old thing. The police said there was a four-wheel drive outside, all ready. They knew what they were doing all right, had it all planned. The rotters.'

He glanced at his wife, and she relaxed visibly. My heart warmed to them. All the money in the world couldn't relieve them of their concerns, but I could see how close they were and knew they'd come through this together.

I looked around. 'So where was the safe kept?'

'In the study,' Lorna replied. 'It backs onto the herb garden. The gate there takes you straight out onto open land. That's where they found the tyre-tracks.'

'So, Sean, do *you* think the village is actually being targeted, as the police have said?' asked Abercrombie.

Suddenly fearful, my heart thumping, I turned to Sean. 'You didn't say anything about this?'

I thought of my little house, unsafe, insecure. The back door was the original, with none of the fancy locks insurance companies tell you to buy. I'd had the front door replaced because it faced the sun and needed it, but the back door - and my MacBook, my precious work, just sitting there.

He smiled apologetically. 'The police think you're being targeted, yes. They think it's a gang, or even gangs, from Manchester.'

'Oh ...' A feeling like cold blancmange slipped down my spine.

Lorna shuddered palpably. 'Dearie me, what a thing. A nice little village like this. Why can't they just stay where they are, get proper jobs like everyone else?'

Abercrombie shook his head. 'State of the economy, not enough jobs around. And now they're taking on all these foreign workers – well.'

'But only because they work hard and take less money,' said Sean. 'Let's face it, some people just can't be bothered putting in an honest day unless they get more than they do on the social. Anyway, these gangs usually start young, don't they? It's often nothing to do with lack of work. They just get involved in crime and drugs, and that's it – lives wasted.'

'To be fair,' I said, 'if their fathers had had decent jobs, their sons might have stood a better chance. It does all come down to the state of the economy in the end.'

'Quite right,' Abercrombie mumbled through his moustache.

Sean neatly changed the subject. 'So – could I just ask where the dogs were when you went out that night?'

Lorna replied. 'Well, we left them outside, chained to the kennels – where they are now. Rusty and Diesel had been sick all day, a tummy bug of some kind, poor things, and we didn't want all the mess everywhere. You can understand.' She looked at me keenly, asking for my support.

'I understand,' I nodded. 'I'd have done the very same thing.'

'Do you own a dog?' she asked.

'No. No, I don't. I'd love one, but I spend too much time away from home, or I'm busy at my desk all day, so it wouldn't be fair.'

'That's true. It's not how many people think, unfortunately, but yes, it is something to consider. Although they are such good company.'

'Could you show us where the safe was kept?' asked Sean, still scribbling.

She waved towards the kitchen door. 'We've had one put into the wall now, but I can show you where the old one was.'

'Please,' he replied.

The study was beautiful, with Georgian-style French windows looking out onto the herb garden and the old wall beyond. Deep shelves lined the walls, books of all shapes and sizes arranged in no particular order, vertically and horizontally. A huge desk created a centrepiece, a Colonial swivel-back chair in green leather completing the scene. There was an aura of old money about the place – cosy, secure.

'What a beautiful room,' I said.

I could just imagine working here in the summer, but a real summer, not the dull, dreary kind we'd been having. The windows would be flung open, the birds would be singing, and a soft warm breeze would be winging its way to my bare feet.

I could dream.

'Thank you - that's very kind of you,' Lorna was saying. She pointed to a corner on the outer wall, left of the desk and a fair distance from the French windows. 'It was over there, the safe.'

Crouching down, Sean studied the carpet. The fibres had been flattened into a large square, the colours still rich and vibrant.

'Just like that?' he asked, slightly bemused. 'Not nailed down or anything?'

'No,' replied Abercrombie. 'Never thought it needed it. It was a heavy old brute. We'd had it for years.' He turned to Lorna. 'What do you think – about thirty?'

She nodded. 'We should have got a more up-to-date one, but you don't think, do you?'

Her husband shook his head mournfully. 'You just go on, business as usual. Year in, year out.'

'What kind of business were you in?' asked Sean.

'Still am, my boy, still am.' He puffed out his chest proudly. 'I'm in property. We don't buy now, of course, just rent the stuff out. Manchester mainly, a couple of stores in London and Edinburgh, and some villas in Portugal.'

Sean and I avoided each other's eyes carefully. Rich? We didn't know the meaning of the word.

'Very nice, Mr Jones.' I smiled.

'Abercrombie. Please.' He smiled back pleasantly, his teeth too white for his age, but attractive for all that. 'But don't think for one minute that I just sit here and wait for the money to come rolling in. Oh, no. I work hard. And we do our bit, charities and all that. That's how we managed to be out that night, the night of the blasted burglary. An auction in aid of the Children's Hospital.'

Sean had his pen poised. 'Sorry, where did you say it was - the auction?'

'Sheffield. Cutlers' Hall.'

Sean checked his notes. 'Oh, yes. Sorry – I did write it down.'

'It was a lovely evening. Such beautiful people,' murmured Lorna. 'Completely spoilt by those dreadful people …'

'Okay, darling.' Abercrombie took her hand quietly. 'It took us a while to settle back into the house, you know. Such a shock. We didn't go out for weeks afterwards. Too scared at what we might find when we came home. But we're alright now, aren't we?' He kissed her hand with a flourish. 'We set the alarm now, and everything's fine.'

'What happens with the dogs at night-time?' asked Sean.

'Well, they're working dogs, really ...'

'Apart from Rusty,' insisted Lorna.

'They stay outside,' continued Abercrombie, 'unleashed, so they can roam.'

'That must set your mind at rest,' I said.

He nodded. 'Yes, it does. Let's hope the bastards never come back, though.'

I smiled wryly. 'Well, they got what they wanted here, but it obviously wasn't enough. So they had to go stealing handbags from Memorial Halls.'

'Was that where it happened?' asked Lorna. 'Not during a play, was it?'

I nodded. 'The dress rehearsal.'

'How awful. But won't there be some kind of insurance? The Memorial Hall must surely have something like that?'

'To be honest, I didn't even think about it, and I doubt whether it would cover personal things like that. Anyway, I claimed from my own insurance, so it was okay in the end.'

But Sean, ever the practical, brought us back to the matter in hand.

'So what was in the safe, Abercrombie – just cash?'

Walking to the window, Abercrombie stared into the garden.

'A right mess they left me with.' He turned back, his face red and angry. 'Over three thousand pounds in cash. But mainly it was investment jewellery - beautiful antique stuff. There were also my gold bullion coins and business documents. Sales ledgers, VAT invoices, receipts and so on. My accountant's still sorting it now. Fortunately, all our deeds are safe with the solicitors, or I don't know what we'd have done.'

'Abs darling, come on,' Lorna said, taking his arm affectionately. 'Let's get back to the kitchen. I'll make us a nice cup of tea.'

'It's okay, Lorna, I'm fine.' Sighing deeply, he shook his head. 'I try not to let these things get me down but - bugger it - why can't they just leave well alone?'

Sean was scribbling. 'I take it you were insured?'

'Of course. Stupid not to be.'

'Is it okay if we take a look outside?' I asked.

Lorna smiled. 'Of course. Take your time. No rush. Will you have time for another coffee, do you think?'

'That would be lovely - thank you,' I replied.

'Good. Come through when you're ready.'

She unlocked both French doors for us before returning to the kitchen with Abercrombie.

The air outside was warm, but damp. Sparkling birdsong filled the air. We made our way through the herb garden, the strong bittersweet scent of rosemary filling my nostrils as we brushed against its woody leaves. Unlocking the old gate, its paint peeling off in tiny green ribbons, Sean stepped into the open field beyond. There were a few cows in the distance, and low cloud covered the hills behind. Sean crouched down to survey the soil, which was thick and gooey after all the rain we'd had. Careful of my shoes, I stood in the gateway.

'They certainly knew what they were doing. Must have had it planned well in advance,' he pondered.

'Do you think it could have been the workmen?'

'I don't know. But I have to wonder why the dogs weren't left to roam when they went out for the evening.'

'Lorna said. They were sick.'

'Mmm.' He shook his head thoughtfully. 'It would take a criminal mind to organise all this. I suppose one of the men might have known someone, passed on the information.'

I sighed. 'Sean - if the police haven't been able to trace anyone, how are *we* supposed to?' I placed my hand against the frame of the gate, pulling back quickly as I stabbed my palm on the splintered wood. 'Aren't we just wasting our time and everyone else's?'

He gave me that boyish grin he has, and kicked at the turf. 'Maybe. Maybe. But I have a feeling here.'

'What?'

'I think we may be dealing with two factions. Maybe connected. Maybe not.'

'How do you mean?'

'Can you see this type, the type who can lift a safe, who can organise something as big as this – can you see him stealing your bag from a dress rehearsal? Or taking jewellery from an old lady, or all the other little things that have happened?'

I thought about it. I supposed, rightly or wrongly, stereotyping or not, the kind of person able to carry out this kind of burglary wouldn't be the type to get away with entering a village hall when a dress rehearsal was on. Particularly *our* dress rehearsal. He'd have stood out like a sore thumb.

'I suppose not,' I acknowledged. 'But, as you said, information could have been passed on. They might have got someone else to do their dirty work.'

'It is possible.'

'So – what do we do now?' I asked.

'We go back, drink our coffee, get the builders' details, then go look for some crooks.'

I smiled. 'You know what, Sean? This is fun.'

3

I peeked through the bedroom curtains. There'd been yet another rainstorm. The sky was grey, the gardens were heavy with mist, and my lovely petunias were hanging low, their heads sad and sorry. A miserable Monday morning. The first week of July.

The room felt cold, damp, and Ed had only just got back from buying African wall art in Pretoria. Tired out, he was still in bed, fast asleep. Pulling on my dressing gown, I scrambled downstairs to turn on the heating and make tea.

When I returned, Ed had woken up and was sitting reading, his glasses perched on the end of his nose. They made him look old, incongruous somehow, sitting there in our place of lovemaking.

I took a cup to his side of the bed. 'Here you go.'

He kissed me. 'Thanks, darling.'

We sat for a while, drinking tea; he reading while I worked at my laptop. My best ideas come first thing in the morning.

'Right - time to get up.' He threw back the duvet suddenly, upsetting my concentration.

I frowned. 'Ed!'

'Sorry.'

'It's okay,' I shrugged. 'I'll be down in a bit, anyway.'

He smiled. 'Don't worry. I'm quite capable of getting my own breakfast.

'I know.' My fingers were back at the keyboard, tip-tapping with the resonance of a runaway train.

'Tell you what - if I make you another cuppa, you can carry on working.'

I grinned. 'It's okay. I need to get up soon, anyway. Loads to do.'

'Okay. But my meeting's at one, so I need to get a move on.'

Pulling off his pyjamas, he walked naked to the shower. Following him with my eyes, my train of thought now completely destroyed, I saved my work and switched off.

Downstairs, I made more tea and ate some cereal. Ed joined me soon afterwards, freshly shaved and ready to go. The morning paper hadn't arrived, so we listened to the news on the radio. Which wasn't good. There'd already been news of some idiot extremist killing innocent children in their classrooms. Why do people end up like that? What on earth does the rest of the world do to them?

Grabbing the last piece of toast, Ed picked up his laptop and overnight bag, kissed me quickly, and left to catch the train to St Pancras.

*

It was now half past eight, so I slung on my sweatpants and trainers and headed out for my walk. I used to jog every morning, but a slight niggle in my left knee forced me to slow down. I'd been to see Phil, the hunky physio at the gym, who said it was *probably* to do with my age and it just needed strengthening with exercise. But the age thing was not something I wanted to think about. Actually.

Heading up the hill, away from the village, I walked quickly, my heart racing, my breath coming fast. The air was cool, the ground damp. Passing the last of the houses, I carried on up, into the countryside. A deep mist clouded the road ahead of me. Cows mooed softly in the fields on either side. Suddenly a car, a scruffy red Nissan, approached from behind, and I paused to give it room to pass. The driver waved and I realised it was George, the barman at the Flying Toad. A relaxed jovial type, happily married to wife Bertie, he adored both her and her home-made food in equal amounts. I waved back, laughing.

Walking always clears my head. This particular day, however, and despite my best endeavours, my thoughts kept returning to my mum. I visited her once a week, always staying for the day to keep her company. She lived half an hour's drive away, a lovely old 1890's house she and Dad bought after my sister Josie and I left home. But I'd begun to worry about her. There'd been no medical opinion or anything like that - we'd managed to keep it all hush-hush so far. But I thought she might be suffering some form of early dementia.

It was the theft of the tea service that had finally convinced me there was something dreadfully wrong.

*

The last Monday in March, it had been. I'd just come home from a week in St Ives. I go there to proofread, when I've finished a novel and need to read it through without interruption. There's a small cottage I rent on The Digey, an old fisherman's place with ragged stone steps leading up to a thickly painted, bright blue door. Beachcomber, it's called. The owner, Bethany Thomson, lives not far away in Penzance, so can let me in at a moment's notice. It's lovely, with Porthmeor Beach at the end of the cobbled street, Brambles tearoom for delicious coffee, and local shops just around the corner. There's even an Albert Wallis print on the sitting room wall (my favourite St Ives artist), and always fresh air and good food. So, relaxed, focused on my work, the problem of Mum's *thefts* had never entered my head.

Until I'd come home, unpacked my case, and filled the washing machine. I hadn't seen Mum in over a week, so texted to let her know I was popping round the following morning.

*

Happy to have finally finished my new novel, I'd driven fast, heater on, warm scarf around my neck, and Chris Evans on the radio. I remember Madonna's *Material Girl* was playing as I switched off the engine outside Mum's house.

I knew there was something wrong as soon as I opened the door. There was a tension about the place, no *Hi, April - I'm in the kitchen.*

No. I found her on the sofa in the sitting room, still in her nightie. Unwashed. Unfed. In tears. Lottie, her very cute cross-breed terrier, was still asleep, curled in her basket on the floor. Calming myself, I put my arm around my mum.

'What is it, Mum? What's wrong?'

She waved her hand as if brushing away a fly.

'Oh, you don't want to know about my problems.'

'Yes, I do. Of course I do.'

Lottie woke up then, running and jumping onto Mum's lap. I took hold of her hand. Her skin felt crisp, papery, like a dried rose petal.

'Come on, tell me what's wrong.'

But her lovely face just crumpled into tears.

'How anybody could do this to me, I'll never know. Taking all my things. Precious, they are. Memories.'

Then it clicked. 'Oh, Mum. Not that again.'

'You see?' Pulling her hand away, she wiped her eyes with the long sleeve of her winceyette nightie. 'Nobody believes me. You all think I'm old and senile.'

'Okay - what's gone missing?'

'It hasn't.'

'What?'

'When I got up this morning. First thing I noticed was the cellar door open. You know I never leave it open – I don't like Lottie going down there. So I went down, just to check. And I found it.'

Idiotically, my heart thumped as irrational thoughts of a dead body, its gnarled hands clutching at the stairs, raced through my mind.

'Found what?'

'The tea service.'

'What?'

'I found the tea service. You know - the one that went missing last week.'

'No, Mum. I don't know.' Now I *was* confused.

'I went down there the week before last to alter the clock - you know, to put the hour forward. And that's when I noticed it. Someone had taken it. That lovely tea service your Auntie Carol bought us when we got married.'

I was stunned. 'But, Mum - you hated that tea service. You're the one who put it down there after the teapot broke.'

'No reason for someone to steal it.'

'I don't understand.' I was ready for a coffee. Or maybe something stronger. 'Why didn't you say something at the time?'

'I did.' There was a slight - a very slight - hesitation. 'I'm sure I did. I rang Jo. I told Jo about it.'

'Did you? Well, she's not said anything to me.'

'Well, she wouldn't. You're always so busy, aren't you?'

'Mum, I've only been away a week. And I was working - you know that.' I stood up, determined to put this thing to rest. 'Come on, we're going down the cellar, and you're going to tell me exactly what's happened.'

More tears. I felt dreadful.

'Oh April, can't we have a nice cup of tea first?'

'No, Mum.' I took her arm, quaking slightly. It's not often I tell my mother what to do. 'We're going down there now, then I'll make you a nice cup of tea and some toast. And then we're going to take Lottie for a nice walk. You'd like that, Lottie, wouldn't you?'

Lottie jumped down, tail wagging, eyes smiling, mouth panting eagerly.

*

I remember the spout of the brown and orange flowery teapot breaking off years ago. Dad, bless him, had glued it back together, but it was never quite the same. So the entire tea service, not just the teapot, was relegated to the dark recesses of the cellar, to a shelf just behind the old sideboard, itself a symbol of times past, the dark varnish thick and syrupy as treacle. The cellar is warm and light, and houses the central heating boiler, the one and only reason Mum goes down there. Twice a year, when the clocks change. Spring forwards, fall backwards - that's how we remember it.

It wasn't as if we'd ever actually used the tea service. It merely served as a display piece on the kitchen dresser and, to my mind, could have continued to do so. It looked kind of right there, its warm vibrant colours set against the ageing pine. But Mum, always the perfectionist, and despite it having been a wedding present from Auntie Carol, decided it would never look right once the teapot was broken.

However, this wasn't the first incident of its kind.

It had started in the January, the day Mum discovered her jewellery box missing. She'd rung Josie, saying that the cleaner, Caroline from Help the Aged, must have stolen it, complete with jewellery. A few weeks later, she lost her front door key, complaining again to Josie, but to no-one else.

You see, both the jewellery box and the key went missing shortly after Caroline and Josie had visited. Now it's hard enough for Josie to get to see Mum as it is, what with work and everything. A self-employed landscape gardener, she'd been as busy as Gatwick Airport on an August bank holiday. Her husband, Joe (yes, I know - apparently that often happens with Libran couples - they can have similar names, a balancing of the scales or something - and just to add to the confusion we call Josie Jo, too) is the head teacher at their local primary school in Hartleton. Their home, a cottage nestling into the hillside right next door to the school, is compact but beautiful, with a garden to die for. Well, it would have, considering Josie's occupation. And how they fit into it with three children and an Old English sheepdog, I'll never know.

Rebecca, their middle child, and Daisy, their youngest, still attended the primary school next door. But Vicky, the eldest, had just started at the local comprehensive. It was a big move for her, unsettling for the whole family, what with having to drag her out of bed each morning to catch the bus, and making sure she'd not forgotten anything before leaving the house. So the last thing any of them needed was Mum on the phone shouting and bawling, accusing the cleaner of stealing her jewellery.

However, not a word of this reached my ears until Josie rang, just before I went to St Ives, prior to the theft of the brown and orange tea service. No - let me make it clear from the start - the *alleged* theft of the brown and orange tea service.

I must be honest, when I did learn about the cleaner I didn't know what to think. So - maybe she *had* stolen Mum's jewellery box. Then maybe she felt guilty, took it back and put it into the wardrobe, which is where Mum eventually found it. How were we to know, one way or the other? Age UK is supposed to be a charity, yet they charge ten pounds for an hour's cleaning, giving the poor cleaner seven pounds fifty. But when I suggested to Mum she change her cleaner, she seemed to have forgotten all about the theft.

'It gives me someone to talk to …'

*

I continued my walk through the mist, pausing briefly to stare at the cows. The thing was, you see, I just knew Mum would never make up something like that.

Let me tell you about my mum. A speech therapist by profession. Many years ago. Yet even now she has that air about her. Intellectual. Efficient. Controlled. I can still see her, walking along the hospital corridor towards me, her white coat flapping open to reveal a light, summery dress, even in the depths of winter, hospitals being what they are. With elegant high heels adding necessary inches to her chunky legs, and a warm, caring smile for everyone she passed, she was happy, relaxed. Without a care in the world.

Dad died at the age of fifty-five, a heart attack, and she'd never met anyone else, never needed anyone else. So when she wanted to look good, she wanted to look good just because she could. I remember vividly her shiny orange fingernails and matching toes. They would fascinate me as a child, like orange-flavoured candies, boiled to a sweet hardness. And bright orange lipstick.

But all that had stopped. It had been a gradual thing, this not caring about her looks, and when I finally noticed, and bought her a new lipstick - Clinique, her favourite - it merely disappeared, never to be seen again.

Unlike her jewellery, which of course *was* seen again. Josie called round weeks after its disappearance to find Mum sitting at the table in tears, a box of long, dangling earrings, chunky bangles and rings fit for a queen, opened up in front of her. She'd found it at the bottom of her wardrobe.

I rang Josie as soon as I got home from Mum's. But it was Joe who answered.

'Joe – is Jo there?' My voice was hoarse from crying.

'April? What on earth's happened?'

'It's Mum - I've just been to see her and - I don't know what to do.'

My whole world was falling apart, my rock, my island in the sun, the one person in the entire universe to whom I could run at any time, and who would always make things right. You think *I'm* the writer. *She's* the one who always knows what to say, and exactly when to say it. Always.

'Sorry, April, she's just popped out. Shall I get her to call you?'

'Please …'

'Is there anything I can do?'

'No. No. Thanks, it's alright. Just get her to call me.'

Josie rang back an hour later, by which time I'd stopped crying. A little.

'What's happened?' she asked, anxiously. 'Is Mum alright?'

I swallowed hard. 'She - I think she's losing it, Jo.'

'Do you mean all this forgetfulness?'

'It's - it's more than that, though.'

'Come on, take a deep breath and tell me what's happened. Slowly.'

'She told you about the tea service being stolen?'

'Yes ...'

'Well, she's found it.'

'Really? Well, that's good news. She was really upset - she rang Joe in tears.'

'No, that's just it - it *isn't* good news. I found it exactly where it had been before it was stolen. Well, if it had been stolen.'

'Sorry, April, you're not making sense.'

'When I got to the house this morning, she was upset, saying it had all been put back. I took her straight down to the cellar and honestly, Jo, I swear - it's never been moved. I lifted up the teapot, and the dust was there, exactly where it should have been. If it had been moved, you'd have been able to tell.'

'Oh.'

Her voice was a squeak. It's not often Jo's lost for words.

'I don't know,' I continued. 'What do you make of it? Is it some kind of game, do you think? To get our attention? Are we all too busy with our own lives, and she wants us to sit up and take notice?'

'Maybe. I don't know.'

'I mean, you don't think she's got some kind of dementia, do you? I know she's not that old, but I can't think what else it could be, I honestly don't.'

'Sorry, April. I'm not taking this seriously enough, am I?'

'It's okay – don't apologise. But we do need to sort this out. For Mum's sake, as well as ours.'

'So, right - let me get this straight. You think Mum's imagining that things are being taken from the house, but they're still there?'

'I think that's what's happening, yes.'

'And we're sure no-one *is* taking them?'

'Yes. I think so. Well, obviously - the jewellery box is still there, and the tea service.'

'She did lose her front door key a few weeks ago and that hasn't turned up yet, but that's an easy thing to lose. But what if – just what if someone did steal the key, took Mum's things, then put them back again?'

'Why on earth would anyone do that? There's no point.'

'Well – maybe it *is* the cleaner. She might be doing it on purpose, to confuse her, make her think she's going senile.'

'Why would she, though? That's silly.'

'I don't know. Yet. But I'll think of something. She's all right. She's not ill. Something's going on, I'm sure of it.'

I wasn't so sure. 'Okay, then. So how do we prove it?'

There was a pause.

'I know.'

'What?'

'We change the locks, then if someone *is* stealing stuff, they can't get in.'

My mind went into overdrive. 'And even if they're not, Mum will know the locks have been changed, so she can't accuse anyone of stealing anything, anyway. Brilliant.'

'Except for the cleaner.'

'Except for the cleaner.'

'We'll have to change the cleaner, then. Help the Aged or whatever it's called will understand, won't they?'

'Well, yes, but will Mum? She likes to chat to Caroline.'

'She'll get used to the new one.'

*

My morning walk was taking me along an old cart-track, up towards the farm. I waved to Molly, the farmer's wife, watering pots of orange-red geraniums in the garden, her lovely old sheepdog by her side. Walking more quickly, my breath coming in short, sharp gasps, I felt the blood pulsating through me, right to the ends of my fingertips.

I tried hard to imagine how Mum must have been feeling. It seemed almost as if part of her mind had switched off momentarily. While it was in that mode, she moved something - the jewellery box, for example. Then, after her mind had switched itself back on, she couldn't remember having moved it. All she knew was that it was missing. But then again, was she merely dreaming it? Was she dreaming that things had gone missing, only to be confused when they turned up? Maybe old age was making her forgetful, rather than throwing her into the depths of dementia. We all have our off days, don't we? I know I do, when someone's name momentarily escapes me, or I leave the keys in the ignition overnight. Usually when I'm tired or stressed. Like then, really. Stressed. Worried. I love my mum, you see. She's always been there for me. And the uncertainty of all this - well, I was finding it very hard.

It was at its worst in the middle of the night when I couldn't sleep, when the guilt of not being able to help her wrapped itself around me, like the hot arms of a sickly child.

4

BACK home, my face hot, my mind refreshed, I took a shower, dried my hair, dressed in joggers and tee-shirt, and made warm, fragrant coffee before settling down to work.

My office, my most favourite place in the world, looks out over the Hope Valley below – soft green fields splashed with trees, sheep gathered like bits of magnetic cotton wool, and the river, a stream of silver in the sunshine. Like a child's drawing.

The room itself, however, is wonderfully conducive to work, everything on tap. It has a complete wall of books - reference books, novels, poetry, all sorts. There's even a set of Winnie the Pooh stories - don't ask me why. It's all there to provide inspiration when I need it, I suppose.

Although I find the best way of finding the right word is to get up, go to the kitchen, and make toast and marmalade. No, really. I have this theory that the walk there and back does something to the brain. It works every time.

Anyway, my office is very palatial, no expense spared. An oak desk, my faithful MacBook, and deep wall to wall carpeting in a dark and mysterious purple. Then there's my chair - a swivel carved in warm oak with arms and cushions, my cosy sky-blue working cardigan slung across the back. No phone. No biscuit tin. No music. Just me and my computer. Divine. I can switch off, then switch on again with the precision of a light-bulb. Talking of light-bulbs, I also have candles. Not just in my study, but all over the house. I'm Aries; I just love them.

Today, however, I wasn't switched off for very long at all. The phone in the hall was ringing itself off the hook.

*

It was Toni. She'd been burgled. She'd only been to her mother's for two nights.

Standing there in the hallway, the receiver in my hand, I went ice-cold with shock.

This thing was becoming a nightmare, a horror film, a London Blitz. Toni was the last person who should be burgled. She didn't need the hassle, the upset, and least of all the expense.

'Are you okay?' I asked. Silly question, I realised.

'I don't know. No, not really ...'

'How did they get in?'

'The bedroom window - Jack's. It's a total mess, stuff everywhere. I've had to cancel all my appointments and everything.'

'You've rung the police?'

'They're on their way. We've only just got back from Mum's. It's as if they knew we were away.' Her voice trailed off in a whisper of fear.

'You want me to come over?'

'No. It's okay.'

She did. I knew she did.

'Give me ten minutes to finish what I'm doing. And put the kettle on.'

'I can't. They've told me not to touch anything.'

'I'll bring a flask, then.'

*

Toni owns a small, detached bungalow in its own grounds. Mike, her ex, a high-up manager at *Santander*, bought it for her as part of the divorce settlement, so there's no mortgage or rent, just the council tax and utility bills to pay. He'd also paid off the business loan on her salon, a small place she and Alistair Bridges, the dentist, shared, a small lift leading up to his surgery. Nevertheless, with two children to feed and clothe and a car to run, she struggles to keep up.

It's a pleasant property. The garden to the left of the house is narrow, barely there at all, fenced off from next door by a hedge. But the garden on the other side is lovely, a wide expanse with small, circular flagstones and a weeping willow sheltering the smooth lawn beneath.

Pushing open the garden gate, I walked up the short path to the front door, but ignored it, turning right, towards the willow tree. The kitchen door is on this side of the house, and it's here I usually found Toni. But as I pushed my way through the long, trailing branches of the willow, I nearly trod on someone's hand. A tall bony chap in police uniform was kneeling on all fours, inspecting the lawn carefully. Behind him, upright, stood an attractive forty-something woman. The guy looked up at me suspiciously.

Ignoring him, I offered my hand to the woman. 'April Stanislavski. I'm a friend of Toni's.'

In plain clothes, slim with short grey hair and pale blue eyes, she shook it, scrutinising me. 'Good morning. I'm Detective Inspector Forbes. And this is Sergeant Evans from Bakewell Police.'

I nodded to him. 'Pleased to meet you.'

Concentrating on the lawn, he merely grunted in reply.

I turned back to DI Forbes. 'So - have you found anything yet?'

She looked at me questioningly.

I smiled. 'It's okay. I'm also a friend of Sean McGuire, Senior Crime Reporter at the Sheffield Star. I understand you've asked him to help with your enquiries, and he's asked me to help out.'

She nodded. 'Oh, yes - April - he did mention you, asked if it would be okay. As long as everything's treated in the strictest of confidence.'

'Of course,' I replied.

'I do trust Sean. He is very professional.'

'I've known him a long time. We were at school together.'

She smiled. 'Come on, then. Over here ...'

Taking me past the rear of the house to the narrow patch of soil on the other side, she paused beside a huge rosemary bush. Overgrown and neglected, it practically filled the gap between the house and the boundary hedge. There was just enough room for one person to squeeze through.

'Footprints,' she revealed. 'Look - just beside the bush. Trainers, I think.' She looked at me pointedly. 'We need to keep this area clear.'

'I'll keep my distance,' I promised.

She then pointed towards the soffit, a flat piece of wood that lies beneath the eaves of the roof. A large coach lantern hangs from the wall beneath it, its leaded lights shaded yellow. But it was broken, two of the glass panes smashed, the door hanging loose.

It would have been a beautiful piece before its demise.

'Mrs Ryan's pretty cut up about this. Apparently, it was quite expensive.'

I nodded in agreement. 'It looks it.'

'The chap was obviously trying to get to the bulb. We'll be checking it for fingerprints.'

Sergeant Evans joined us, his walk ungainly and stilted. 'I've organised for Rob to come out, but it won't be until later. After his tea, he thinks.'

'Thanks, Will. Rob's the fingerprint expert,' she explained. 'I know it must be very difficult for Mrs Ryan, but we're doing everything we can. He's burgled so many places now, he's sure to make a mistake at some point.'

I wasn't so sure about that. I thought he'd been doing very well indeed. But I smiled and nodded.

'Let's hope so.'

Making my excuses, I returned to the kitchen door. As I knocked, however, it opened of its own accord. To reveal complete devastation. Drawers pulled out, cupboard doors hanging off hinges, piles of tins, broken bottles, smashed crockery, all heaped onto the floor like a pile of recycled rubbish. I tiptoed inside, calling out.

'Toni? Okay for me to come in?'

I found her in the dining room, in tears, on the phone to her mother. She motioned for me to stay where I was, so I stood at the entrance, my heart reaching out to her. But eventually her tears subsided and she said goodbye.

'I know, April,' she cried. 'I shouldn't have rung. She'll only worry. But I was so upset.'

'She'll be fine. But it looks to me like *you* need a stiff drink.'

'I need a tissue ...'

Pulling one from her bag, she blew her nose, wiping her face before the hall mirror, its golden frame catching the light from the window.

'Come on outside,' I said, pulling a flask from my bag and waving it. 'I have coffee ...'

'Thank you, that's great.' She reached carefully into a kitchen cupboard, trying not to touch anything. 'And what about this - I have brandy ...'

I pushed the brandy into my bag with the flask, and we went outside. Toni followed, her arms folded across her chest as if to comfort herself. We sat at the table in the back garden, surrounded by greenery, holly bushes, yew bushes, and tall conifer trees. It was turning into a lovely day, considering the rain we'd been having. I poured coffee and brandy into two plastic cups. The warming brandy smelt delicious, bringing out the caramel and vanilla tones of the coffee.

I pushed a cup along the smooth oak surface to Toni. 'Here you go, m'dear.'

'Thanks.'

But her hands were shaking. 'Are you okay?'

She nodded tearfully. 'I'm fine. Really. I've sent Abi and Jack round to Oliver's. His mum rang as soon as she heard the news. They're going down to the pool.'

The village has had the use of an outdoor swimming pool for over a century. Now heated, it requires constant funding, but the fund-raising, the jumble sales and the galas, I'm sure, help keep the community spirit of Millerstone alive.

'Oh, they'll have a great time,' I replied. 'Kids find things like this exciting. They'll be telling all their friends.' I realised suddenly it wasn't just Toni's hands that were shaking; she was shivering all over. 'You sure you're okay, Toni? You're shivering. You want to go back inside?'

She shook her head, her red curly hair glistening in the sunshine. 'I'm fine - just a bit shaken, that's all.'

DI Forbes and Sergeant Evans appeared suddenly.

'That's all for now, thanks, Mrs Ryan,' said DI Forbes. 'The fingerprint chap will be round later. We'll be in touch.'

Toni nodded. 'Thank you. Thanks for coming so quickly.'

'Here's my card. If you should find anything …'

'Thank you,' she nodded, taking it.

'Goodbye now.'

'Goodbye. Thank you.'

We watched them carefully negotiate the weeping willow before leaving the garden.

'Have they told you about the footprints?' I asked.

'Mm.' She stared at me, her face pale, her green eyes big and round. 'They wondered if it was one of the kids, but their feet aren't that big. Besides, I don't think they are trainers - they've got too much tread. They look more like proper running shoes - I know because Mike wears them. And they've found another one that matches it - on one of the garden chairs. Looks like the chap stood on it to get to the outside light. Cost an arm and a leg, that light did. Mum bought it for us, so we could light up that side of the house with the sensor. A lot of good it did.'

'I suppose that's the trouble with bungalows – everything's low down, easy to get to.'

'I know.' She sipped her coffee, breathing in the aroma deeply. 'This is just what I needed, April. Thank you.'

'The brandy definitely helps, mind.'

'Thanks, anyway - thanks for being here.' She gazed up at the house. 'I need to get an alarm, don't I? God knows how much that'll cost.'

'Oh, they're not that bad these days - not like they used to be. At one time only the rich and famous could afford one.'

'I could do without it, though. I've already got a massive credit card bill on its way from the holiday,' she sighed.

'You needed that holiday,' I insisted.

She and her mum had taken the kids to Devon for a week at half-term. They'd stayed in a hotel, no expense spared. But it was just what they all needed, and the kids had had a whale of a time.

'I suppose I could always ask Mike to lend me some.'

'No, don't do that. I can help if you like. Just until you get straight.'

But she shook her head vigorously. 'April - no. You should never mix business with pleasure. It's really kind of you, but no. Thank you.'

'Well, if you're sure. But the offer stands.'

My phone rang suddenly, and I pulled it from my bag.

'Hello?'

'April?' It was Sean.

'Hiya. How are you?'

'Fine, thanks. You?'

'Okay. So what can I do for you on this lovely sunny day?'

'I've got an appointment with Mr and Mrs Royston tomorrow. You remember they had a burglary three weeks ago? I thought you might like to come along.

And I've just been to see the chaps who worked on the Jones's place ...'

I interrupted. 'Sean - you're not going to believe this, but there's already been another burglary. My friend's house was broken into last night. I'm there now.'

'What? You are joking ...'

'Unfortunately, no.'

'Could I come over, do you think?'

'When?'

'Now?'

'Hang on a minute.' Covering the phone with my hand, I winked salaciously at Toni. 'How'd you like a gorgeous hunk to call round and inspect your damage?'

She grinned, her dimples making cute inroads into her cheeks. 'Any time. Who is it?'

I spoke into the phone. 'That's fine, Sean. But she's a single mum, so be nice to her.'

He laughed. 'You trying to marry me off, April Hutton?'

The use of my maiden name took me back years. I've been Turner and Stanislavski since then, Turner being my married name, Stanislavski my pen name, obviously after the Russian method actor. Weirdly, his real surname was Alexeyev, but he adopted Stanislavski as his secret stage name because acting was, in 1884, the domain of the lower classes.

61

But I grinned, attempting my *Miss Piggy* impersonation.

'Who? Moi?'

'I'll be round in half an hour.'

I checked my watch. 'Actually, could we make it around two? We need to have lunch and it will have to be at my place. In fact, why not meet us there - it's easier to park - and we can walk down together?' I gave him my address.

'Okay then, I'll see you at two. Bye for now.'

'Bye, Sean.'

'So. Who exactly is this gorgeous hunk?' asked Toni.

'An old friend from school. Sean McGavin. He works for the Sheffield Star. He's doing an article on the Millerstone burglaries, and I'm helping out.'

'Wow.'

I shook my head forlornly. 'We've not exactly found the culprits yet though, have we?'

*

Abi and Jack are lovely kids. Thoughtful, but extremely verbal. Which is how kids should be, I suppose. Abi at thirteen was turning into a real beauty with long dark hair and serious brown eyes, fingers forever locked around her phone. The typical teenager. But Jack, at ten, was still a kid with curly red hair and freckles, always making me laugh. Toni and I were in my kitchen, making egg mayo sandwiches at the table, when he came bounding in, a skateboard tucked beneath one arm.

'Jack – wipe your feet. Or take your shoes off. Or something!' exclaimed Toni, scraping thick creamy butter onto bread.

I turned from peeling the eggs. 'It doesn't matter - don't worry about it.'

He ignored us both anyway. 'Mum?'

'Yes?'

'Did you ask the policeman why there've been so many burglaries in Millerstone? Olly's mum says there's been loads.'

'No, I didn't. I should think they've got better things to do than stand chatting to me.'

I smiled. 'Well, I happen to know a newspaper reporter who's looking into all these burglaries, and he's coming to your house this afternoon. He might just have a theory, you never know.'

His face lit up. 'A reporter? A real one? Like on TV? Cool!'

Toni grinned. 'Now don't go getting all excited; he probably won't stay long. And anyway, you're going straight back to Oliver's after you've eaten. Right now, please take your shoes off, wash your hands, and come help set the table.'

We ate egg mayo sandwiches. There was tea in the pot, and I'd bought a lemon drizzle cake from the local deli at great expense. But well, I didn't have kids round for lunch that often.

'So when's the reporter coming round, Mum?' asked Jack, through a chunk of bread.

'Two o'clock. And I want you both out of the way.' She looked across at Abi, engrossed in her phone. 'Abi – put your phone away, please.'

Abi looked up, her eyes still and calm. 'I'm just trying to sort out the weekend, Mum. It's important.'

*

Sean arrived at two o'clock, as promised. Sending the kids back to Oliver's, the three of us set off to walk down the hill to the village. The place was buzzing with tourists, their shorts, tee-shirts and hats adding bright summery colour to the wonderful backdrop of ancient stone buildings. Mountain bikes and motor-bikes had been parked up outside cafés, slow-moving cars fought for space along the narrow road, and the scent of heavy roast dinners and fresh coffee filled our nostrils.

I shook my head thoughtfully. 'You know, any one of these visitors could take it into his head to come back at night. And there are so many strange faces around anyway that no-one would think to question them if they were hanging about. They could easily watch for folks going on holiday, or going out for the night. It doesn't take much doing, if you think about it.'

Toni pulled a face. 'I know. I was stupid. The least I could have done was leave a few lights on. But we were only away a couple of days – I didn't think.'

I could have bitten off my tongue. 'Sorry, Toni - I didn't mean it like it was your fault.'

But Sean was pragmatic. 'If they want to get in, they'll get in. Let's be honest – they'd soon work out if you've got lights going on and off.'

Reaching Toni's 1920's bungalow, situated on a short cobbled street behind the post office, I pushed open the gate.

'Anyway, don't go getting upset all over again,' I said. 'What's done is done.'

Toni unlocked the front door, while Sean and I followed, stepping gingerly onto the carpet, careful not to touch any unnecessary surfaces. But as he poked his head into the kitchen, he pulled back quickly.

'Whoops, maybe not. What a mess. How did they get in?'

'Through the small bedroom window,' I replied. 'Jack's room, bless him. The chap used the garden fork to prise it open.'

'Shall we stay outside then - have a look round?' he suggested.

We walked the perimeter of the house, ensuring we didn't do anything to confuse the fingerprint chap when he arrived. Not only had the burglar tried to force open Jack's UPVC window, he'd had a go at the kitchen and bathroom windows too. Careful not to disturb anything, I showed Sean the footprints beside the rosemary bush.

'The police think these belong to the burglar.'

He knelt down, studying the ground carefully. 'Mm. Interesting.'

I expected him to stand up again, but he didn't, he just carried on staring. Until I had to say something.

'Okay, Sherlock - what is it?'

He stood up then, rearranging his jacket carefully. 'Interesting. I'd say a size seven or eight, not huge. And not a heavy person. Could be a youth. And facing towards the rear of the house, which suggests he entered the garden from this side, the narrow side.' He nodded to Toni as she gathered round. 'I would say that's pretty unusual, wouldn't you?'

'How do you mean?' she asked.

'Well, I'd bet ninety-nine point nine per cent of people enter the garden from the other side, near the weeping willow. You've got flagstones there and it's wider, more accessible, the natural way to go.'

'Yes, you're right!' she exclaimed, her face turning pale. 'God, just the thought of someone sneaking round.'

Shrewdly, I changed the subject. 'What's happening with the insurance company – are they sending someone out?'

'Tomorrow. I've got to rearrange all my afternoon appointments. It's a total pig.'

'Do you want me to come over?'

'No - thanks - it's okay.' At the sound of a car approaching the house, she hurried off. 'This'll be the fingerprint man ...'

A small, skinny chap with a long neck, his great leather bag like an old-fashioned doctor's, he followed Toni to where Sean and I were chatting beside the rosemary bush.

We shook hands. 'Hi - Rob Jellis - pleased to meet you. Very sorry about the burglary, but we'll catch him - you see if we don't.' Briefly, he took photos of the footprints. 'Now then, could you show me the point of entry?'

We showed him the damage to Jack's bedroom window, then the mess in the kitchen. He kindly dusted for fingerprints here first, so we could clear up and make tea. An hour later, he found us still in there, sitting at the small red table.

'All done. Thank you very much.'

Toni looked up, anxiously. 'Did you find anything?'

'A footprint on the chair, a few in the soil. No fingerprints, though. Must have been wearing gloves. Do you know if anything's missing?'

She shook her head sadly. 'I've not looked. The police told me not to touch anything.'

'Well, when you do, let us know if you find anything unusual, anything that shouldn't be there. You'd be surprised how often they drop something, leave something behind.'

'Oh.' She turned pale.

'It's okay, love - they won't come back, if that's what you're thinking. More than their life's worth.' He picked up his bag. 'Right, I'll be off. You find anything, you let me know.' He handed her his card.

'More than their life's worth?' she muttered. 'I'll be standing with a bloody rolling pin ...'

I smiled. 'Come on, Mr Jellis – I'll show you out.'

'Thank you, that's very kind.'

It was only when I returned that I noticed the rapport, the hint of a sparkle, between Sean and Toni. Her face, as pale as a sheet of paper all day, was suddenly glowing, pink and radiant. I was really pleased for her.

'So - you think they knew you were away?' asked Sean, scribbling away as if nothing had occurred.

She nodded. 'Yes.'

'Had you booked through a travel agent or anything?'

'Oh, no – we were only visiting Mum in Manchester. A couple of days, that's all.'

'Did anyone know about it? Paper shop, milkman, neighbour?'

She shook her head. 'No. Nobody. Mr Foster next door usually has the key when we're away, but I didn't give it to him this time – it was only for two days.'

'Okay.' He scribbled away.

'I really think they were watching us,' she said, her voice suddenly timid, tired.

I studied her carefully. It wasn't like her to be so fearful. This had really got to her. But Sean caught hold of my thoughts.

'I doubt it. I think it was a one-off, some kid trying his luck and succeeding. We need to find out what was stolen, what they were after - the motive.'

I filled the kettle. Again. Concerned about Toni, I tried to lighten the situation.

'Motive? Money - what else? Probably junkies wanting a quick fix. But they won't be back. Once you've put in a burglar alarm, metal bars across the windows, installed CCTV and an electronic eye across the doorway, they won't be interested. Oh - and the life-sized cut-out of your mum in her bra and pants.'

This vision was just too much for Toni, and she doubled up with laughter.

'April,' she giggled, 'don't.'

But her laughter was infectious, and before long we were holding our aching ribs like silly schoolgirls.

Sean shook his head in mock despair. 'Come on now, ladies, we have some serious tidying-up to do. Is there a toolbox anywhere?'

The very thought of it was enough to calm us down.

*

Three hours later, the house clean and tidy again, Sean had gone back to work, the children were sitting in front of the TV, and Toni and I were in the kitchen, making a list of the missing items. A grey jewellery box sat on the table before us.

'At least they left this,' she said, picking a ring from the top tray. 'It was Mum's – the one Dad gave her on their wedding day. She's passed it to me now, and no doubt I shall pass it onto Abi when I'm old and grey. It's diamond. Beautiful.' She placed it onto her finger, but its sparkle was disappointing and sad. 'And my pearl earrings are still here.' She showed me a pair of beautiful pearl studs I'd never seen her wear. 'But all the bracelets and chains Mike bought me - all gone.'

'The insurance will replace them, don't worry.'

'It's not the same, though, is it? Having to go into a shop and buy stuff on my own. It's not exactly someone buying it as a wonderful surprise, or because they love you, is it?'

I touched her arm in sympathy. 'I know.'

'The weird thing is - they didn't take this.' Lifting the tray, she pulled out a slim, white gold, diamond-encrusted bracelet. 'It looks nice, but it wasn't that expensive really, just a little trinket Mum bought me off the shopping channel. But you'd think they'd have taken it, wouldn't you?'

'They might have thought it was silver, or fake, or something. Which suggests they can't have been very bright ...'

5

I awoke the following day to a splitting headache.
Fresh air was what I needed. Right then, right there. I
pulled on a tee-shirt, hoodie, sweatpants and
trainers.

We were only into the second week of July, but
dry, crunchy leaves had littered the roads overnight.
A chilling breeze skittered them around me as I
walked, head down. But the wind made my eyes and
nose water, exactly what I needed to clear my
sinuses. Wiping them with a tissue, I waved to
George driving by in his Nissan.

Passing the last of the houses, I walked quickly up
the hill towards the fields. An overnight mist still
clung to the air, thick, seemingly impenetrable, and I
wondered how long it would be before I'd have to
wear my hi-viz jacket again. *Probably two weeks*, I
thought, grinning to myself. At Molly's, I paused to

wave, but she wasn't there, so I returned to the main road, forcing my legs to the very top of the hill. I tend to linger here a few minutes; the view of the village with its stone houses and winding river is spectacular on a pleasant day. But today I couldn't see a thing, so turned back, allowing my feet to jog a little down the hill, soon reaching the plateau, halfway to my house. Here, I paused to catch my breath, not something I usually had to do, and I realised how tired I was, how much in need of the holiday Ed had promised me. Although at that moment the very thought of having to pack a case was enough to make me want to throw myself onto a beach, comatose.

Walking more slowly, I approached the curve of the road, at the junction with Birley Lane. There's a bench opposite that overlooks a field, although it was hard to define through the haze. But I *could* see the man, a tall man, the dark silhouette of a man, standing beside the bench. I felt him watch as I approached, could practically hear him breathing. My heart thudding with sudden, inexplicable fear, my head screaming in pain, I forced myself to run past him, down the hill, my eyes focused on the ground ahead. Until I was way past the junction. Once I felt safe, once I could see more clearly, I slowed to a crawl, listening and looking. But there was nothing. No-one. Not a sound. Not a whisper.

The mist had wrapped everything in cotton wool. Completely spooked now, my breath coming fast, I ran home for all I was worth.

Locking the front door with shaking hands, I ran up to the bathroom, threw off my clothes, and stood beneath the hot shower, rinsing off the awful fear nestling inside my bones.

But my headache had gone.

*

Dressed in comfy jeans and a pale blue linen shirt, I felt alive and human again. But the phone was alive too. First there was Sandy, my agent, arranging a get-together at her office on London's Albert Embankment.

Sandy is amazing. She worked for a couple of daily tabloids in her youth – well, in her twenties and thirties. But now, married and much more affluent, she runs a small agency for a very select list of clients, myself being one of them. I happened to get lucky, I guess. She was only just setting up in business, eager for new authors, when I sent her my very first synopsis. She's a sweet lady if you're on the right side of her, but if you cross her, then beware. I can tell you - I've seen it.

I was there a couple of years ago, discussing the title of my latest novel (it was already being used by another author) when this chap just barged into her office, and without an appointment. Rachel, Sandy's secretary, asked him to leave very politely, but he pushed her to one side as if she were a bag of feathers.

'Fuck off!' he shouted. 'Just fuck off, or I'll bleeding well smash your head in!'

Rachel had to back away, bless her, while he ranted and raved at Sandy because she hadn't replied to his emails, hadn't answered his phone calls, and wouldn't see him in person. In short, he was a total bastard. I sat there, on the wrong side of her desk, totally amazed by this performance. Thankfully, he just ignored my presence.

Sandy, however, was as calm as a lake at midnight.

Turning to me, she murmured, 'Excuse me one minute, April.' She then proceeded to walk round the desk in her very high heels, raise herself up like a tiger ready to pounce, and whispered, 'I *will* fetch the police.'

The mere act of whispering stopped him in his tracks.

'What?' he retorted, puzzled.

Gesturing towards the door, she repeated herself, loudly. 'I said. If you don't get the hell out of here, I will call the police. Rachel! Nine nine nine!'

He scattered like a scorched rat.

Sitting down, Sandy merely smoothed back her hair as if looking into the mirror, and continued our conversation.

'Now then, where were we?'

As I said, an amazing woman.

So I agreed to meet up with her the second week of August, upon my return from holidaying with Ed. I needed to do some shopping anyway, so why not? I was already planning my itinerary:

1. Book into a small hotel.
2. Meet Sandy.
3. Shop.
4. Have my hair done.
5. Shop.
6. Visit the Victoria and Albert's latest.
7. Shop.

It's a hard life.

So, having arranged everything with Sandy, I was just making myself coffee before returning to work when my phone rang again. This time it was Toni.

'I need to ask a favour, and I know it's a biggie, but would you be able to babysit for me tonight? Please? It's just ...'

Her hesitation said it all. 'You've got a date.'

'Yes.'

'Wow! Who?'

There was silence, hesitation. But I knew.

'Sean?' I asked.

'How did you know?'

'Easy-peasy.'

'April ...'

'No, I'm pleased for you. He's a good-looking guy.'

'Thank you.' Her voice was a smile wrapped in rose petals.

But I was puzzled. 'Why me, anyway? I mean, your mum usually sits, doesn't she?'

'She can't get over at such short notice. It's just, he's been given free tickets for the Lyceum – Harold Pinter. And he's got no-one to take.'

I thought quickly. 'Okay. I don't want to be too late back, though.'

'Thanks, April, you're a love.'

'Don't worry - I'll bring some work round. What time do you want me?'

'Half-six? I'll make sure the kids are in their rooms before I go.'

'That's fine. See you later, then.'

'By the way, the police rang. Apparently, they've got this special agreement with the council. If you're classed as vulnerable and you've been burgled, they'll fit you a free alarm system.'

'You're not vulnerable, are you?'

'Yes, I am - because I live on my own with two young children. So I'm getting a free alarm. Worth five hundred quid.'

'Wow. That's amazing.'

'I know. It'll save me a fortune. And I'll feel so much better about leaving the house.'

I was just returning to my office when the doorbell rang. Slightly annoyed at yet another interruption, I turned back, opening the door to blazing sunshine, the chill wind having disappeared with the mist.

'Hi.'

It was the postman, whose name I've never discovered, but who tells everyone he has a black cat named Jess in his van. Turns out it's a stuffed cat, a toy. No. Really.

'Morning,' he replied, holding out a parcel. 'Just sign here.'

I signed. 'Thank you.'

He pointed to the sky with his nose, shiny brown with enlarged pores. 'Nice morning now.'

I followed his gaze. 'A good thing, too, I think.'

'Going to rain this aft, though. That'll clear off any mist that's lingering.'

I pulled a face. 'You're a bringer of good news, aren't you? I don't know which I hate most – the rain or the mist.'

'Well, won't matter to me. Me and the missus - we're off to Spain on Saturday.'

I sighed, visions of myself and Ed lazing on a warm, sandy beach in France filling my head.

'Sounds lovely. Have a good time, won't you?'

Closing the door, I took my parcel into the kitchen. I'd ordered a new bikini and swimsuit online and couldn't wait to see them in the flesh. I was pulling open the wrapping when the phone rang yet again. This time it was Sean, ringing to discuss Toni's burglary and how I thought she was handling it.

'She seems fine, Sean. Looks like you've taken her mind off it quite nicely.'

'Oh – we were given some complimentary tickets from the Lyceum. I just didn't fancy going with Simon from work again.'

'Well, it's very kind of you. But in the midst of your chatting her up, did she manage to tell you exactly what she'd had stolen?'

'No.'

'Bracelets, necklaces, a few rings.'

'Jewellery. Again.'

'But only the yellow gold. They left the white gold and the silver. Sean, it's as if they couldn't distinguish between the two.'

'I wonder why?'

'Stuff with precious stones in, too – they just left them. They want easy money, stuff they can push inside an envelope and post to one of these Cash for Gold places. No trail.'

'It's all easy to carry away, too.'

I paused, my mind ticking away. Sean's too, I discovered.

'Sean?'

'Mm?'

'Are you thinking what I'm thinking?'

'Somebody local.'

'Someone who wouldn't be noticed if they were seen walking along the street, jewellery clinking away in their pockets.'

'So I was right about the Jones's. I don't think it was the same person. And I've just spent ages arranging a meeting with their damned builder.'

A sudden realisation hit me. 'It's just one person, no helpers, isn't it?'

'What makes you think that?'

'Dunno. A gut feeling.'

'You could be right.'

'I don't know - I'll work on it.'

'Okay. So what are we doing about the Roystons?'

'Can I let you know? I'm going away on Saturday for a couple of weeks and …'

'Oh. Anywhere nice?'

'France. With Ed.'

'Very nice. Tell you what, I'll go and see them myself, let you know what's happening when you get back.'

*

Just one hour later, my work on hold, I'd packed. *Strike while the iron's hot* is a command that often comes in useful, I find. And I knew that if I'd packed at any other time, when I wasn't quite in the mood, it would have taken hours. And I mean *hours*. My new bikini, a scarlet two-piece with tiny spots and frill details, was gorgeous, sexy yet demure at the same time. Ed wouldn't be able to resist. The swimsuit, on the other hand, was kind of nautical-looking - navy blue and white stripe with a halter-neck fastening. I liked it - it was ideal for long swims or for when the sea was a bit on the chilly side. All of a sudden I was getting butterflies, as excited as a child with a fluffy new kitten. Pulling my passport out of the bedside drawer with a flourish, I placed it inside my overnight bag.

I made up for my lapse in concentration, though, because the afternoon was spent writing the plot for my new novel. Toni's burglary had inspired me. My next romance was to feature a legal secretary, studying to become a chartered legal exec. She falls madly in love with the policeman investigating the many burglaries in her area, but when she's hit on the head by the burglar, she runs to her neighbour, a student doctor, for assistance. The student doctor falls for her. He proves that her policeman lover, using information gleaned whilst working for a company selling security systems, is in fact the burglar. Our heroine, distraught, turns to the student doctor for consolation. Studying together in the comfort of his attic bedroom, they fall in love, and agree to marry upon qualifying. The End.

*

I walked down to Toni's at six o'clock, laptop in bag. Tall conifers sheltered my way as I walked down Jaggers Lane, and the rain foretold by the postman had been and gone. That, and the warm sunshine, made the ground smell rich and earthy, like ginseng tea. I breathed in deeply before turning onto the main road, past the old stone house on the corner. The couple who lived there were keen gardeners and there was always some kind of display to brighten up the village. Today the house was laden with hanging baskets, heavy with pink and white petunias, and the earthy scent was swept away, replaced by another, deep and heavily perfumed. I savoured every last drop of it.

And so it was with a light heart and a silly smile that I entered Toni's kitchen, now all neat and tidy and clean.

'Hi, Toni.'

Busy placing dirty dishes inside the dishwasher, she looked up. 'Hiya. We've just had pizza and salad - something quick.'

'Sounds delicious.'

She stood up, her slim red dress showing off her fabulous figure. 'Not exactly healthy, but well …'

'You look nice.'

'Nervous.'

'Oh, Sean's lovely. You'll have a fabulous time.'

She grinned shyly. 'I know. It's just - I've not been out with anyone in ages.'

'Toni, he's a lovely man. I've known him for years, remember.'

Her eyes glistened with hope. 'Thanks, April.'

I checked my watch. 'He's a bit late, though.'

'Is it that time already?' She checked herself in the mirror. 'The kids are in Abi's room. Jack needs to be in bed for half seven, please. School tomorrow.'

'Fine.'

'We've fastened tape around his window. I mean, it's locked and everything, it's just the plastic that's damaged. But he'd never have slept in there if we hadn't done something, bless him.'

'So what did the insurance chap say?' I asked, sitting at the table.

'They've organised for someone to fix the damage to the windows, and I've got to send in photos of my jewellery. It's a bloody pain, actually, having to go through everything. I don't have the time. I can't even remember some of the stuff I've been given – you know, cheap bits that didn't cost a lot, but all add up.'

'That burglar has a lot to answer for.'

'Bloody idiot.'

I grinned. At least she was angry now, and not so upset.

'Aren't they all?'

The doorbell rang.

'That's Sean,' I said. 'Have a good time, girl.'

*

My evening was highly productive, once Jack had stopped pestering me for drinks and snacks and had finally gone off to sleep. Abi was very good and just looked after herself. But I'd promised Sandy a two-page synopsis, which isn't as easy as it sounds, even after all these years. Deciding what to leave out of the plot is pretty hard, and each book feels like my very first baby until it's been adopted by Sandy. Then it's out of my hands.

But tonight I was doing well. Sitting in Toni's warm lounge, curtains closed, candles burning brightly on the stone mantelpiece (I knew she wouldn't mind), I analysed and dissected my plot with the tenacity of a steamroller. By eleven o'clock, however, I'd finished and was ready for bed. Anxious to get home, I peeped through the curtains. No car, no sign of Sean. Just a man at the rear of the post office. Dressed in dark clothing, he was leaning against the wall, smoking. But as he turned towards me, I let the curtain drop, a sudden irrational trembling seizing me, a dark uncertainty of fear. Turning back into the room, I then reprimanded myself, mentally slapping my face. I was a coward, a coward in need of a strong man, a drink, a bar of Green and Black's, anything to dispel the cloud of dread threatening me. What on earth was happening to me?

Determined to shake it off, I gritted my teeth, turned off the lamp I'd been working by, and returned to the window, determined to see his face. But he'd gone.

I turned back, definitely needing a drink. But it would be a mug of hot, sweet tea. As I walked into the kitchen, however, I realised with a sudden understanding that he'd reminded me of the chap I'd seen that morning, the one beside the bench opposite Birley Lane. Was someone following me? Was it the burglar, having found out I was looking into things? Or was I finally becoming paranoid?

It was eleven thirty when Sean's Audi pulled up. I rushed to the door, unlocking it quickly.

Toni looked radiant.

'Thanks, April,' she said. 'How's everything been? Kids okay?'

I nodded. 'Fine. Abi was brilliant. Jack took a little persuading, but once he was in bed, he just zonked out.'

Sean followed us into the kitchen, throwing his jacket onto the back of a chair.

'Aren't they all like that?' he said. 'Ruby was just the same, insisting she wasn't tired, didn't want to go to bed, and then when she climbed in – like a tiger cub.'

It was good to see Toni smiling so happily. 'We're having a glass of red, April. Fancy some?'

Unwilling to dampen her spirits, I accepted a glass. If I'm honest, though, my true reason for accepting was that I didn't feel quite ready to walk home in the dark. I find a little Dutch courage always helps.

'How was the play?' I asked.

'Brilliant. Quite emotional. Very well done.'

Opening the Shiraz, she poured me a glass.

'Thank you,' I murmured. 'Well, here's to more trips to the theatre, you two. I'll babysit whenever you like – well, if I'm available.'

Toni raised her glass. 'It was really good of you, last minute and everything, but I'm sure Mum'll do it in future. And I wouldn't want to impose.'

Unwilling to spoil their evening, I didn't mention the chap standing outside. Anyway, it had probably been my overactive imagination making something out of nothing. So, at midnight, having had two glasses of delicious *Calvet Fitou*, I was ready to make my way home. By which time I'd persuaded myself I was in danger of becoming middle-aged and paranoid, and that the chap outside was only someone from the village waiting for his girl. Sean did offer to run me home, but I convinced both of us that I'd be fine, that it wasn't far, and that I needed the walk. So, with a cheery wave to the cosy couple, I set off.

*

Halfway up Jaggers Lane, however, I was really regretting my decision. The beautiful hanging baskets on the corner house looked dark and threatening. Two of the street lamps on Jaggers Lane weren't working, so the light from the main road threw long shadows ahead of me. The tall conifers that had sheltered me on my walk down began to sway in the wind, and there was a shuffling sound in the hedge close by. Terrified, my blood pounding through my ears, I stopped and turned. To hear a voice, a loud whisper.

'Hi there.'

My heart jumping into my mouth, I ran as fast as I could. Back to the light. Back to Toni's.

Sean's car had gone, but the house lights were still glowing. Running straight through the branches of the weeping willow, I knocked loudly on the door, but there was no reply. Pushing down the handle, I opened it. Toni was there, sitting there at the table.

She looked up, guiltily. The long sparkling necklace dangling from her hand froze in mid-air.

'Oh. April.'

'Sorry, Toni. Sorry to burst in. I did knock.'

Pushing the necklace inside the jewellery box, she jumped up. 'No, no, it's fine. I thought you'd gone home, that's all. Come in.'

'Sorry. I couldn't – I couldn't go home. There was a man ...'

I recounted my tale of the man opposite Birley Lane, the one outside the post office, and of the noise I'd just heard on Jaggers Lane. By which time she'd put the kettle on, and I was drinking hot sweet tea.

'Is it the same person, do you think? I mean, is there someone following you?' she asked.

'I don't know.'

But the mere action of her putting my thoughts into words was enough to set me off, and silly, stupid tears filled my eyes.

She hugged me. 'Look, you must stay here the night. I insist. You can have the put-you-up in the dining room. If that's okay?'

I could have kissed her. 'I'm so tired I could sleep anywhere. Thanks, Toni.'

She hurried to the door. 'I'll go and find some bedding, then. Won't be long.'

It was only then that I noticed the jewellery box, the necklace protruding slightly, on the worktop above the washing machine. I stared at it, puzzled. I couldn't recall having seen that after the burglary.

Toni returned suddenly. 'Can you come and help me? I can never pull out the bloody put-you-up on my own.'

But she saw my face, followed my eyes. And smiled quietly.

'The necklace. Beautiful, isn't it? Abi found it in her room when she got back from school. Why it was there, I've no idea, because it had been in my jewellery box. I guess the chap must have dropped it when he was searching round. To be honest, I'd forgotten all about it. It's one Mum gave me years ago. It's only cubic zirconia, but it brushes up well and I like to wear it with my black stuff.' She shrugged animatedly.

But I was puzzled. There was something not quite right about this. Why had she looked so guilty when I walked in? Could she really have forgotten about it?

But I was tired, still slightly drunk, and ready for bed.

'Your mum'll be pleased you've found it, then.'

'She will. But right now I need some sleep. Come on, let's sort you out.'

*

I tossed and turned, my mind a whirligig of thoughts and emotions. Round and round and round. I'd been truly disturbed by the chap outside Toni's house. Was he the one I'd seen earlier? Was someone following me, watching me?

I sat up suddenly. If he was watching me, then maybe he'd discovered Sean and I were helping the police, were trying to get a lead on the perpetrator. Maybe we were actually onto something, after all.

Settling back down again, my stomach churning, I realised I definitely needed a new back door.

6

St Pancras, London

ED threw my case into the car. Eleven days had passed since I'd packed it, eleven days of overexcitement, waxing legs, spray-tanning, and the application of crimson-red gel nails. And now it had finally arrived, my long-promised holiday, our first ever as a couple. The first of many, I hoped. I'd been promised peace, relaxation, beautiful scenery, mountains, lakes. Nirvana on legs.

He kissed me seductively. 'How was the journey?'

'Fine, thank you. Nice and relaxing.' My arms around him, I snuggled into his warmth. 'Coffee, magazines, the works.'

We'd arranged to meet up at St Pancras railway station. Ed was working in London, so it was easier to meet up there than for him to drive home and back down again. I was to meet him in the station car park, which had worried me slightly. I'd imagined a huge place full of nondescript cars like his, me walking around forever trying to find the right one. But I'd had no need to worry. Someone hopping on one leg with a blindfold over their eyes would have seen Ed's Volvo. The fluorescent pinks and greens of the enormous windsurf fastened to the roof were about as subtle as a spaceship on a Spanish beach.

He caressed it proudly. 'What do you think?'

I smiled. 'Very nice.'

'I've only just bought it. Think you might like a go?'

'Yes. Okay.'

Why not, I thought? What harm could it do? It might even be fun.

*

We travelled long and hard. A ferry ride, autoroutes, and tiny country roads, until finally, my legs stiff, my mouth thick with service station coffee, we pulled up at the chalet Ed had rented. It was nearly midnight. The sky was coal-black, and the lake beside the chalet a still, dark pool stretching into oblivion. I fell into bed exhausted, ready and raring for a wonderful holiday.

The following morning, excited as a knobbly-kneed nine-year-old, I pulled open the chintz curtains dramatically, imagining green mountains, white goats, a glistening lake, beautiful wooden chalets, lace at the windows, painted ornaments made from local forests, the bread and cheese of Heidi on the table. I had not imagined, for one second, the stagnant pool of slime that lay before me. Nor had I envisaged the oppressive mountain of dark forest bordering the bank opposite.

Definitely. Not.

Swallowing my disappointment, I showered and dressed, determined to cheer up, to go outside and look around properly. Big mistake. For it was then that I saw the row of huge red and white electricity pylons lining the hill behind us. Like soldiers marching toward Hell. This, the dark forest, and the stagnant lake, were all I could see for miles.

Ed placed his arms around me. 'Beautiful, isn't it?'

I nodded. 'Not quite what I expected.'

'Wait until you're out there on the lake, the water at your feet, the wind in your hair. We're going to have a wonderful time.'

'Can't wait,' I murmured.

Our chalet was one of a row lining the bank. The others were owned, I was to discover, by middle-aged Parisian couples meeting up for a spot of fishing. Laughing and chatting, they were like one big happy family. And although the plump, purple-haired woman next door smiled and waved as she hung out her washing, I felt very much the outsider.

So, anxious to begin my holiday in earnest, I donned my new navy swimsuit.

We were in the Jura region of France, which is supposed to be beautiful. And maybe it is. The bits I couldn't see. But that first day became a sign of things to come. The windsurfing was a non-starter, the board much too heavy, although I tried and tried until my back ached. And I didn't fancy swimming; green algae clung to the water like leeches. In fact, it soon became clear there was really nothing for me to do.

Ed was so happy on his board, coming in occasionally for coffee or a meal and enthusing about the wonderful time he was having. But, all alone and miserable, I fervently wished for a hot air balloon to come and whisk me away. Nothing to do, nowhere to go, no cute villages to visit, no shops, no quaint cafés for morning coffee, no restaurants for romantic evenings out. Just miles and miles of lake and forest.

I was like a bird without air.

There was a double-door American-sized fridge in the chalet, completely full, every eventuality catered for. Ed had told the owners I was veggie but, honestly, their idea of veggie was a lump of Comté, some grated parmesan, and a paper bag full of mushrooms. He'd arranged for a new delivery of food the following weekend, so it became obscenely clear that he had no intention of moving, of going anywhere. So, no shopping, no sightseeing, no going out for meals. He was out there all day, surfing up the lake, down the lake, then across the lake. I was expected to sit and watch, taking the occasional photo or two.

We did have a lovely meal outside the chalet on the Monday night. I'd cooked a rather nice mushroom stroganoff. But there was no 'What would you like to do tomorrow? Shall we go somewhere?'

So I did what I had to do. I fluttered my eyelashes, played seductively with my hair, and snuggled up to him.

'What shall we do tomorrow then? A bit of sightseeing? It's just, I'm getting a little bored of sitting here all the time, Ed.'

'Really?'

He was utterly, genuinely, astounded. Honestly.

'Oh, come on, April.' Gesticulating wildly towards the lake and the forest beyond, he stood up to emphasise his point. 'Just look at that, it's beautiful out there. And you've got rest, relaxation, fresh air. How can you say you're bored?'

'Can't we just do a bit of sightseeing or something? Please?'

'Well. Okay. But there isn't really anywhere to go – no big cities or anything. I think the nearest place is Paris.'

Oh - yes! My heart skipped a beat.

'Ed, that would be fantastic. When?'

But his face fell with the force of a house-brick. 'You are joking, right?'

I shook my head, tears threatening.

He sat down again. 'Sorry, April darling, but it's hours away. And really, I don't want to be doing any more driving. I get enough of that at home.'

'I'll drive.'

From the look on his face, that wasn't a good idea either. Not in his car. Control freak.

'Come on, April. What would you do if we went to Paris? You've seen all the sights, done all the shopping. Can't you just relax for a couple of weeks, take the weight off?' Pulling at my hand, he jumped up. 'Come on, why not put on that sexy red bikini and try out the windsurf again? You might get the hang of it this time. And it's dark, so no-one's watching.'

I pulled back. 'No, Ed, I've just eaten. And anyway, it really is too heavy for me.' Guiltily, I blinked back my tears. 'Sorry.'

'Well, do you want to hang out, do a bit of writing - just relax?'

He massaged my shoulders seductively, but I shrugged away.

'Sorry, Ed. This just isn't working.'

'There's not really a lot to do around here, is there?' he agreed. 'I suppose we could go for a walk, if you like. What about it?'

We went for a walk that evening, but the scenery was repetitive and our conversation the same, I'm afraid to say. So it was never suggested again.

The next day, after a restless night, I found the air suffocating, hot and sticky. Oppressive. I'd have loved to have gone for a swim, but the water was so still, so disgustingly green. Deciding Ed was never going to leave the place until the holiday ended, I turned to my writing, beginning work on a brand new story.

Apart from that, my only distraction was Marie, a local girl, employed to come in every morning to clean the chalet and make the bed. I'd make coffee for us both. It was nice to have someone to chat to for half an hour, and Marie's English was good, but after enquiring about her family, where she'd gone to school, and what she liked doing, there wasn't much else to talk about. In any event, that wasn't why I'd gone on holiday. I'd imagined lazy, sun-filled days, meals in off-the-beaten-track restaurants, lovemaking in the afternoon, clear water, fresh vibrant air.

But all my complaints about the holiday were as nothing compared to what happened the following week.

*

It was Tuesday evening, I was sitting on the bed, and I was trying to write. But it was difficult, the atmosphere so dense my tee-shirt and shorts were sticking to me. I was sure I could feel a storm brewing.

And I was right.

Ed was making a veggie *salade Nicoise* in the small kitchen.

'Wine?' he called out.

'Mm – yes, please.'

But instead of bringing me a glass of red, he appeared with a bucket of ice. Silver, heavy, handles on either side, and a bottle of *Laurent Perrier* perched inside. Surprised, bewildered, I looked up, saving my work and closing my laptop.

'What's this?'

He placed the bucket upon the bed.

'I ordered it 'specially.'

'Wow.'

'April,' he began, grinning sheepishly.

'Yes?'

My heart thumped madly. I felt suddenly sick.

'There's something I need to ask.' Kneeling down, he took my hand.

I knew exactly what was coming. 'Ed ...'

I was shaking all over; I did not want to hear this.

'We've only known each other a short while, but I've come to realise just how special you've become, how you enrich my life, how much I love you. But you must already know that.'

My heart missed an awful, sickening beat, and I must have gone deathly pale. But I forced a smile.

'April - would you please, please, do me the honour of becoming my wife?'

Despite my sudden frailty, I felt like hitting him over the head with the champagne, and running. Fast. But how to get out of that bloody awful place? I'd have to take his car. I panicked suddenly, my eyes darting towards the door.

'April?'

He was beginning to worry. I could see it in his face. His eyes pleaded with me, stupidly, like a child caught with an illicit bar of chocolate. Pulling my hand away, I took a deep breath, trying to calm down, forcing myself to think logically.

'Ed, you're a wonderful man, but - it's too soon.' I lowered my eyes, unable to look at him. 'I've been hurt before, as you know, and I really need to know someone for a long time before I could even think about settling down again.'

I looked up, feeling terribly, horribly guilty. The pain on his face pierced me to the heart, but the thought of going somewhere like this year after year – I just couldn't do it. His idea of bliss was, I'm afraid, not mine. His utopia of non-stop water-sports was equivalent to my idea of being stuck in a traffic jam. For ten years. I took back his hand, tears rolling down my face.

'I'm really sorry, Ed. I just …' but I couldn't finish the sentence.

He stood up, his eyes red and weepy. 'It's okay. Don't worry about it. I can wait.'

But for how long, I wondered? It may be never. I may never be ready. Which would have been unfair, on both of us.

We drank the champagne anyway, and our lovemaking was especially sweet that night. Because I knew it would be for the last time. I couldn't hurt him like that, keeping him waiting. He was far too nice.

*

I left the next morning in a highly expensive taxi. I'd woken up early - I say woken up, I hadn't really slept at all - and arranged it all on my phone. Ed woke up just as it was arriving. I'd expected to feel upset, but actually I felt numb. What's that song by Pink Floyd - *Comfortably Numb*? I suddenly understood the phrase. It was the exact description. I felt nothing, and it didn't bother me. I'd written a note explaining everything, but even so the parting was bad.

'Why?' he kept saying. 'Why?'

'I can't do it, Ed. I can't marry you. And I can't keep you waiting. I'm so, so sorry.'

Still in his striped, old-man, pyjamas, he pleaded with me, pulling at my hand.

'You don't have to marry me. It doesn't matter. Only please don't go, April.'

But the numb feeling had worn off by the time the taxi finally reached the *Gare du Nord*. Instead, I felt terrible. I bought a ticket to London St Pancras, but then had four hours to kill before the train was due. I desperately needed something to distract me, some kind of panacea. The word panacea is taken from Greek mythology, by the way, Panacea being the goddess of cures. Or maybe you knew that. Anyway, she was just the person I needed at that very moment.

Walking out of the station, I quickly found the *Boulevard Haussmann,* having been there before, and chose a table at the first café I found. Sitting at a small pavement table watching people pass by is my idea of Heaven. Always. Besides, I was starving. I ordered salad with pear and blue cheese, followed by *tartelette a l'abricot.* Delicious.

Wonderfully satiated, I walked along to *Le Printemps,* the local department store, spent nearly three hundred euros (and did I care?) on a pale pink shirt in shantung silk, and returned to the *Gare du Nord.* Just in time for my train. I slept most of the way to St Pancras, changed for Sheffield, then for Millerstone. By which time it was seven thirty, and was I glad to see home.

*

Ed had been messaging me all day. Ignoring him, I had in the end switched off my phone. Now, however, I needed to talk.

I texted Colin.

I've come home. Need to talk. Please ring asap.

But I needed someone there and then - a real-life person who could give me feedback, make me feel better, or even tell me what an idiot I'd been. I rang Jo.

'April,' she said. 'How's the holiday?'

But I couldn't reply. I just burst into sad, sorry tears.

'What is it? Where's Ed?' she asked, confused.

'I'm home. I've come home.'

'What? What's wrong?'

'I've left him. He's still out there. But it was awful, Jo. He just ignored me - practically the whole time - didn't take me anywhere. We just stayed in this rotten old chalet thing with a lake and a mountain. God, it was so boring. I wish I'd never gone, and I've really been looking forward to it.'

'Oh, you poor thing. But what a swine - I'd never have thought it of him. Do you want me to come over?'

I shook my head at the phone. 'No, it's okay. Sorry, Jo. I just had to talk to someone.'

'Don't be silly, sweetie, that's what I'm here for. But if he's still in France, how on earth did you get home?'

'I got a taxi, then the train.' I yawned involuntarily.

'You must be exhausted. Look – eat something, and try to get some sleep. It'll all seem so much better in the morning.'

'I will. Sorry, Jo ...'

'Stop. Now. Just get yourself to bed, and I'll ring tomorrow.'

'Mm.'

'And don't worry - everything will work out fine. You just take care of yourself.'

Not believing her for one minute, I put down the receiver, locked all the doors, and made my way upstairs. Rinsing my hot face with cold water, I ran a bath and soaked for half an hour with a novel opened up on the soap rack.

Sinking into my very own, very lovely, bed, I felt calmer and much less shaky. Sleep filled me quickly and suddenly, giving me the wonderful peace I'd been craving all week.

But my mobile rang an hour later. Poking my hand out of bed, I checked the time - ten o'clock - and made sure it wasn't Ed before answering.

'Hi, Colin.'

'Hi there. Just got your message. You okay?'

I rubbed my eyes wearily. 'No. Not really. Sorry to be such a pain. I just needed some TLC, that's all. Are you still in Dunfermline?'

'Afraid so. Why are you back home, anyway? Is everything alright?'

He sounded so caring, so loving, his voice like a massage, a marvellous, soothing rub around the temples.

'Can I see you?' I asked.

'April? What is it, what's happened?'

'I've never had such an awful time …' but the huge lump in my throat threatened to engulf me, and I couldn't speak.

'Where's Ed?' he asked.

I swallowed back the tears. 'Still there. I left him this morning. I got a taxi to Paris and caught the train home.'

'Crikey. It must have been bad.'

*

Colin turned up at eight o'clock Saturday morning, having travelled home the previous night. I'd recovered a little by this time, but was still very, very glad to see him. I was still in my pyjamas as I answered the door, but that didn't appear to bother him. Gathering me up, he carried me upstairs, placed me onto the still warm bed, and kissed me.

'Is this alright?' he asked, cautiously.

I nodded, tears filling my eyes. It was more than alright. It was what I wanted more than anything in the world.

We made love for the very first time, carefully, slowly, taking it easy, making it last. His hands caressed, his lips cajoled, his words soothed. I felt like Cleopatra in the arms of Mark Anthony. Cared for. Loved. Truly wanted. And afterwards, I slept like a baby.

Just after eleven, the phone rang, waking us up. It was Josie.

'Hi,' I said.

'Hi, there. Just ringing to see how you are today.'

'I'm fine, thank you.' Colin was placing his arms around me, his body curling itself into my back. 'Really, really fine.'

'You sure? You sound like you've only just got out of bed. Are you not sleeping?'

Colin's fingers were gently stroking me in all the right places.

'I'm still in bed, as a matter of fact.'

'Is Ed there?' she asked, cautiously.

Unable to concentrate now, I wriggled away. 'No. No. It's Colin.'

There was a pause while she thought about it. 'Boy - you're a fast worker, my girl.'

Guilt tugged at me as I sat up, pulling the duvet around me. 'Mm - yes.'

'I won't ask.'

'Sorry, Jo.'

'Actually, sweetie, there *is* something I have to tell you.'

'What?'

'Now don't go getting upset all over again, but you have to know.'

'What, Jo?'

'It's about Ed.'

'What?'

'You are so, so much better off without him.'

'Why?' I whispered, fearfully.

'It would appear he's a serial proposer. Been turned down twice in the past two years. I've only just found out from that friend of Joe's - you know the one?'

I recalled him, a frog-faced chap who liked fast cars and sunglasses. A half-cousin of a half-cousin of Ed's, I think.

'Yes, I remember him.' I squirmed. 'Actually, he's been turned down three times.'

'What?'

'That's why I left. It kind of forced the issue. My God, I couldn't believe he could be such a selfish

106

bastard. Dumps me in the back of beyond, leaves me to just get on with it, then bloody well proposes.'

'You're joking. What a prick! Look - I know it's difficult for you, sweetie, but you are definitely better off without him.'

Actually, it wasn't that difficult. Not at that very moment.

'Mm, I know,' I replied.

'Anyway, have you got anything planned for tomorrow? We're having a barbie, and we'd love to see you. We thought you'd be busy unpacking from your holiday, so it'll be a nice surprise for the kids. Mum's coming, too - I managed to talk her into it.'

I wasn't sure I was ready for Mum just yet. There'd be the same old moans about how I'd messed up my life, getting married to the wrong guy in the first place, having no children, writing what she called 'sordid' books, and going from one man to another. I wish.

Then I realised that's exactly what I'd just done. I grinned.

'Okay, yes, that'd be lovely. Can I bring Colin?'

'What?' he mumbled, behind me.

I turned round. 'Want to come to a barbecue tomorrow, at my sister's?'

'Does that mean I'm staying the weekend?' he whispered, nibbling at my ear.

Josie was saying, 'If you can put up with Mum's comments on relationships and you, then yes - no problem.'

'Okay. What time?' I asked.

'Two?'

'Okay, brilliant. See you then.'

Exhausted suddenly, I allowed my head to fall to the pillow.

'Now then, were where we?' murmured Colin.

7

Millerstone, Derbyshire

COLIN was so unlike any man I'd ever known. Kind, caring, thoughtful. He wasn't drop-dead gorgeous or anything, but he could melt your heart with a wink of the eye.

Now Jeremy, my first husband, was the tall, dark, handsome type. And he knew it. Just like Ed, I now realise. You'd think I'd have learned my lesson.

Jeremy was a lecturer in English and Creative Writing in term-time, a singer/songwriter through school holidays and weekends. That's how we met. I worked as a low-paid loss adjuster for an insurance company. I'd written a few short stories, all of which were unpublished, and I needed to learn more. I wanted to write, to make money from writing, to simply invent characters, storylines, from the comfort of my own home. But not only was I naïve about a writing career, I was inexperienced romantically, too.

Jeremy, however, much more mature at thirty-two, had been around, so to speak. He was extremely handsome in a Richard Gere sort of way, and he completely blew my mind. The night he sang *The Way You Look Tonight* to a rapturous audience in a local pub was the night I lost my virginity. In his back garden, of all places. He owned a small, neat terraced house in a leafy suburb of Sheffield; quiet, middle-class. The garden was long and narrow, with an old hammock swing along one wall and ivy growing along the other. I went home with him after the concert, fully intending to make love to him. I'd just turned twenty, my parents and Josie were on holiday in Norfolk, so there was no-one to question where I'd been all night. To be honest, I can hardly remember it now. My first time.

I do remember the curious scent of dry grass after two weeks of hot weather, the sound of cars in the distance, the hard ground beneath the quilt, and the warm air caressing my body. But that's about it. A quick fumble really, and it was over. Jeremy never was a brilliant lover, too interested in his own needs, if you know what I mean. But I had no-one to compare him with at the time. Now Colin …

Colin was definitely not tall, dark and handsome. No. Kind of mousey, tall but not strikingly so, and not particularly good-looking, not in the classic way. Apart from his eyes, with those long dark lashes. I always fall for the eyes. So big and green you could swim in them. But did he make me melt. Like chocolate over a pan of boiling water. When he put his arms around me, I felt as if I'd come home. And when we made love – it was everything it should be. His innate gentleness in the real world came through. He thought about my pleasure, my needs, my body. Every single inch of it. Even before his own. He loved me. I knew he loved me. I knew he would always love me.

Jeremy was the complete opposite. Looking back, I can see he was too old for me. The only melting I was in danger of was from placing his slippers too close to the fire. I think he was a kind of father figure, to be honest. His musical ability impressed me too, I suppose, and his writing. Although he was never published. And that was only the first bone of contention in our marriage. There was definite competition between us, which should have been healthy, but wasn't. Oh, the tears I shed over that.

I was very lucky with my career, you see, finding an agent with my very first book, even though it seemed to take forever at the time. Using Jeremy's old *Writers and Artists Yearbook*, a tome that had seen better days, I wrote to agent after agent, dreading the stamped, self-addressed envelopes dropping through the letterbox afterwards, my own handwriting an obvious giveaway. And when they did arrive, these white slates of sorrow, I'd hide them in my undies drawer until Jeremy was out of the house. Then I'd tear them open, pull out the inevitable rejection slips, rip them up angrily, and steel myself to try again. One day, however, I found a letter I'd placed there and forgotten about. Tucked beneath some white cotton panties, it had lain there for weeks. It was from my agent, Sandy, asking to see the full manuscript. And that, as they say, is history. I've never looked back. Apart from a failed marriage and one or two (okay, okay, more than two) lousy relationships, life has been pretty good.

We all make mistakes. Petty ones. Great big gangling ones. But what I want to know is, after all the blunders I'd made already, how could I have been so mistaken about Ed? Why had I not seen him for what he was? He'd have been quite happy for me to sit around, prepare meals, organise the cleaning, chew my nails, and fester, for a whole two weeks. With no thought for me at all, barely a nod in my direction. How could I have been so wrong? I couldn't believe we'd spent a whole year together and he still didn't know where I was coming from. And I certainly didn't know what made him tick.

What a complete waste of time. Oh, dear. Yet another notch on the bedpost of life.

*

But on this beautiful Sunday morning I was with Colin. We'd awoken to glorious sunshine, just the kind of day for a barbecue. It was late; ten thirty, to be precise. Dashing out of bed, I showered and dressed in my favourite Levi's and an old blue embroidered top. Colin had tiptoed downstairs while I was in the shower. I thought he was making breakfast, but he had in fact left the house, run to the village greengrocers, and returned with an enormous bunch of pink lilies, two of which were already flowering. As I came downstairs, they were sitting there, still wrapped in cellophane, poking out of my huge white enamel jug, with a breathless Colin sitting beside them.

I shook my head in pretend horror. 'What on earth?!'

He grinned. 'I know. Romantic or what?'

'Just a bit.' I breathed in their scent. 'Thank you - they're beautiful.'

I kissed him, and he pulled me onto his lap.

'And so are you.'

Giggling, I suddenly noticed his clothing.

'You've still got your pyjamas on.'

'I've got a jumper on top,' he pointed out.

'Mmm.' I shook my head in disdain.

'It's okay, no-one knows me.'

'It's a good job. Because you're crazy.'

'You're *so* right,' he whispered, kissing me again, gently at first, then ferociously, his hands exploring. 'Crazy for you.'

'Oh - no - I promised Jo ...'

*

The barbecue was a tremendous success, Josie's garden a profusion of pink roses, red geraniums, blue anemones and various colour of snapdragon. Joe stood guard over the barbecue, an old striped pinafore covering his jeans as he waved the tongs around with the military precision of a cheerleader. But it all smelled delicious. The stuffed peppers cooking as we arrived looked amazing, and my aubergine parcels, made especially by Jo, tasted delicious.

Mum looked good too, in black trousers with an ivory and copper geometric top, and there were no snide remarks about Ed. Josie had warned her; I was sure Josie had warned her. So I introduced her to Colin, and Mum - in fact, everyone - drew him straight to their hearts. Daisy, Josie's youngest at seven, and Rebecca, at ten, were absolute darlings, taking hold of his hands and pulling him towards the swing at the back of the garden.

'Come on, Colin, you can push us.'

He looked back at me, grinning, his legs facing one way, his head the other.

Smiling happily, I sipped my wine. What Colin didn't know was that Daisy and Rebecca had never - would never have - asked Ed to push them on the swing. He just wasn't that kind of person. Ridiculing myself for my own stupidity, my enormous mental block as far as men are concerned, I turned to Mum, who was chatting to Vicky, Josie's eldest.

Vicky's face had always been demure - long, lean, and graceful. But lately, having had the obligatory brace fitted, she'd morphed into a caricature of the great white shark in *Jaws* whenever she smiled, bless her. She was smiling now, at Mum.

'It's great. My fave lesson is music. Mrs Wilson is just so cool. She plays everything, all my favourite bands and things.'

Mum smiled too, her kind eyes wrinkling with pleasure. 'That's wonderful, but don't tell me which ones - I'm sure I won't have heard of them. Now in my day, it was Elvis and Frank Sinatra. Real singers. Proper songs.'

'Mum, don't be such a fuddy-duddy,' I said. 'I bet if you listened to the radio sometimes - which I'm always suggesting you do - you'd quite enjoy today's music. It really isn't that different.'

Tut-tutting, she waved me away with her hand. 'Don't talk to me about today's music. That new cleaner they've sent me - she's always putting the radio on. Can't hear myself think sometimes.'

It was Josie who'd organised the new cleaner with Age UK. She'd also had Mum's locks changed. And, so far, Mum was fine. Nothing going missing. Nothing being moved.

But Vicky's reply to Mum's monologue was rather sweet, I thought.

'But Gran, she might be a bit shy, you know - if she's new. Maybe she doesn't know what to say to you, so she puts on the radio instead.'

'Well, she never will know if she keeps listening to that thing and never says a word to me,' replied Mum, twisted her hands together as if washing with soap. 'I did like Caroline. Now I could talk to her.'

'How can you say that?' I asked indignantly. 'She stole your jewellery box.'

'But she didn't steal it, did she? Because I found it, didn't I? Mislaid it was - that's all.' Her lower lip began to tremble.

Vicky turned to me, puzzled and upset.

I caught hold of her hand. 'How about bringing out some of that delicious strawberry tart, and some cream? You do know it's Gran's favourite, don't you?'

'Okay. No probs.' Jumping up, she ran inside the house.

I needed to change the subject quickly and carefully. So I risked the subject of men.

'So, what do you think to Colin, Mum? Isn't he lovely?'

She watched as he pushed the swing. Henry, Josie's Old English Sheepdog, and Lottie, were nuzzling at his knees, trying to get in on the act. But he just laughed them away.

'Colin?' said Mum. 'Is that his name? I knew a Colin once.' But then she stopped, her eyes glazing over.

Fear clutched at me, and I had to stop myself from shaking her.

'Mum? Are you alright?'

Her eyes focused again. 'I'm fine, April. Thank you, dear. Why?'

'Nothing.' My heart racing, I pushed my fear far, far away.

At that moment Vicky came out with a thick slice of strawberry tart, a spoon, and a jug of thick cream.

'Here you go, Gran – do you want me to put the cream on for you?'

Leaving Mum with Vicky, I went to help Josie in the kitchen, a warm, friendly place made from oak and always smelling of cake. She'd seemed to have spent most of her time that afternoon making endless cold drinks and cups of tea. I found her rinsing glasses under the tap, her hands and arms gnarled and freckled from too much gardening.

'Hi,' I said.

Shaking back her long dark hair, she turned. 'Hiya.'

'Why don't you go and sit with Mum for a while? I'll carry on here.'

'He's nice, isn't he?' she smiled, nudging me with her elbow. 'I'm not surprised you left Ed for him.'

'I didn't. Not really.' I picked up a tea-towel and began to wipe.

'Oh? What happened then?'

'We've kind of been friends for a while. He just happened to be there when I walked out on Ed.'

'He's not as good-looking, though, is he? But then he doesn't fancy himself either, doesn't think he's the bees' knees.'

I stopped drying. I'd never really seen Ed in that way.

'Is that how he came across?'

'Sorry, love – didn't mean to upset you or anything. I mean, I'd never have said that while you were still seeing him.'

'It's okay. You're right, I suppose. He does think he's irresistible. It's just – I've never realised before quite how useless I am at spotting decent men.'

'There aren't that many out there - that's the *real* problem.'

118

'You two are alright though, aren't you - you and Joe?' I asked.

'Yeah. Worse luck.' Seeing my face, a visage of shock and confusion, she burst out laughing. 'I'm joking! No, I just think sometimes it would be fun to play the dating game again.'

'No. Believe me, Jo, it's not fun. Not at our age. I'd love to have been married as long as you have, with kids and dogs running around the place.'

She smiled sweetly in an attempt to make me feel better. 'Hey, it's not all guns and roses, you know. We have our moments. But come here.' She hugged me with her soapy arms. 'You'll find someone. Colin's nice.'

*

Colin left at six for the long drive back to Dunfermline.

I caught up with some correspondence, left a message on Sandy's phone to tell her I'd returned from holiday, and ran a bath. I needed an early night, preceded by a good book. However, life is never as simple as having a bath and going to bed with a good book.

At least - not my life.

Ed was at the door, ringing the bell like a madman. Still dressed, thankfully, and unable to avoid the inevitable, I answered.

'Hi, Ed.'

I felt nothing. He *was* nothing. To me.

'Hi, April.'

He looked pale, shaken, dark rings beneath his eyes like devil's horns.

'Come on in,' I said.

He stepped inside. 'Sorry about this.'

'It's okay.'

But it wasn't okay. My mind was a twirling time-bomb of indecision.

He followed me into the kitchen. It was cool and dark, so I switched on the light. Then wished I hadn't. The cellophane from my lilies was still there, poking out of the bin, huge fingers of plastic pointing towards my guilt. Thankfully, the lilies themselves were in the sitting room, beautifully displayed on the hearth. All I could do was hope Ed didn't put two and two together. I waved towards the table.

'Sit yourself down. Cup of tea?'

'Please.'

He sat, his hands twisting and turning in despair. I felt terrible - I'd never seen him like this. Not knowing what to say to him, I babbled on about Josie's barbecue.

'We had a lovely time. Mum enjoyed it too, nearly back to her old self, chatting away to the kids and stuff.'

But when I took his tea to the table, he pulled at my hand.

'Sit down, April. Please.'

I sat.

'I'm sorry, Ed. Sorry for walking out on you like that.'

'It's alright.' He let out a long, deep sigh. 'I'm sorry for the rubbish holiday, for ignoring you. For being a total idiot.' He took hold of my hand. 'Can we start again, do you think? I've learned my lesson.'

My stomach churned with the speed of a V8 engine. I knew what I needed to say, and there was no way of avoiding it. But I couldn't. I felt like a huge great fish, caught in the net, floundering, with no way of escape.

'Please, April, we could be so happy. We could get married - I was thinking maybe a Christmas wedding. We could buy a beautiful house - in Millerstone, if you like.' He pulled at my hand again, but it felt like he'd taken hold of my throat. 'I promise to treat you well, the way you deserve to be treated.'

'Ed …' but I couldn't say it.

Suddenly fearful, suddenly perceptive, he let go of me. 'I am extremely well-off, you know. It's just - I have all this money, and no-one to help me spend it. We could have such a wonderful life together.'

That was it. That was the key that opened the lock. That's what made me see red. Screeching back the chair, I stood, my arms folded, my back sturdy and straight.

'You think that's all I bloody well care about? Money? Do you know me at all? Do you really think I'm that shallow?'

'No.' He shook his head mournfully. 'No.'

'Let me tell you something, Ed Berwyn - you don't know me at all. I could live on tuppence if I were with someone who made me happy, someone who really, truly loved me. And anyway, I make more than enough to look after myself. Obviously,' and I waved my arms at the furnishings, the bespoke cabinets, the blue Italian tiling from Messina. 'I don't need your money, or anyone else's for that matter. And if you think that's why I fell for you, then ...'

I opened the door, ready to show him out. But he remained sitting, a slab of flesh petrified into submission.

'I - I - I didn't mean it like that.'

'Didn't you? Well, shall I tell you why I did fall for you? I *thought* you were the kindest man on the planet. I *thought* you were fun to be with. Exciting, sexy, charming. I did not realise you were a serial proposer - that you couldn't live without a bloody woman in your life.'

That shocked him. You should have seen the look on his face. You think Munch's *The Scream* is weird?

'What - what do you mean?' he stammered.

'You know damn well what I mean.'

And he did. He collapsed inward, like a balloon.

'It wasn't like that.'

I lowered my voice, determined not to reveal my anger, not to scream like an old fishwife.

'Need someone to darn your socks for you, do you?'

'April. Don't.'

'Sorry, Ed. This is it.'

He stood up then, sorry tears in his eyes, and left.

Closing the door behind him, I felt nothing. Empty. Anaesthetised. And I'd only had one glass of wine at the barbie.

Maybe I needed another.

My hands shaking suddenly, I stood before the wine rack and pulled out the first bottle of red I came to. It happened to be a rather expensive Chateauneuf-du-Pape. I poured a glassful, right to the brim, and sipped. Delicious.

Taking my glass, I headed upstairs, eager for my bath, wanting to float in strawberry-scented bubbles up to the neck. But my phone bleeped suddenly. It was Sean.

Dr Jani burgled. Address, Yew House, Far Lane, round the corner from you. You okay to meet up tomorrow at six?

I texted back.
Yes. OK.
Brief and to the point. But right now I just needed to soak in bubbles, slap on some creamy body lotion, and climb into bed.
Suddenly, I was very tired.

8

DR Aashika Jani was a tiny woman, a native of India. Her dark hair, now greying, was drawn back into a tight bun. Her dark skin and soft, deep brown eyes reminded me of the cocker spaniel my best friend had had at primary school. She'd called him Theo after some book she'd read, and he was the soppiest animal you could ever wish to meet. He even let her sit on his back to watch TV.

Dressed in a crisp white shirt and black trousers, Dr Jani bowed her head gently before she spoke.

'Welcome. I am so pleased to meet you.'

We followed her through the wide hallway into her lounge, an enormous, airy space with a deeply-polished wooden floor and tall ceilings. The maroon Persian rug looked so soft and luxurious, we felt guilty walking across it. But Dr Jani motioned for us to sit down upon the cream couch, its cushions protected by a long throw of deep turquoise silk. A delicate tinkling at the open window revealed glass chimes hanging in the breeze. Unwittingly, I released a sigh from deep within.

Dr Jani didn't sit down, but stood before the stone fireplace opposite. A silk rug hung upon the wall above, an ivory-white elephant against a background of blue. The elephant looked down upon us, its eyes old and wise, serene, beautiful, while its trunk curled high in the air as if to say *Hello*. I couldn't take my eyes from it, and found myself looking at the elephant instead of Dr Jani.

But Sean took charge of the situation, opening his case and pulling out his notepad.

'Thank you for seeing us at such short notice, Dr Jani. My colleague here is April Stanislavski, a writer who's helping me investigate the village burglaries.'

Smiling at me, she again nodded.

'I am very pleased to meet you. Will you be writing about them, is that it?'

Dragging my eyes away from the elephant, I replied.

'No. Sean's just got me along as his sidekick. Because I know the area, I think.' I shook my head emphatically. 'No – Sean will be doing all the writing.'

'Would you like a drink at all? Tea, coffee?'

'No - thank you, Dr Jani. I'm fine.'

'I'm fine too,' said Sean. 'But to get down to business - would you mind giving us some details of the burglary?'

She sat down now, upon a small red armchair beside the fireplace. Nodding calmly, she folded her delicate, almost childlike, hands, upon her lap.

'Of course,' she said. 'What is it you would like to know?'

There was a slight lilt to her voice, but other than that she spoke English perfectly. And I wouldn't have minded her being my doctor in a crisis. Her voice was so gentle and soothing, I'm sure she could have sent people to sleep without the anaesthetic.

'Well, I understand it happened on Saturday afternoon,' replied Sean.

'Yes. I was at work. I'm an ophthalmic surgeon at the Hallamshire. I was there all day, from seven in the morning 'til six in the evening. The traffic was very bad,' she added, by way of explanation. 'Then I came into the house to find the back door had been forced open. Luckily, the boys were with their auntie for the weekend, otherwise ...' and she shook her head sadly.

'How old are your boys?' I asked.

'Fifteen and seventeen. They like to play football with their cousins.'

I smiled. 'Do they follow a team?'

'Not really. They prefer to play rather than to watch. They only get to play at school these days, though. The village team doesn't get enough players; they all prefer their computer games. Such a shame, it is so good for them, to run around in the fresh air.'

Sean interrupted his scribbling. 'Dr Jani - what exactly did the burglars take? I know it was jewellery of some kind.'

She tugged at her wrist. 'All my bangles. My rings. Some necklaces, too. Twenty-two carat gold, all of it. My husband was always so generous.'

Her hands returned to their composed posture upon her lap.

'It must all be very upsetting,' I replied, sympathetically.

'It is. We are on our own now, me and the children.' Her voice became a hush, a whisper of a breath. 'Mesha, my husband, died in a car crash two years ago.' Her voice became louder, her hands gesticulating wildly now as they released their angst into the air. 'So you see - there is no way to replace those things. They have no value once they are gone.'

I felt for her. 'I'm so sorry, Dr Jani.'

But her extreme sorrow filled me with a new energy and I determined, no matter what, to find the cowards who had done this. Sean coughed quietly, clearing his throat. Her grief was obviously getting to him too, not that that surprised me. It was a low cloud hanging over all of us, a long shadow in the midst of the room.

Sean stood up. 'Would you mind showing us the back door, Dr Jani - and exactly where the jewellery was kept?'

'Of course.'

She led the way into the kitchen, an array of sleek white cabinets beneath vermilion tiles. The floor - spotless - was of the same beautiful red. A delicious aroma of garlic, coriander, and some kind of meat emanated from the orange *Le Creuset* casserole on the gas. The back door, half UPVC and half glass, had been boarded up, a heavy wooden chest placed behind it. She looked at us, nervously.

'I was here on my own all weekend. I did not get much sleep.'

'I can understand that,' I said. 'Couldn't you have gone to stay with the children's aunt?'

She shook her head emphatically. 'Oh, no, no. I did not wish to leave the house unattended. No, that would have been asking for trouble. Much trouble.' Her accent had become suddenly thicker, a singsong of crochets and quavers. 'But the window company - they are coming tomorrow. I had to work today, you see.'

Sean was scribbling again. 'So. They came in here and …'

She pointed towards the hallway. 'There. Through there. Straight up the stairs they went. I will show you.' She turned to us. 'I will not ask you to remove your shoes – I am having the carpets cleaned, anyway. Goodness knows what they brought into the house.'

We followed her upstairs. The entire house was beautiful, airy, elegant. Peaceful. And I know it's awful to say this, but I wasn't surprised such a lovely house had been burgled.

We followed her into the main bedroom, also a haven of tranquillity, with pure white curtains and a bed to match.

'Dr Jani,' I pondered, 'you have such a very beautiful home. Why have you never had an alarm fitted?'

She stared at me with those huge, intelligent eyes. 'But - we have never needed one. And they are such noisy things. The man next door - he has one. If we are outside, we hear it bleeping on and off every time he goes in or out of the house. But the policewoman who came on Saturday - she suggested I have one fitted. I have promised to think about it.'

'Okay,' I replied. I didn't pursue the matter; Dr Jani was astute enough to make up her own mind.

Sean was studying the bedroom. 'So where exactly was the jewellery kept?'

Opening the top drawer of a deep chest, she pulled out what appeared to be a small roll of pale blue velvet with two beaded strings dangling. As she opened it out, we saw it was in fact a jewellery bag with three zipped pockets. All unzipped. All completely empty.

'Everything. Gone.' Her hands were shaking.

'Did they take anything else?' Sean asked, carefully.

'No. Nothing.' Suddenly pale, she pushed back a strand of hair and made as if to leave the room. 'I need to go downstairs now. If you don't mind.'

We followed her down.

'Are you alright? Can I get you anything?' I asked.

She shook her head. 'I am fine, thank you. I just need to sit.'

But her hand was still clinging tightly to the banister.

'Shall I make you some tea?'

'I am fine. Really. Thank you very much. I just need to sit for a while.'

She returned to her chair beside the fireplace while Sean and I stood at the doorway, unwilling to tramp across the Persian rug again.

'Is there anything else we need to know, Sean?' I asked. 'I mean, I think maybe Dr Jani needs to rest.'

She nodded gratefully. 'Sorry. It has been such a very great shock.'

'Don't worry about it. I fully understand.'

And I did. I understood completely. Dr Jani had no-one to take care of her - which was unquestionably the main problem. The burglar, that selfish, uncaring, pig-ignorant burglar had done no more that drive home the fact that her husband was no longer there.

Sean nodded. 'I think I've got everything for now. Thank you, Dr Jani.' Walking carefully around the edge of the Persian rug, he crossed the room to shake her hand.

She bowed gracefully. 'If you need any more information, you have my telephone number.'

'I do. And thank you very much for your time,' he said.

'Dr Jani,' I said. 'I only live just around the corner. So if you ever need some company, just ring me. I'm in the book.'

She smiled, her face pale, her eyes still wide with fear. 'Thank you, that is very kind of you. But my sons are home tonight. I will be fine.'

We left then, climbing into Sean's car, upset and overwhelmed at what one human being could do to another.

Sean checked his watch. 'A quarter to seven. Fancy a bite to eat? The smell in that kitchen made me hungry.'

I had planned on a mozzarella salad and an early night. But suddenly I needed some company myself. 'Okay. That'd be lovely.'

*

We headed towards the Flying Toad, notorious for its steak pie. I personally go for the savoury mushroom pie, which I've been told is just as delicious.

George was at the bar. 'Evening, April, how's things? You been at that there rehearsing again?'

'No, not tonight. I'm just out with a friend.' I introduced him. 'Sean, meet George. George - this is Sean, an old friend from school.'

George laughed. 'That's what they all say.'

The Flying Toad is a traditional pub, all hand-pulled beers and leaded glass. Named after the famous Toad's Mouth Rock that guards the road into Sheffield, the food is excellent. Jeremy and I used to drive there for special occasions. I remember we came out one Valentine's Day, when they gave me a red rose and a free glass of sparkling. A lovely place.

We ordered food from George and sat down near the window, two pints of Guinness on the table. I'd noticed Sean had ordered the mushroom pie too.

'Did you order the mushroom because you're veggie, or because you just fancied it?'

'I'm veggie,' he replied, sipping his Guinness.

I looked across, surprised. 'I never knew that about you.'

'Well, you do now. Actually, I didn't used to be, but my dad had a heart bypass a couple of years ago and it got me thinking. To be honest, I don't really miss the meat, and it makes me eat more healthily in general. I feel better for it.'

'Well, good for you.' I raised my glass. 'But the mushroom pie's so yummy, some carnivores eat it instead of the steak – according to George, anyway.'

'Really? Well then, I can't wait to get tucked in.' He looked at me closely. 'So, how are you? What happened with the holiday?'

I sipped my Guinness carefully, surveying him. I knew that merry twinkle in his eyes. He was up to no good, trying to get all the goss. A true reporter. I pulled a face.

'Can we not even go there? Sorry, but I'm not quite ready. Not at the moment.'

To be honest, I wasn't sure I ever would be ready. What a huge, enormous, bloody stupid mistake. Again.

He peered at me over his glass. 'Okay. In that case, we'll talk about Dr Jani.'

'Oh, what a lovely lady. And that house.' I sighed deeply.

'Beautiful, wasn't it? And that blue rug above the fireplace was just amazing. I couldn't take my eyes off the thing.'

'Me, too.'

'Talking of burglaries, did I tell you I've seen the Jones's builders?'

'I didn't think you were going to bother.'

Dr Jani's burglary and my quarrel with Ed were still whirlpools of mud at the back of my mind, but, suddenly relaxing for the first time that day, I sat with my hand wrapped around my Guinness, and I listened.

'Well, I decided that if one of the builders lived locally, we might be able to put two and two together, maybe find some sort of connection.'

'And?'

'They all live the other side of Sheffield. None of them can afford to live round here.' He stared at me, mock-sardonically.

I laughed. 'Hey. You either got it, or you don't.'

He leaned towards me. 'Well, not all of us can make our money writing smutty sex scenes, April Stanislavski.'

I giggled. 'Sean McGavin, that is not true. You cut that out, right now.'

But Holly, the waitress, was carrying our food across, so we needed to behave like adults. Calmly picking up my beer, I sat back.

'Saved by the pie,' Sean grinned.

'So lucky.'

An hour later, our stomachs satiated, we returned to the subject of Dr Jani. We were on sparkling mineral water by now, as Sean had to drive home.

I looked at him curiously. 'Why is it that Indians always buy twenty-two carat gold - do you know?'

'As a matter of fact, I do. I am not Sheffield Star's Senior Crime Reporter for nothing.'

'Go on, then.'

'Well, according to Hindu mythology, during the creation of the universe the creator deposited a seed in the waters, made from his own body. This became a golden egg. Ever since, golden ornaments have been worn for specific ceremonies and occasions. Gold is considered to be pure as the result of the evolution process, passing through fire as it does. And twenty-two carat is the purest you can buy.'

'Wow. You *do* know your stuff.'

'Well, one gets to know these things when one is Senior Crime Reporter. One is not Senior Crime Reporter for nothing.'

I laughed. 'Alright, alright.'

We left the pub half an hour later, Sean to drive home, myself to walk off the calories I'd just consumed. Sean did offer me a lift, but I was looking after my figure. A girl's gotta do what a girl's gotta do.

Walking up Jaggers Lane, I pulled my jacket around me. The weather had turned suddenly autumnal. After a beautifully sunny day, a cold wind was blowing the leaves off the trees and forcing grey clouds to scurry across the darkening sky. Increasing my pace dramatically, I was out of breath by the time I reached my gate.

Throwing on my pyjamas, I sat at my laptop, my big blue cardigan around my shoulders. I had some ideas I needed to get down, just a few paragraphs, before I forgot them. But I couldn't concentrate, my mind too much on other things. Which is totally unlike me. My writing is the one thing that clears my head, helps me relax, forget about the outside world.

I knew what part of the problem was, though. My walk up Jaggers Lane had reminded me of the guy I'd seen outside the post office. What had he been doing there? And was he the same guy as the one standing opposite Birley Lane? I'd mentioned him to Toni, but all she could do was remind me about the old school that used to be there.

The land opposite Birley Lane, now just a large field, was given to Millerstone's poor in 1719 by Bartholomew Ashington, Esquire, to enable the building of a school. Here, Edge Green School was built. Opened in 1721, the building consisted of a schoolroom with two small rooms at one end. But it ceased to be used as a school in 1810 when a new school was built down in the village, This was more central, easier to get to. Edge Green School subsequently fell to the ground and was moved from the site in 1827.

Toni was suggesting, jokingly of course, that the man I'd seen was the ghost of Bartholomew Ashington, Esquire. Rumour has it that a man can sometimes be seen near that field. According to legend, he's dressed in a long circular cloak that he pulls around him when approached. He's been said, on different occasions, to be wearing a hat, a pigtail, a cravat, and/or tall riding boots. Allegedly, he guards the entrance to the field, although no-one quite knows why. It is just a rumour and I didn't believe it was my guy for a second. But I must admit, as I sat there with twilight flickering through the window and a crescent moon deep in the sky, it did fire my imagination. Okay, okay, I know that doesn't take a lot of doing. However, I did determine to look into the finer details of this rumour, maybe think about some kind of romance, a novel to tickle the senses.

But there was still the question of the guy outside Toni's house. Tapping at the edge of my desk, pondering, surmising, I finally decided he was just someone waiting for his girl, and dismissed him entirely from my mind.

The other part of the reason I couldn't concentrate, I realised, was Mum. Someone I could not dismiss so easily. She was always there in the background, a constant worry, a wound that wouldn't heal. I mean, she'd seemed alright at the barbecue, apart from the little incident where she went off into her dreamworld. Afterwards, I'd promised to call and see her on Wednesday. So I decided I'd take flowers - red roses, her favourite.

Dad had always bought them for her. From Marks and Spencer's if he could get them, because they lasted longer, and he'd bring them home from work, hidden behind his back. Not because it was a special occasion, either - just because. He was a builder by trade, specialising in renovation and refurbishment. He travelled the country, but more often than not worked within a radius of sixty miles or so, enabling him to come home at night. Then, once a week, he'd go and buy flowers during his lunch hour while the other chaps sat in the van eating fish and chips. It didn't matter that he didn't get a full hour's rest, or that he had to gobble down his lunch, as long as he could take home some red roses.

That's true love for you.

9

WEDNESDAY morning. The sun was shining again, and my walk was pure heaven. I even jogged back down the hill, so joyous was I at the feeling of warm sunshine upon my face.

But my elation was short-lived; my phone rang as soon just as I walked into the house. It was Josie. Mum had fallen over. Josie had called the doctor and driven over immediately. As far as she could see, there was nothing broken, but she didn't want to move her without the doctor's say-so. But I had to smile. Even as Jo was talking, I could hear Mum in the background, chatting away, going on about how we all make such a fuss.

I showered and dressed quickly, then called at the greengrocer's on my way through the village. Red roses, of course.

Knocking on Mum's door, I removed my sunglasses and walked in, straight through to the sitting room. Josie greeted me, looking harassed but not upset.

'The doc's just gone. She's alright, just a little shocked, nothing broken.'

Mum looked pale, jittery. She was sitting upright on the sofa, still in her pink winceyette nightie, a cushion supporting her back, her legs stretched out beneath a grey blanket, and a cold cup of tea on the small table beside her.

'Oh, April, how have I come to this?' she moaned, as I gave her the flowers and hugged her.

Picking Lottie up, I sat with her on my knee, her eyes big and sad. 'It's just a fall, Mum. Nothing broken.'

She smiled. 'Thank you, darling. Red roses - they're beautiful.'

'So what happened? Can you remember?'

'Of course I can remember. What do you think I am - senile?'

Josie grinned at me from the doorway.

'Sorry, Mum,' I said.

'I was only at the sink, washing up. I turned round, and then I slipped. I grabbed hold of the sink, but I just went. That's all. There's nothing wrong with me, nothing wrong at all.'

Placing Lottie onto the armchair, I knelt beside Mum, patting her hand. 'Calm down, Mum, I was only asking. The main thing is, you're alright. So what do you think happened – had you spilt something?'

She looked suddenly shamefaced. 'I think so. I'd burnt a pan, so I left it soaking on the cooker overnight. You know how you do. But when I carried it across, I splashed water on the floor. My hands aren't as steady as they used to be, you know.'

'I know, I know. It's okay,' I said, soothingly.

'I should have mopped it up, though.'

'Accidents happen, so don't worry about it. You're alright, you're fine.'

She nodded miserably, her eyes on the floor. 'I know.'

I cupped her chin in my hand. 'Mum, look at me. Smile. You've had a fall, that's all there is to it. You could have knocked yourself out and been there for hours. But you didn't.'

'I know. And I've jolly well learnt my lesson.'

'Yes. Next time - mop it up.'

She smiled her lovely smile. 'Next time, mop it up.'

'Good. Right. Cuppa, anyone?' I asked.

'That would be nice,' Mum said, indicating the cup on the table. 'This one's gone cold, with the doctor coming and everything. He's checked my blood pressure, though, and all is well.'

'That's excellent, Mum. So it's all good news. I'll put the kettle on, then. Shall I put these into some water?' I picked up the roses.

'Yes, please. They are beautiful.'

'I'll come,' said Josie, following me.

Mum's kitchen. Always so clean and tidy as we were growing up. Always full of the scent of baking at weekends – she even made her own rice puddings. In between meals, however, there was never a pot or a pan out of place. She hated to see stuff drying by the sink; she'd always dry up with the tea towel and put everything away. Then she'd wipe down the surfaces and bleach the cloths in the sink to kill the germs. Maybe it was working in a hospital that did it, I don't know.

But now. Now. Hardly any food in the house. Used teabags on the side, jam with the lid off, milk left out of the fridge. Dirty knives and spoons lying around. And these days she had a dishwasher to hide everything in.

What was going on with our mum?

'How long is it since Dad died?' Josie asked.

I worked it out on my fingers. 'Seventeen years. Why?'

'Do you think she's just lonely?'

I smiled. 'That would explain everything.'

'Maybe we should find her a companion.'

'What?' I searched for kitchen scissors in the drawer.

'A friend. You know, one of these online dating places.'

Cutting the stem ends from the roses, I shook my head. 'No chance. Can you imagine Mum meeting up with a complete stranger in a bar, full of other oldies meeting up with complete strangers in a bar? No, I don't think so.'

Josie placed clean mugs onto the surface, tidying up and placing the dirty ones inside the dishwasher. 'But that's what she needs, isn't it? A nice man to take care of her.'

Placing the roses into a cut glass vase, I tried to think of all the nice men I'd known. Not many.

'She doesn't need a man, particularly. Just someone who can listen, understand.'

'Someone to cuddle up to on a dark night. Someone to hold her hand when she's sad, and kiss her when she's happy.'

I grinned. 'You ever thought about writing, Jo?'

'Yeah. I should write my memoirs. The Life and Times of Josie Robertson, Gardener to the Stars.' She waved the dishcloth through the air, as if to highlight the words.

'Really?'

'Mm. I do Jim Allsop's old place, you know.'

Jim Allsop is an ageing songwriter. Rumour has it he'd written for the Yardbirds before they became famous. Anyway, he'd obviously made plenty of money out of it, because he owned a farm just outside Millerstone, on the way into Sheffield. A kind of local celeb, he kept himself to himself, so I was surprised he'd even let Josie onto his land.

'Wow.'

She grinned. 'Did I not tell you? How remiss of me.'

'Yes, it is. Actually. What's he like, then?'

'Old. No, he's actually very nice, a bit gnarled, a bit doddery. But on the whole, a real gentleman. He always sends lovely presents to the kids at Christmas.'

'Oh, that's sweet.'

'I know.'

I arranged the roses artistically. 'How long is it since Mum retired, Jo?'

'She's seventy now, so it must be five years, mustn't it?'

'So she's been on her own, not working, pottering around, for five years. No wonder she's fed up with herself. *I* would be.'

'I suppose so.'

'She needs a hobby.'

'She needs a man.' Jo threw the dishcloth into the sink with aplomb. 'Come on, let's go and sort her out.'

I carried a tray of tea and Digestives through. Mum was sitting with her feet on the floor now, stroking Lottie, watching *This Morning* and laughing at the satirical wit of Phillip Schofield. It was lovely to see.

We munched our way through half a packet of biscuits, then I made toast and jam. Starving, having not had any breakfast, my normally healthy diet went completely out of the window.

'Mum?' I ventured.

'Yes?' She was still watching the telly.

'Have you ever thought about doing any volunteering or anything? A charity shop or something?'

'Ooh, no. I'm getting too old for that sort of thing. Maybe in my heyday.'

'What?' I exploded. 'Is this my real mother talking? My mum, who always said she would never get old, never stop painting her nails, or doing her hair, or wearing high heels? 'Where's she gone, Mum?'

Sudden tears appeared. Guiltily, I watched her wipe them away.

'Oh, April.'

I hugged her, stroking back her fine silver hair as if she were a child. 'Mum. Don't. I'm sorry.'

She pulled away. 'No. No. You're right. I don't always feel like it, though. I'm just so tired all the time.'

'It's because you're on your own all day, not working, not doing anything. You ought to get out and meet people.'

'What – at my age?'

I stood up abruptly. 'See? Can you hear yourself?'

'How about me and April having a look round – see what's out there?' asked Josie.

I nodded. 'There's the Women's Institute in Millerstone. And badminton for the over fifties.'

'Ooh, a load of women with too much time on their hands,' moaned Mum.

'But Mum, isn't that you, now you've retired?' asked Josie. 'Sorry to be blunt, but at least they're doing things to help other people, or keeping themselves fit.'

She looked suddenly crestfallen. 'I know.'

'What about a charity shop, then?' I asked. 'You could make yourselves cups of tea, have a good old natter. What do you think?'

She peered at me over her cup. 'Is there one around here, then?'

'There'll be loads on the High Street – they're everywhere these days.'

She nodded quietly, introspectively. 'Alright.'

'Okay. But first we need you to rest and get yourself back into tiptop shape.'

'How do I do that then? Join the gym?'

I smiled. 'No, Mum, unless you really want to. But a nice walk in the country would do you good. How about we take you and Lottie out somewhere next week, once you're feeling better? We could go for a pub lunch.'

'Now you know I need to watch my figure.'

'But Mum, you hardly eat anything.'

'How do you know whether I eat anything or not?'

'Well, look at you. You're all skin and bone. And there's hardly any food in the house.'

'I'm fine. I've just lost my appetite a bit, that's all. People do as they get older.' She began to sob.

Those tears. Again.

'We're not telling you off, Mum,' Josie said. 'We're just worried about you.'

'If you've lost your appetite,' I said, 'then that's all the more reason to work it up again. We could drive you over to my house, put on our boots, and go for a good old walk. That'd do the trick.'

'Okay. I'll see how I feel.'

*

We made Mum beans on toast for lunch, and insisted we eat it in the garden. While Josie cooked and Mum washed and dressed, I dashed to the shops to buy freshly baked carrot cake from the local Deli. It was always delicious, nearly as good as Mum's own.

And by the time we'd finished fussing over her, Mum was smiling, preening, nearly back to her old self. She just needed some company.

'Mum,' I said, thinking *carefully does it*. 'When does the cleaner come?'

'She comes on a Tuesday morning. First thing. Switches the radio on, so I can't hear myself think. And it's no good, you know - I have to get myself up and open the door to let her in and ...'

'But Mum, what's wrong with that? You should be getting up in a morning. It doesn't do to be staying in bed all day.'

'I don't stay in bed.'

'No, but you don't bother to get dressed, either.'

'Well, what's the point? I'm not going anywhere. It's not like I've got to get up and go to work, is it?'

Josie butted in. 'That's why we've suggested a charity shop, Mum. Something to do, something to look forward to.'

'I know.'

'So if the cleaner comes on a Tuesday,' I persisted, 'why was the kitchen in such a mess when we arrived?'

'Oh, she only does one room at a time – it takes her that long. I think it's the kitchen *next* week.'

'But Mum, you're quite capable of cleaning the kitchen yourself. You always used to be so spotless when we were little, always afraid of germs, of us getting upset tummies.'

'I know,' she nodded. 'But you're not here now, are you? There's only me and Lottie to think about.'

'Oh, Mum.' I took hold of her hand. 'We're always here for you, you know – you only have to pick up the phone.'

'But you're both so busy.'

'Never too busy to talk to you,' insisted Josie.

'Look - I'll ring you,' I said. 'Every day, I'll ring you.'

'Don't be silly, April. You've got your own life to lead, all those books you write.'

'But I'm worried about you, Mum. I think you're feeling lonely now you've stopped work.'

'If you like, I'll look into the local charity place and see if they need anyone,' offered Josie.

Mum nodded over her tea. 'Okay. But I'll see.'

Josie stood up suddenly. 'While I'm here, Mum, I'll do you a bit of weeding. Your borders are full of dandelions. And I'll mow the lawn as well. When's the last time you did it?'

'Oh, Bill down the road sometimes does it for me. I do pay him. But his wife's been ill, quite poorly, so he's not had the time just lately.'

Josie's face crumpled as warm tears filled her eyes.

'Oh, Mum - I never thought. Sorry. What must you think of me? A professional gardener for a daughter and I never bother to come and do yours. I'm so sorry.'

'Josie, don't,' I said. 'We're both to blame. I never notice things like that, either. I didn't know Bill was doing the garden. I thought Mum was on top of things.'

'I *am* on top of things,' Mum complained. 'I've just been off it for a while, that's all.'

And so it was that I ended up at the bottom of Mum's garden, pulling up dandelions and thistles, the knees of my jeans green and my fingernails black. But as I stood up to the sound of teacups clinking outside the kitchen, I suddenly noticed the windows of the house next door. Black bin liners had been stretched tightly across the upstairs windows. You could only see them from the bottom of the garden, and I guess it would only be obvious when the sun was shining. But suddenly I was on my guard.

Stretching out my aching back, I wandered down to the house. Mum had brought out tea and biscuits – ginger, my favourite – placing them onto the patio table.

I sat down, picked up a biscuit, and dunked it.

'Mum,' I said, 'who's living next door these days? Is it still that couple with the twin girls?'

Making herself comfortable, she shook her head. 'No, they moved a couple of years ago. He got a job in Birmingham somewhere – some kind of council job, it was. I know they were very excited about it all.' Sipping her tea, she looked up quizzically. 'Why?'

'So who lives there now?'

'You don't see them around much, to be honest. I think they must be gay or something. Not that I have anything against gay men,' she added hastily. 'But there's no woman that I can see. And I would have done. I mean, there's never any washing hanging out or anything. Not even on a day like this. And I'm home most of the time, as you know.'

I followed her eyes. The sky that day was the most beautiful blue, the colour of a baby boy's blanket. Not a cloud anywhere. I sighed. Why did it all have to be spoilt by the vision that was now filling my head?

'What is it, April?' asked Josie, concerned. 'You look upset about something.'

I smiled. 'No. It's nothing. I'm okay.'

'You sure?' she insisted.

'I'm sure.' But I was so engaged with my thoughts that the second biscuit I dunked softened so much it fell into my cup. 'Oh, damn it. Now look what I've gone and done.'

Josie laughed, I laughed, and soon even Mum was laughing. The afternoon was turning out to be so much better than expected.

*

A little later, I helped Jo while she was unravelling the lead to the lawnmower.

'Jo?' I said.

'Yes?'

'Could we not just get some of that stuff to put onto the dandelions? You know, that stuff you paint on?'

'I suppose so. It would stop them coming back next year. But it's expensive.'

'I'll get it.'

'No, you won't,' Mum retorted. 'It's my garden.'

I smiled. This was definitely my old mum.

'But Mum, it's for me, not you. So I don't have to ruin my nails.'

'It's a good job I don't think like that,' retorted Josie.

'There's that garden centre down the road, isn't there?' I said. 'Is it still open?'

'It is,' Mum nodded.

'Right.'

'Get some poppy and meadow seeds while you're there,' Josie said. 'We'll fill in that gap with them.'

There was a gap at the side of Mum's house that didn't get much sun. The only things that seemed to grow there were daffodils and dandelions. Josie was right; it did need more colour, something that would grow easily.

'Good idea,' I replied, gulping down my soggy-biscuit tea.

I decided to walk to the garden centre. It wasn't that far, and it meant I had to pass the house next door, the one with the blacked-out windows. The windows at the front of the house hadn't been blacked out, however. There were curtains up, and brilliant white netting that stretched across the glass. So I walked slowly, taking notice, listening and watching. There were no cars outside, no sounds anywhere, and no evidence of life. But then, it was the middle of the afternoon; they were probably at work. It was this conviction that made me more daring. Sherlock Holmes, I thought, eat your heart out.

Throwing caution to the wind, I pushed open the small gate, walked up the path to the front door, and looked up. The upstairs windows, a small window and a bay, the same arrangement as Mum's, could also have been blacked out, but the net curtain made it difficult to see. Shielding my eyes from the light, I put my face to the bay window on the ground floor, peering through. The net hid everything, but I did notice one definite thing. The glass was dripping with condensation.

I walked over to the front door. Thickly painted in midnight blue, it looked unkempt, unloved, the paint beginning to peel, the fake brass letterbox chipped to reveal yellow at the edges. Opening it, I peered inside. An interior door formed a porch between me and the hallway, so I couldn't see anything, but there was a faint whirring sound, like that of a fan heater. Other than that, it was deadly quiet. My heart was pounding, but I called out.

'Is anyone there?'

I had a feeling there wouldn't be, but was still terrified someone might answer and I'd need a good excuse for loitering.

No-one did.

Heaving relief, I let go of the letterbox and walked down the side of the house, the same side that needed Mum's meadow seeds. This land had been grassed over, the grass uncut, full of weeds, and smelling of cat wee. I trod carefully.

The rear of the house was hidden from Mum's by tall fencing and some kind of bush growing alongside. I could hear Josie and Mum chatting to each other and calling to Lottie, who could probably hear me on the other side of the hedge. Bending down so I wouldn't be spotted, I tried the handle of the back door. It was well and truly locked. Weirdly, there was also a letterbox on this door, as if it had once been a front door. Nervously, I peered through.

A sickly sweet scent hit me, the dark and sinister aroma of warmed air and fruity vegetation. Weekends in Amsterdam with Jeremy had attuned my nose to the distinctive scent of cannabis, and this was similar, but much, much stronger. I pulled back quickly, aware of my fingerprints upon the letterbox. So I was right about the windows.

The upper rooms were definitely being used to grow cannabis.

Right next door to my mum's house, as well.

10

THE following Friday saw me back at the Flying Toad, George welcoming me in.

'Hi, April, it's good to see you back. After all this time.' He winked cheekily, no doubt referring to my meal with Sean.

I smiled. 'Okay, okay. It was a business meeting.'

'If you say so.'

I'd lived in Millerstone for thirteen years, had known George for ten. I moved there from Sheffield after Jeremy and I split up. I wanted to start again, away from *our* friends and *our* neighbours. We'd been falling apart for over a year, and I knew it. He definitely knew it, having treated me like dirt from Day One and then having an affair with one of the secretaries at the uni. Not that I came out of it squeaky clean. I'd guessed he was cheating on me and had asked him the question, but he fervently denied it. Too fervently.

So I got my own affair.

I didn't begin it on purpose. There was no retaliation or anything like that. It just kind of crept up on me, I was so very unhappy. By this time I'd given up work as a loss adjuster and was working from home, writing. My morning run in those days would take me up Little Fox Lane, not far from our house in Stannington, at the top of which I'd pause to catch my breath. An absolutely gorgeous Georgian property stood there, with an old rickety garage, stables and about three acres of land. I'd always loved it. It was up for sale, empty, for over a year before the *Sold* sign finally went up. During that year, however, I'm afraid I took great advantage of my husband's infidelity.

*

Dino Simioni, the owner of the property, would visit the house once a week to tidy up the garden, check on the old water pipes, and ensure the heating was on if necessary. A busy man, a self-employed architectural engineer, he'd arrive early at around eight o'clock, then leave at ten. And that was when we made love. There was no furniture or anything. We were on the floor, on a big, blue inflatable bed he smuggled in just for the occasion.

I'd met him on one of my runs. He and his wife had separated and she'd moved out of the city and into the countryside with the kids, which was why the house was up for sale. Dino had moved into an apartment, not far from his office.

It was a near tragedy, actually, the way we met. It was raining, pelting down. The rain had started ten minutes into my run, falling so fast it was like a waterfall. I should have turned back, but I was already drenched and the air was still warm, so I continued. Soaked to the skin, I didn't stop to catch my breath at the top of Little Fox Lane as usual, but ran straight on, past Dino's gate, intending to turn right and up a small track that would take me back down the busy road home. But I didn't see his silver Audi pulling out of the driveway. Running straight at it, I managed to pull back just in time.

The brakes screeched in protest as I stood there, dripping like an idiot, watching as he wound down his window.

'I'm sorry. Are you alright?' he called.

His thick Italian accent made my stomach tumble.

'I think so. You nearly got me, though.'

I tried smiling to show I was okay, but it seemed to come out all wrong. I wasn't okay; I was in shock and shivering.

'I'm so sorry,' he cried. 'Let me just park up.'

Reversing into the drive, he pulled on the handbrake noisily. I knew I should have just run home to get warm. But I didn't. I waited to see what would happen.

It was curiosity that killed the cat.

As he climbed out of the car, I noticed first his eyes. Deep, dark, brown. Then his hair. Dark with greying sideburns. He wore a slim grey suit and tie. Very sophisticated.

He waved me towards the house. 'Come on, out of this horrendous rain. I'll make us coffee and get you warm.'

I shook my head. 'No, no, I'm fine. Thank you.'

'You sure? It's good coffee.'

'I'm sure.'

'You're not going to sue me or anything?'

He smiled with concern, his smile like sunshine, lighting up his face. The day actually deserved a rainbow, the coming together of rain and sunshine, I thought. And it was just what I needed at that moment; a rainbow to lift my spirits, to remove me from my problems, my philandering husband, my dithering, inescapable thoughts. I returned the smile, rubbing at my arms to warm them.

'No, I won't sue. It was my fault, anyway. I couldn't see properly. The rain.'

'I know,' he nodded.

I held out my arms. 'Look - no broken bones or anything.'

But then I began to shiver violently.

He came up to me, pulled off his wet jacket and placed it around my shoulders, coaxing me into the house.

'Come on, come on, I insist. I'll light the fire.'

So that was it. A mad, passionate *affaire*. No real love, just sex, although he was very romantic. He would whisper to me, sweet nothings in Italian, and make warm croissants with fresh coffee after our lovemaking, the odd little chocolate or soft Amaretti biscuit on the side. Amarettis. Ahh. An almond tang so powerful, I still can't eat one without thinking of sex.

We'd meet every Wednesday morning without fail. There'd be a log fire burning in the grate, the bed blown up on the floor, white silk duvets above and below us. The bed was supremely comfortable but, to be honest, we'd end up on the floor more often than not, the silk so soft and the mattress so unforgiving. And we'd just slide, laughing our heads off. It was fun, pure fun. And boy, did it feel good. I'd been so miserable. Jeremy was out most nights, allegedly singing in a pub somewhere, but I was so busy with my brand-new writing career I could only go along at weekends. I'd applaud at the right time, chat to the friends of other musicians, and drink the proverbial Guinness. But the gap between us - I knew it - was widening, and I needed more than he was able to give. Not his fault, particularly. He wanted to be a writer, a writer who knew his facts, his history, writing about wars and economies and the battle for peace. He just never made it. And to be faced with someone, someone he thought he loved, writing cheap chick-lit to wild acclaim - well, you can understand.

So we drifted on.

The affair lasted eleven months before Dino sold the house. We were never found out, except once, nearly. Very nearly. The house was on the market for eight hundred and fifty thousand, a lot of money for a five bedroomed house. But it *was* gorgeous. Having been converted into an out-of-town gentleman's club in the Fifties, it had retained its *old boy* charm, with the original oak staircase, oak panelling in the library, and a large orangery that had once been used for dining. The estate agents had agreed as part of their contract to show people round on Dino's behalf. They had the keys and the code for the alarm, so could arrange everything.

One rather misty Wednesday morning, about the middle of May, I met up with Dino as usual. The fire was lit, the bed inflated. He'd even lit candles and placed them across the drawing room floor. Pulling me towards him as I entered the house, he pulled off my sweaty running shirt and began kissing me ferociously. He always tasted of toothpaste and liquorice, I don't know why. Suddenly, to our horror, we heard the sound of a car engine. Then silence as someone switched it off. It was still early, eight o'clock, so we never thought for one minute that someone was coming to see the house. But then we heard voices, car doors slamming, sudden laughter. Shocked and pale to the bone, Dino peered through the curtains. I will never forget the panic on his face. It's not as if he could have hidden me in the wardrobe until they'd gone. Potential buyers want to see every nook and cranny. Meanwhile, I was pulling on my clothes, snuffing out the candles, deflating the bed, and rolling up the duvets, my heart thumping hysterically.

'Where do I put these?' I whispered.

He turned, his face ashen. 'Leave them. I'll think of something.'

How we got out of that one, I'll never know. I think it was Dino's barefaced cheek more than anything. He put on his jacket, straightened his tie, tidied away the candles, and kissed me goodbye.

'As soon as they've gone, run.'

Tall and poised, he walked outside to greet them, while I peered, terrified, through the window. The car was a Mercedes with the estate agent's initials DHR1 on the plate. Donald or David, or whatever his name was, was strolling towards the front door, briefcase in hand, chatting animatedly to a couple in their forties - a very well-to-do couple in their forties - when Dino approached them. They paused while he talked, gesticulating with both arms in that classic Italian way he has. Persuading them to turn back, he took them across the narrow lane and pushed open the old green gate, the entrance to the paddock, while they followed. As they disappeared from view, I took a deep breath, pulled at the door, and ran for all I was worth.

The following week, Dino explained all. He'd merely told them the insurance company required him to sleep at the house for two nights a month to ensure full cover remained in place. Smiling, he described the look on the estate agent's face, obviously rather put out at this invasion into his domain. But he'd acquiesced in the end, and so the morning ended well. It was a close call, though, and one I never, ever, want to repeat.

*

Dino and I became good friends, phoning each other, emailing, and meeting up occasionally, even after the house was sold and I'd left Jeremy. But we were never meant to be in love, just lovers. I never loved him, and he knew it. I just needed someone, a man outside the world I lived in, to make me feel special. I wanted a creature of passion, of frivolity, a being who wasn't Jeremy, I suppose. Dino was upset when my marriage broke up, blaming himself, but I soon put that to rest. He was Catholic, you see, his family hailing from Bellagio, Lake Como. He often talked about the place, his childhood, his family, how his parents sent him off to York in England, paying for him to study architecture. I came to realise he'd become a very lonely person after his divorce. Yet he loved to talk, and I loved to listen. The only contact he had with his family was when he picked up the children, two girls, alternate weekends. Eventually, though, he found someone else, a maths teacher, someone he could love properly, and we stopped communicating. He's probably married now with two more children. No, I'm pleased for him. I suppose we fulfilled a need in each other just when we needed it. That's life, though.

*

But I'm becoming maudlin, feeling sorry for myself. And I shouldn't be. I married someone who wasn't right for me, and that's that. The thing is, when I met Jeremy, I was a vulnerable youngster, he much older. I thought he was mature, knew everything, would look after me. I allowed him to dictate what I wore, what I ate, what I read. At that age it's cute having the man you love help choose your clothes, your books, etc. But you try living with a dictator for a few years. It seemed to become worse instead of

165

better, and when I started pulling back, saying no, I wouldn't do that, or no, I wanted to do this - that's when he started his sordid little affair. How the marriage lasted so long, I shall never know. I mean, I knew him for five years before we married, but it all seemed different then, like he was taking care of me. Maybe he *was* a father figure. Not that I needed one. At least, not consciously. But who knows what goes on in the deep, dark recesses of our minds? It was only once we began living together, after we married, that the whole thing became so transparent. I was thirty years old when we eventually divorced.

Anyway, I digress. Again.

As I've already said, I was at the Flying Toad, thanking George for my Guinness. I wandered through to the back room where the Village Players gather to read plays, decide which to perform, and to rehearse them. The others were already seated, chatting noisily. Alfie, a pure white shirt showing off his golden tan, pulled back the chair beside him.

'Here you go, April. It is good to see you, my darling.'

I smiled. 'Thanks, Alfie. Did you have a good holiday?'

'Wonderful, it was, darling - absolutely wonderful. Two weeks in Turkey with my Francis. And wall to wall sunshine.'

'Sounds delightful, Alfie.'

'I went there just after uni, you know, the very same place. My boyfriend at the time was quite well-off - his parents left him the business. And he spoiled me dreadfully. But just look at the shirt, April.'

Standing up, he performed a pirouette, his hands tucked beneath his chin. The shirt *was* rather nice, with a large purple peony on the back. I applauded loudly, and the others joined in. Deep down, however, I envied him slightly, my holiday having been a damp squib of boredom and sorrow.

'It's lovely, Alfie,' I said.

'Thank you, darling. You're a treasure.' Clapping his hands together, he called, 'Right, please, could I have everyone's attention?'

The noise quietened to a low murmur and I looked around, suddenly noticing Emilisa Meadows-Whitworth at the end of the table. So Lorna Jones had been right - she was coming back.

'Welcome back, everyone,' continued Alfie. 'It's so lovely to see you all, and I hope we're all having a good summer.' There was a murmur of approval. 'Now, first things first. You may already know this, but I have the pleasure of welcoming Emilisa Meadows-Whitworth back into our fold.'

He waved towards her, waiting for her acknowledgement. Which she gave; a nod of the head, a smile.

Alfie continued. 'As many of you know, Emilisa was with us for many years before leaving, for personal reasons, shall we say. But she is back. And with a vengeance. She has offered to direct our forthcoming play, a one acter called The Mystery of Sir Hugh Tompkinson. It was written by a local author in 1957, would you believe. But it's very amusing, a whodunit, and I'm just *so* excited. So. Over to you, Emilisa, darling.'

Applauding her dramatically, he sat down again.

She stood up, the heavy scent of *Yves St Laurent Opium* making its way towards me. My nose wrinkled involuntarily.

'Thank you, Alfie dear, that was a wonderfully warm welcome.' Her voice was deep, slow, like black treacle. 'And I'm so happy to be back here, doing what I love to do most. I do hope I can give this marvellous play the justice it deserves. Now – if you would just take a script from the pile on the table.'

Alfie passed me one, the cover plain white, the book thin and uninteresting. I opened it with interest.

Emilisa continued. 'The play was first performed at the Lyceum in Sheffield in 1959. A very witty murder mystery, it is set in the 1920s. A country house party is in full swing, but the owner of the house has an ulterior motive ...'

There was a murmur of approval as she continued to read from her notes, delicate reading glasses perched across her perfect nose.

'Sir William's brother has been missing for three years, since the end of the First World War. All the house party guests were his brother's friends or acquaintances at the time of his disappearance. All are suspected of having some knowledge of the disappearance. It is the final evening of a week during which the host has been watching each and every one of them. Each character could be a suspect. We come to discover that they all have their secrets. So how does Sir William discover the truth? And is his brother still alive? We are left at the end of only one act to make up our minds. We are left dangling. But if we have paid attention, ladies and gentlemen, we shall have the answer. It is thought-provoking, intellectual, intelligent. I hope you will love it.' Smiling, she peered over her glasses. 'Think *Downton Abbey* for costume and setting. It is going to be just divine, I know. Obviously, I need to meet up with everyone again, get an idea of people and so on, character-wise.'

Percy Wainstone, the only guy with the *Winston Churchill* figure in the company, held up his hand.

'I'm available, Emilisa. Just to let you know.'

She smiled graciously, and I noticed how her lips didn't move quite where they should have. A little Botox in evidence, maybe.

'Thank you, Percy. And to set your mind at rest, I already have just the part for you. You would be marvellous as the Brigadier, I know it.' She picked up a pile of notelets, passing them around the table. 'Now, if you could all let me know your availability.'

I registered the parts available and the date rehearsals would begin. But I wondered how we were going to pull off a one act play, all by itself.

'Emilisa?' I called.

She smiled. Definitely Botox.

'Yes, April?'

'Why are we only doing a one act play? Is it quite long?'

There was a schoolgirl giggle from my right. Gemma Jameson, her lovely dark hair fastened up in a cocoon of disarray, covered her mouth hastily.

'Sorry, April,' she whispered.

I grinned.

But Emilisa ignored her. 'I was going to come to that, April. Because this is such a tremendous play and I really wanted to do it, we have two choices. We either do two one act plays, which would entail two lots of costumes, scenery, et cetera, et cetera. Or we have short evenings on the Thursday and Friday, with tea and coffee afterwards. We thought a little get-together for everyone, maybe raffle tickets, and then a Grand Auction on the Saturday night. We're all trying to raise money for the swimming pool, aren't we?'

There were nods of agreement, mumbles of appreciation. We'd heard the pool was in danger of closing again, due to Government cutbacks.

'I've assumed you'd want to go with the latter, so have asked Diane Downing and her Women's Institute to help with the auction. They are the experts on these things. It might take some extra organising as far as the play is concerned, clearing the decks and so on, but I'm sure it will be fine. It might even be fun. So thank you, everyone.'

'Thank you, Emilisa, and welcome,' said Alfie. 'Now, if we could turn to our scripts. Gemma, could you play Lady Isabella, Sir Hugh's ex-girlfriend? Percy, Brigadier Worthing? April, Miss Forsythe, please. You'll love her – she was Sir Hugh's secretary, but she has a shady past.'

11

London, SE1

SANDY'S office is small, but smart. The pale blue sofa and walls of the reception area calm you, welcome you, invite you into her domain. This domain - a neat beige office, is about two metres square. Tiny. How she does any work in there, I'll never know. Maybe she doesn't; maybe the majority is done at home. I would ask, but it might sound rude. Besides, that small piece of property must have cost a fortune. Part of a block of twenty-four offices, each with its own doorbell, its own pristine sign beside the door, the corridors streamlined and hushed with soft cream carpeting, it looks very expensive, very understated.

Rachel, Sandy's secretary, is also petite. With dark shiny hair, she looks Chinese, her mother from Hong Kong, her father British. But she's British, so her

English is impeccable. This particular day, she welcomed me in like an old friend, ushering me into the reception area and closing the door behind me.

'April - it is so lovely to see you again. Sandy's waiting for you. Would you like coffee?' Her soft brown eyes curled up at the edges as she guided me towards the office.

'Coffee would be lovely. White, no sugar. Thank you.'

Sandy stood as I entered, her arms outstretched, her ample bosom clothed in a fitted navy suit and pure white shirt.

'How lovely to see you, April.' She kissed me on both cheeks, continental-style. 'How are you? You look wonderful, as always.'

We sat down either side of her desk, a large, tidy affair taking up a fair-sized chunk of the room.

'Thank you, Sandy. You, too.'

'Oh, no. I definitely need to lose weight.' She pulled at her jacket. 'These beach holidays do me no good at all.'

Her figure is in fact impeccable. Large bosom, small waist and hips. She always looks fantastic.

I grinned. 'You look amazing. And don't mention beach holidays to me. I'm in desperate need of one at the moment.'

She looked puzzled. 'Oh? Well, Rachel is arranging coffee, so we'll soon have you feeling fresh as a daisy. Anything else you'd like? Croissant, bagel?' She made as if to press the button on her intercom.

'A glass of water would be nice.'

'It shall be done.' She buzzed Rachel before sitting back into her chair, eyeing me carefully. 'What happened with the holiday, then? Sounds to me like you didn't make it.'

I groaned. 'It wasn't quite the relaxing break I'd been expecting.'

'Don't tell me. He sat at the bar all day, leaving you alone on the beach.'

'If only. No. No beach, no bar. Just a filthy lake and a row of weird chalets.' I shook my head in disgust. 'Don't ask.'

She looked at me, thoughtfully. 'And the bloke?'

'Gone. We're finished.'

'I'm sorry.'

'It's okay. We obviously weren't right for each other.'

'Some men are total bastards, are they not?'

I nodded. 'Some are, some aren't. This one - this one has proposed to three women in the last two years. Including me.'

Her eyes nearly left their sockets. 'What? When? On this holiday? He *proposed* on this horrendous, awful, holiday?'

'He did.'

'The bastard.'

But the look on her professional, pristine face was an absolute picture, a contrast of puritanical dismay and quiet pleasure, and I began to laugh hysterically.

'Sorry, Sandy,' I said, wiping the tears from my eyes. 'That was just so funny.'

'Isn't it true, though? They are bastards, most of them. Why we women have anything to do with them, I'll never know. Mother nature, I guess – reproduction of the species and all that.'

Just then, Rachel walked in with a tray of drinks. Picking up the glass of water, I downed it in one.

'Thanks, Rachel, I needed that.'

She stared at me. 'Are you okay, April?'

'Just a fit of the giggles. Ignore me – I don't sleep too well in hotels.'

She picked up the glass. 'You want more water?'

'No, I'm fine with coffee. Thank you.'

'Okay, if you're sure.'

Bemused, she closed the door behind her.

Sandy smiled succinctly. 'Right. If you're sure you're okay?'

'I'm fine, Sandy. And don't worry - I am so over him. A cliché, I know, but he really is yesterday's bad news.'

She nodded. 'So, about our campaign ...'

Two hours later, we'd planned our next onslaught on the buying public. It was to be a two-parter, a historical romance, the period yet to be decided.

However, I was acutely aware that my idea of using Bartholomew Ashington and Edge Green School was fitting into the plan quite nicely. This little seedling just needed the chance to sprout.

We said our farewells, and I found myself out on the street, starving hungry and eager for a walk. Continuing along Albert Embankment, the scent of summer high in the air, I paused now and again to watch the boats sail lazily by, the Thames a muddy green. Twenty minutes later, I'd arrived at the Garden Café, a delightful place in the grounds of Lambeth Palace Gardens. There was only one table free, so I sat down, ordering goat's cheese and walnut tart with salad, and a pot of Darjeeling, from a waitress who was the spitting image of Leslie Caron in *Gigi*.

Munching away, I was happy, full of ideas on how the book would begin. I was thinking maybe a death, a funeral.

I'd nearly finished my meal, however, when an elderly woman approached, one gnarled hand holding tightly onto her walking stick.

'Mind if I sit here?'

Swallowing quickly, I shook my head. I could hardly refuse, could I, sitting there all on my own, at the only table with an empty chair?

'No, help yourself. I'm leaving in a minute, anyway.'

'Thank you. Very kind.'

She sat, leaning heavily against the table, her brown pleated skirt folding neatly around her, and ordered a filter coffee from Leslie Caron, her voice upmarket and tight.

I smiled, indicating the remainder of my salad. 'The food is very good.'

She shook her head. 'I never eat at this time of day. They only bring me my breakfast at ten o'clock.'

I indicated puzzlement with a tilt of the head, so she explained.

'I stay at the Bentley. I have a permanent room there. They're all very nice to me, though.'

The Bentley, I knew, was a Hilton Hotel. Very posh. So, even though I wasn't quite in the mood for conversation, I felt I should talk.

'How long have you lived in London?'

'All my life. I was born in the East End, although I know I don't sound it.' She paused as the waitress brought her coffee on a tray, a cream jug and sugar bowl to one side. Pushing the jug and sugar bowl away, she pulled a face. 'Awful stuff. I always take my coffee black. Gallstones, you know.'

Lovely, I thought, eating a chunk of juicy red tomato. Then she leaned towards me, conspiratorially. 'I used to see Diana quite regularly, you know. Before she became the princess.'

I nodded. 'Oh?'

I honestly didn't know whether to believe her or not. She just seemed like a lonely old lady needing company.

'I knew her aunt, Lady Anne. Lovely girl, she was, Diana. Before he got hold of her.'

Drinking up the remnants of my tea, I smiled. 'Well, I suppose it takes two to tango.'

'I know, but such a shame. Beautiful, she was. Why couldn't he treat her like the princess she was?'

Finishing my meal, I left a tip, made my excuses and left. The sun had come out; it was a beautiful afternoon. I felt sorry for the old lady, but didn't really want to get involved in such a conversation. And she reminded me a bit of Mum, on her own, desperate for company.

Why do we children always feel so guilty?

I decided there and then to spend more time with Mum, maybe get her to the doctor's, see if she needed antidepressants or something, anything to help change her life.

*

My hotel was on Rochester Road, bang slap between Victoria and Pimlico underground stations. I'd arrived the previous afternoon, tossed and turned all night for no particular reason, then slept in until eight o'clock. Having stayed here before, I knew it was convenient for Sandy's office, but also for the hairdresser's, a little place I use in Camden Town. I'd already made an appointment for the following day because I hate my hair when it's just been done, so was leaving it until the very last minute. It meant I could nip back to the hotel, wash my hair in the shower, and style it myself before anyone could see. Because no matter which hairdresser I choose, no matter where I am at the time, I always come out looking like a bloody Norwegian prostitute.

This afternoon, however, and despite the sunshine, I wanted to visit the Victoria and Albert. There was an exhibition on, a display of Beatrix Potter botanical illustrations that was only there until December, and I didn't want to miss it. I've always loved Beatrix Potter books and would beg Mum to read them to me, even when I could read myself. There's something comforting about them, something eternal. Peter Rabbit, Benjamin Bunny, Sally Henny-penny. I was going to call my children after them when I grew up but, sadly, it was never to be. The drawings were beautiful, though. Pretty, extremely delicate, amazing to see in the flesh.

I spent the next three hours walking around the museum, pausing only for tea and a scone. An amazing place anyway, that day it was full of bright-eyed children running round in *Mini Boden*, their anxious mothers telling them not to touch, their fathers in the City no doubt oblivious to the work entailed in keeping their offspring safe and sound through the school holidays.

I ate tea at the hotel, before wandering outside to imbibe the atmosphere surrounding Hampstead Theatre. I tried to buy a ticket for the show, but they were sold out. Anyway, if I'm honest, I'm not very good at walking into these places on my own; I always feel like a tramp in a palace. I was tired, too, after my horrendous night's sleep, so I walked back to the hotel, had a long, lazy bath, and went to bed.

The next morning, however, I felt as bright as a button. I had no work to do, just shopping, lunch, the hairdresser's, packing, and home. Crossing Camden Town, I walked down Albany Street, past Regents Park, along Portland Place, to Oxford Street. I walked for miles and miles, or so it seemed. I bought some amazing Christmas pressies for Mum, Josie and the kids, called into John Lewis for coffee, and lunched there again on my way back. Boring, I know. Predictable, yes. I could call into John Lewis anywhere, any time. But I knew the food would be okay, and relatively inexpensive. I'd splashed out a lot on the hotel, so didn't want to eat into my budget too much, even if it was all on expenses.

After lunch, I headed to Harvey Nics. Here I went a bit mad, spending two hundred and fifty quid on some Dolce & Gabbana jeans. Skinny, stonewashed, and fabulous.

It was on my way back to the hotel, however, rushing to be in time for my hairdressing appointment, that I saw it. At the centre of a tiny shop window hung a beautiful silk rug, azure blue, an ivory-white elephant at its centre, its trunk curling high in the air as if to say *Hello*, its brown eyes smiling out at me. A spotlight shone from the ceiling, displaying its colours in all their glory. I could not believe it. I knew exactly where that would go in my house. I would sleep beneath the most beautiful rug I had ever seen. I bought it, no questions asked.

Toni usually does my hair for me. Cathy does it only when I'm in Camden Town. So I sat there for two and a half hours, came out looking like the Norwegian prostitute I'd predicted, and fifteen minutes later was standing beneath a hot shower. Bliss. My hair, however, looked wonderful. Every woman should try it. Fresh, clean highlights are a tonic for the soul. More importantly, they take ten years off you.

So, armed with my new jeans, my rug and my hairstyle, I made my way to the 17.55 at St Pancras.

*

It was as we were approaching Sheffield two hours later that Sean rang.

I forced myself awake. 'Hi there.'

'Hiya. How was London?'

181

'Brill, thanks. Amazing.' I checked my watch. 'I'm still on the train. Is everything alright?'

'Bad news, I'm afraid. Another burglary.'

'Who is it this time?'

'Not just a burglary this time, April. Manslaughter, murder - one of them. A rich old lady on her own, she fell down the stairs chasing him. The cleaner found her, unconscious, this morning. DI Forbes has just rung, and she died in hospital this afternoon. The entire village is in shock.'

I went cold, slippery, limp. 'Oh. God.'

'I know.'

'Oh.'

'A heart attack, it was.'

'Is it anyone I know?'

'Lady Barnstaple, the widow of Lord Barnstaple. She moved to Millerstone about ten years ago.'

'I've heard the name. But how awful.'

'DI Forbes says there's been a spate of thefts since Dr Jani's, but she knew I had a lot on. They've even taken purses from the nursing home staffroom, of all places, then went and lifted money from one of their accounts. Someone had their PIN number written down.'

'No.'

'There has also been some very expensive jewellery taken from people's homes. You know those apartments near the station? You can't get through the door without a key-code, but they've managed it. How they got in is anyone's guess.'

'Houdini.'

'The DI's wondering if it's someone medical – you know, a chiropodist or a masseur or something. They'd have access to the nursing home, although the old folks in the apartments say they never give anyone their codes.'

'You don't know though, do you? They might not like to say, might be embarrassed.'

'That's true.'

'This chap certainly knows what he's doing, doesn't he?'

'It does sound like it. Look, April, can you get down there first thing tomorrow – Lady Barnstaple's, I mean? Do you know where it is?'

12

Millerstone, Derbyshire

LADY Barnstaple lived next to the cricket ground, just before the path leading to the Parish Church. The property dates from the 18th century, stone with mullioned windows and a neat front garden. Once inside, however, I found it had been modernised into an open-plan family home. Probably much smaller than Lady Barnstaple had been used to, but big enough, I suppose.

Sean and I had to squeeze past five police cars parked along the narrow rutted path to the gate, only to find reams of black and yellow tape cutting us off from the garden. Awful stuff it is, signalling to the world the depth of horror inside its sticky web.

I was wearing a pale lemon tunic over white Capri trousers that day, and we were given white plastic overalls to wear. So I must have looked like a banana wrapped in cling-film. Although I didn't find it a bit funny at the time. A uniformed cop at the door ticked our names off a list while we donned hoods, overshoes and gloves. The carpet was also covered with protective sheeting, and I noticed a smell about the place, fusty and damp, as if the windows had been left open for weeks. Gingerly, we walked through the hallway, a wide angular room with a staircase and open-plan lounge leading off.

My stomach churned suddenly and I felt sick. I'd never, ever visited a murder scene before. Yes, I've written about them, described them to the nth degree. But I'd never really seen one in the flesh, except on films.

DI Forbes appeared, greeting us with a sad smile. Her presence made me feel a little better, and I swallowed hard to get rid of the nausea. She led us into the kitchen, past bright red triangular markers that showed where Lady Barnstaple had fallen. Rob, the fingerprint man, was already there, dusting the windowsill.

'Thanks for coming,' she said. 'I know it's not a pretty scene, but we thought it might be useful for you to get an idea of any clues before they're dismissed.'

'That's okay,' Sean replied. 'It's good to get a feel for these things, the point of entry, et cetera, et cetera.'

But I was staring at DI Forbes. She seemed to have aged suddenly. Her face had lost its pertness, its youth. Overnight, it seemed. What a job. I reckoned she was blaming herself for not having solved the earlier cases, before someone was killed. I truly felt for her. I wouldn't have wanted her job for all the tea in China.

'We have a suspect,' she informed us, handing Sean some notes. 'This is all we know at present. He came to collect Lady Barnstaple's Audi last week for a service.'

He scanned the page. 'Tobias Wilkinson. Any prints yet?'

Rob shook his head. 'Bloody gloves. Who invented them?'

'Do we know what happened - how she fell?' I asked.

Rob led us back to the hallway. 'Here, at the bottom of the stairs, there's a bit of loose carpeting – there, look.' He pointed to the third step up, to the rich green Axminster, worn and fraying at the edges. 'I'll give the girl her due. She had some guts, scaring him off like that.'

DI Forbes sighed heavily. 'Our one bloody witness. And she bloody well goes and dies on us.'

'Did she recover consciousness? Was anyone able to talk to her?' I asked.

'She knocked her head as she fell, was unconscious when the cleaner found her. But it must all have been too much for her – the poor old thing suffered a heart attack.'

'Where was the point of entry?' asked Sean, pulling out his notepad. 'And did he get away with anything, do we know?'

'Through the rear window, just behind the dining table,' replied Rob. 'Just broke the glass and undid the lock. He must have made some noise, though, because she came looking for him. And no, we don't know whether he got away with anything. There doesn't appear to be anything missing at the moment - we need to check with relatives. But note - this is the first house burglary where the property's been occupied.'

'Right,' said Sean, scribbling away.

'We've contacted the only next of kin, a daughter living in Oxfordshire. She drove up last night and is staying at the Ashbourne. Apparently, her mother was supposed to be visiting them by train this week, but she was unwell, so cancelled.'

'So he knew she was going to be away, or thought she was,' muttered Sean.

DI Forbes grinned through her fatigue. 'My, you're quick, Mr McGavin. How he knew, though, is anyone's guess. Unless …'

I chipped in, my mind having worked its way through every possible scenario. 'She told the car chap when he came to collect her car.'

'Well done, April,' she smiled. 'Which reminds me – you left me a message last Thursday. Sorry I didn't get back. Too much going on.'

'I was just a bit concerned about my mum's next door neighbour, that's all.'

'Oh?'

'She lives in Totley. It's a nice area and everything, but this house doesn't appear lived in, and I know it sounds a bit – now I don't want you to think I'm doing your job or anything, but it's just – I think they may be growing cannabis.'

She nodded calmly. 'Weed? Really? Well, it wouldn't surprise me.'

Sean was the one who looked surprised. 'Well, well, well. April Hutton. We'll make an Inspector Morse of you yet.'

But DI Forbes was taking this seriously. 'What's your mum's address?'

I told her, and she entered it into her phone.

'So what makes you think they're growing weed?'

'Blacked-out windows. Not much sign of life, although they could have been at work. Two guys living there, according to Mum. But there was this really sickly smell coming through the letterbox.'

'My, you have been doing your research,' she said, grinning.

'You went up to the house?' asked Sean, incredulous.

'Obviously I made sure there was no-one around first.'

'And you didn't say anything?' he said.

'I didn't see the point in making a fuss. I might be totally and utterly wrong.'

'I'll get a team out there,' said DI Forbes. 'Thanks, April.'

I nodded. 'Just thought you should know.'

'Well done. Maybe I ought to call out, get a story,' said Sean.

'Once we've checked it out. Then I'll ring you, promise,' she replied.

'Brill. Thanks,' he smiled, winking at me.

*

The Ashbourne is five hundred years old, traditionally a coaching inn, famous for having been visited by Charlotte Bronte, but now a beautifully relaxing hotel, the food excellent and the service first class. I met the owner once; a tall hippy type with greying hair and a skinny body. Having worked in London's Dorchester Hotel throughout the Swinging Sixties, he'd brought his many talents to the Ashbourne. And it showed.

189

It was still early, about ten o'clock, so the hotel lounge, made up of long sofas and tall armchairs, was nearly empty as Sean and I walked in. I could smell food cooking, but my stomach wasn't quite up to the thought of eating. We had a job to do, and it wasn't going to be pleasant.

Kate Reed, Lady Barnstaple's daughter, stood up to greet us. Tall and slim, with an impeccable taste in clothes, she looked exhausted, her eyes small and red, her face gaunt.

We shook hands, expressed our sorrow for her loss, and sat down to the tea and scones she'd already ordered.

'There's not much I can tell you, I'm afraid. I don't see much of Mum. I run my own business, you see.' Her eyes filled with sudden tears, but she blinked them back stoically. 'Sorry - it's been a bit of a shock. She was supposed to be coming to visit us, to see the children. They're home from university. It's not often she can get to see them ...'

Unable to continue, she merely sat there, shaking her head, tears grazing her cheeks like sharp slivers of ice.

I patted her arm. 'It's okay, Mrs Reed. Take your time.'

Sean pulled out his notebook and pen. 'As I said on the phone, Mrs Reed ...'

'Call me Kate, please,' she gulped.

'Kate – as I said on the phone, I'm Senior Crime Reporter for the local newspaper, but I'm also helping investigate the recent burglaries we've had in this area.'

Pulling a tissue from her bag, she looked round in bewilderment. 'What? Here?'

Sean nodded mournfully.

'But we thought it was such a nice place – beautiful, in fact. Mum only moved here after Dad died.'

'It is a nice place. Usually,' I insisted. 'But people take advantage, don't they? Someone …'

'She should have stayed where she was!' she exploded. 'I said, stay where your friends are, where you know people. But no, she wouldn't listen. She's always loved the Peak District, and now look what's happened.'

'I'm dreadfully sorry,' I replied. I knew how she felt. My mum was just as obstinate, just as selfish. 'But she did make many friends while she was here. Millerstone is a very friendly place, lots of clubs, societies …'

Sean interrupted. 'I'm sure your mum was very happy living here. But I just need to know if there was anyone she was acquainted with, someone who might have taken advantage, who might have known she was going away.'

She looked confused. 'But she wasn't away, was she?'

'No, but they might have thought she was. You see, it's the first time they've burgled a place when someone's been at home.'

'She only delayed coming down because she was ill, a tummy bug, a stupid bloody tummy bug.' Gritting her teeth, her anger and sorrow sat side by side, and her chest heaved with the enormity of it all.

I spoke quietly. 'Kate, we're trying to trace your mother's killer before it's too late, before the trail goes cold. Is there anyone who might have befriended her, someone who seemed inappropriate at the time? Can you think of anyone?'

She shook her head. 'No. Sorry. No-one.'

'So who was she friends with, who did she meet up for coffee with?'

'She has quite a few friends, really. She loves to paint, attending one workshop after another, always on the phone to someone. She'd be out with her camera first thing in the morning.' Pausing, sniffing, trying to take control, she wiped her eyes.

'If it's the local art group, I'll contact them, get some names and addresses,' I volunteered.

'Okay,' replied Sean. 'Thanks.'

Finishing our tea and scones amidst polite conversation, we realised there was nothing more to be said, so bade our farewells and left Kate Reed to make her arrangements.

The Ashbourne was still empty, quiet, subdued, as we made our way through the lounge to the fresh air outside. Maybe our mood was contagious. Maybe word of Lady Barnstaple had crept its way through the door already.

*

Leaving Sean to drive home, I was looking forward to meeting up with Mum and Josie. Today was the day we'd scheduled for our pub lunch, and I thought it might remove the horror of the morning from my mind. But as I walked through the door, there was a message on the answerphone.

It was Mum. She was cancelling, hadn't slept well, wasn't up to it, and would rearrange another time. Immediately, I texted Jo in case Mum hadn't told her, then rang Mum's surgery. With a sigh of relief, I accepted the first appointment they offered me - four o'clock. The only thing I then had to do was persuade her to go.

I rang the Arts Society, as promised, to find out more about Lady Barnstaple. But there was no reply, so I left a message, jumped in the car, and drove straight over to Mum's. There was work I could have done, research for my new novel, and I hadn't found one minute for hanging up my new rug, but in London I'd promised myself to take more care of her.

So I was. Anyway, I didn't want her ending up like that old spinster I'd met. I loved her way too much for that.

Also, I wanted to surprise her, to see exactly how she was when she wasn't expecting visitors. So, even though I did expect the house to be a mess, I was still in for a shock.

The first thing I noticed was the curtains. Still drawn across on such a beautifully sunny day. Pushing open the front door (unlocked) I walked straight through to the sitting room and drew them back. Lottie, asleep in her basket, woke up as I did so.

'Hi, Lottie,' I said, stroking her fur and patting her head. 'How are you?'

Licking my hand enthusiastically, she hopped out of the basket to follow me. I'd guessed Mum was in the kitchen, so waltzed through, expecting her to be making lunch. But no, she'd pulled a dining chair through and was just sitting there, still in her nightie, staring at the washing machine. I could have understood it if there'd been clothes spinning around, because that can be quite hypnotic. But it was completely empty, the door hanging open like an unwashed mouth.

'Hi, Mum.'

She turned as I walked in. Her face was pale, worn, as if she hadn't slept in months. Shocked and distressed, I swallowed hard, hiding my fear, my awful, unwanted thoughts.

'What are you doing here?' she asked. 'I said I didn't want to go walking.'

'Well, that's a nice greeting, I must say.' I kissed her on the forehead. 'I've spent the morning chatting to the police about a burglary, and all that work has made me hungry, so I've decided to come and take my best mum out to lunch. No walking. How about it?'

Suddenly interested in my unexpected arrival, her face lit up. As I knew it would.

'The police? What was it about - your burglary?'

'It was just a theft, Mum, not a burglary.' I placed a finger to my lips. 'But shush, it's all hush-hush. If you go and get washed and dressed, I'll tell you all about it. But only if you can keep a secret.'

*

Mum had fish and chips for lunch, which she utterly and completely devoured. I could tell she hadn't been eating properly. I had an egg salad, with a drizzle of French dressing. I can't remember now what it was called, but it was delicious.

You see, the only way Mum would agree to leave the house was if I took her to her favourite place – a café owned by her old friend Rita. A traditional, red-brick place on the main road going through Totley, not far from the petrol station, it looked like

195

something from the cover of a children's book, the woodwork bright poster green, the door a deep red.

But if you were to meet Rita, you would see she could never have done anything else; she just *had* to run a café. She welcomed, she cajoled, she empathised, her carmine red lipstick a constant smile. What else could she have done with her life? Okay, maybe a nurse or something. In truth, she'd only been running it since her husband died. And that was probably the attraction between Rita and Mum; they'd both lost their husbands quite early in life. I mean, fifty-three is no age at which to find yourself on your own, is it? Rita is African, her parents having come over in the post-war immigration of the Fifties, her mother to nurse, her father to work on the London buses, and she was just the kind of friend Mum needed. Unfortunately, however, she worked full-time, Monday to Saturday.

'So,' Mum murmured, having demolished her meal. 'Tell me about the police, then, about this burglary.'

I smiled happily. She was looking more like her old self - makeup, earrings, nice clothes.

'You probably won't remember Sean McGavin, from school?'

Thoughtfully, she cupped her hands beneath her chin. 'The name rings a bell. Go on, you've met up again, but he's going to prison or something?'

I laughed. Definitely the same old mum.

'No. We have met up again, but he's now a reporter for the Sheffield Star.'

'Is he now?' Her eyes lit up as if to say *now he's the one for my daughter.*

'No, Mum, it's not like that, honestly. We're just good friends.'

'Oh.'

'He's working on a story about the burglaries in Millerstone.'

'Burglaries? More than one?'

'Yes, Mum.'

I didn't say I'd told her this; not remembering it would have upset her.

'What - in Millerstone?'

'Yes.'

'Oh.'

'Anyway, because I live there, he wanted me to help out with some of the interviews. So, basically, we've been helping the police with their enquiries. No more than that.'

'Oh. Right.'

Rita came up to us, a large brown teapot balanced sturdily between both hands.

'Another cuppa, Judy? On the house.'

Mum nodded. 'Mm, please, Rita.'

Chatting away, her bright red lips always moving, Rita poured tea into our cups, walking away with a flourish of her long skirt to see to the next table.

I decided it was time to broach the real reason for my visit. 'Mum?'

'Yes?' She picked up her cup.

'If I tell you something, will you promise not to get mad at me or anything?'

She smiled submissively. 'What is it you've done now?'

'I've booked you in to see Dr Whitby.'

Alarm drenched her face. 'What? What for?'

'Because I'm - we're - me and Jo - we're worried about you.'

Tears filled her eyes. 'You've no right.'

Sympathetically, I took her hand. 'Yes, we have. You're our mum and we love you.'

'But I'm alright, April, I'm fine. I just miss your dad, that's all. I get a bit lonely sometimes.'

'That's just it, Mum, we know all that. We think you might be a bit depressed. Maybe some mild antidepressants ...'

There was no reply. She merely wiped away the tears threatening to ruin her mascara.

'Just for a while, Mum, just to lift your spirits a bit.'

*

Dr Whitby was marvellous.

'I treat the whole patient, Mrs Hutton. Not just the little aches and pains, but what's going on inside the person, up here.' She tapped herself on the head. 'The mind has such an impact on the body's defences, you wouldn't believe.'

Mum smiled her *I'm a professional too* kind of smile. 'I'm aware of that. I'm fine most of the time, it's just that ...'

Dr Whitby pulled an A4 pad from her desk drawer, tearing off a sheet. 'There's a form here, a few tick-boxes for you to complete. It's just to give me an idea of how bad the bad days are.' She passed Mum a pen before returning to her computer screen.

Mum had forgotten her reading glasses, so I read the questions out loud. She ticked the 'yes' or 'no' boxes, one at a time. Her answers didn't surprise me; she was definitely feeling depressed.

Dr Whitby merely glanced at the form. 'Okay, Mrs Hutton, I'm prescribing some Paxil for you, a mild antidepressant. They won't interact with your blood pressure tablets, you might only need them for a few months, but they're highly effective.' Clicking at the keyboard, she printed off a green and white prescription.

Mum looked at me as if to say *how have I come to this?* before painfully accepting it.

*

We called at Tesco's pharmacy on the way back, picking up some food at the same time.

I watched as Mum took her first tablet, sipping at a glass of water in the kitchen, and prayed it would do the trick.

'Cup of tea, Mum?'

Slightly disgruntled by my afternoon's work, she went through to the dining room to sit and open the mail that had arrived. Now, Mum's dining room is usually her pride and joy. An antique water pitcher and bowl, in white china with pink roses, takes centre stage on an oak dresser, taking up nearly the whole of one wall. It's about three metres in length, much longer than the pine one in the kitchen. And there's a refectory table and chairs to match; as shiny as a new conker, that table is. Well, usually. But not now. Now you could hardly see it, piles of magazines, leaflets, letters, littering the surface as if she'd been on holiday for months.

That was the answer, I thought. A holiday.

With this in mind, I made us both a cup of tea and began to tidy up.

'There's no need for that,' moaned Mum. 'I'm quite capable of tidying my own house, you know.'

I paused. 'You're not though, are you, Mum?'

Sorry tears filled her eyes. 'No.'

I put my arm around her. 'This is why we've been to the doctor's, don't you see? Because you *are* capable of doing all this. And you usually do, but you're not doing.'

Tears fell into her cup. 'I know.'

I found myself crying, too. 'Is there anything I can do, Mum? To help, I mean? And what's happened to the new cleaner? Is she still coming?'

'Yes, but she's not Caroline. She's very young, and I can't talk to her.'

'Oh, Mum.'

'And she doesn't know anything about cleaning. She's only doing it for the money – she's got a baby.'

'Do you want me to ring Help the Aged and get someone else?'

'Oh no, I wouldn't want to get her the sack, it wouldn't be fair. Rita's daughter's in the same boat, you know, a single mother with a baby. I don't know - these young things.'

'She wouldn't get the sack though, Mum. They'd just give her another job to do, I'm sure they would.'

She nodded tearfully. 'Okay then, if that's what you think. It would be nice to have Caroline again.'

*

Josie rang to speak to Mum while I was making tea for us. A light omelette, and salad with French dressing, raw garlic rubbed around the bowl's interior. Anything to whet her appetite. Luckily, the eggs were still in the bowl and not cooking when

Josie rang, because all of a sudden I had the most marvellous plan. I rushed into the hall.

'Mum, don't say goodbye yet. I need to talk to her.'

Finishing her conversation, she passed me the phone, walking back into the dining room.

'Hi, Jo.'

'Well done with Mum, April. She's told me what's happened. Do you think they'll do the trick?'

'I hope so. Dr Whitby seems to think that may be the problem, so fingers crossed. But I've been thinking. I think Mum needs a holiday, and I wondered about the three of us going …'

'We're away next week. Majorca.'

'No, no. I mean when it's quieter, maybe in September or something. Outside the school holidays. I thought about asking Colin if we could rent his apartment.'

'What, in Sheffield?'

'No. He's got one in the south of France. St Raphael. It sounds lovely.'

'Ooh. Posh.'

'It probably isn't, it's probably incredibly small. But it's at the seaside, with sunshine and fresh air and lovely food, and French coffee.'

'I'm taking it you want me to come on my own, then? No kids?'

'That's exactly what I want. Mum would have the two of us to talk to, twenty-four seven. We could go just for the week. Do you think Joe would mind, and look after Lottie for us?'

'Mind? As if I care! Sorry, didn't mean it like that. It's just, it would be rather nice to get away, no responsibilities, no making sure the food was on the table and the loo roll was out.'

'My treat,' I added, before she started worrying about the cost. 'And no arguments.'

13

Bakewell, Derbyshire

BAKEWELL police station is a quaint old building, red brick with stone windows. There's a marketplace just across the road, with a special parking area for police cars. Rumour has it the atmosphere inside the station is very friendly, and that many prisoners get to eat fish and chips from the chippie around the corner. But don't quote me on that.

Sean and I had an appointment with DI Forbes at two o'clock.

We'd agreed to meet at half past one, so as not to be late. So to kill time, we wandered slowly through the marketplace. Sean was looking for antiques, but there wasn't much around – just an old lady selling knick-knacks in the sunshine: wine glasses, old lamps, a few ornaments. He did show an interest in a set of champagne saucers, their authentic thumbprint design glinting beautifully in the sunlight. I thought they were rather lovely, reminiscent of bygone times, but Sean resisted. And well, I won't buy anything you can't put inside the tray of a dishwasher. So we walked along amiably, the scent of fish and chips permeating the air around us.

As we turned right, however, I was surprised to find Emilisa Meadows-Whitworth standing there, her stall selling home-made produce for the Women's Institute. And it was a feast for the eyes. Jars of gingham-covered jam, honey, and pasta sauce sat alongside huge trays of oversized cookies, pretty cupcakes, and round loaves of home-baked bread. The long, bleached tablecloth blew in the breeze as I smiled at her.

'Hi, Emilisa.'

She ran a hand through her long dark hair.

'April.'

'I didn't know you were in the WI?'

'Well, we all have to do our bit,' she replied, smiling at Sean behind me.

Smiling guiltily, having never 'done my bit', I introduced him. 'This is Sean, an old friend of mine. We're just shopping for antiques.'

Sean nodded and smiled. 'Hi.'

To ease my guilt, I picked out a jar of heather honey and handed her a five pound note.

'It's okay, keep the change.'

'Thank you,' she replied, pushing it inside her money bag. 'I hope you have a nice day, the two of you.'

We moved to walk away, but my sudden guilt made me turn back. 'Emilisa – this auction thing for the pool?'

'Yes?'

'Is there anything I can do to help – you know, organising prizes and things?'

She looked suddenly tired, depressed; maybe she was taking on too much. 'Thanks, that would be great. Diane's not here today, but I'll let her know you're interested. I'm sure she'll be in touch.'

I smiled. 'Okay. Great. Thanks.'

*

DI Forbes actually worked from the main police station in Sheffield, but had agreed to meet us in Bakewell at my request as it took less time out of my day.

Greeting us warmly, she shook our hands.

'Thanks for coming in.'

I smiled. 'It's fine, not a problem.'

She motioned for us to sit at the table. Sean tried to grin, as if to say *what a laugh, being summoned to the police station*. But his blue eyes were deadly serious.

'I'm arranging coffee,' she continued. 'It's going to be a long afternoon. You alright with coffee?'

I nodded. 'Thank you.'

'I hope you don't mind my taking up your valuable time like this. I realise you're a very busy lady.'

She sat across from us, the wooden table sparse, apart from her Ipad and a thick manila folder in dark orange. The room itself smelt of hospitals, disinfectant wrapped around soap.

'No, it's okay. Who knows, I may even be able to use all this in one of my novels?'

'Discretion being the better part of valour,' she murmured.

'Of course.'

A young woman entered, bringing a tray of coffee from the machine, tubes of sugar, stirrers and packets of oat biscuits.

DI Forbes sipped her own coffee daintily. 'Now April, I understand you have a list of names and addresses for me.'

'Yes,' I nodded. 'All members of the Arts Society. Sean and I can arrange to interview them, but it might be an idea for you to look into their backgrounds first. What do you think?'

'Thanks. That's very useful.' She took the details from me, typed onto a piece of paper. 'But, as I said yesterday, we may already have a suspect.'

Obviously referring to a discussion with Sean, she looked across to him, and he nodded.

'We've been watching him for a while,' she continued, 'and we've had him in for questioning, but there's nothing on him. No evidence, not even circumstantial. Always an alibi.'

Sean interrupted. 'The thing is - we're pretty sure he's the culprit, but …'

I jumped ahead. 'Do I know him or something? Is it still this chap at Millerstone Garage?'

'It is,' she replied. 'He's a young lad, age twenty-three. Tobias Wilkinson, Toby for short. His father owns the garage. Slim, dark, fairly good-looking, has a girlfriend in the village. Likes throwing his cash around.' She looked at me questioningly.

I shook my head. 'No , I don't know him. I may have seen him around, though. I take my Mini there for servicing.'

'He's a mechanic. Will probably take over the business once his father's retired.'

Sean sipped his coffee. 'The DI wondered whether we could call on your services, April. I mean, I don't know whether you ever interview people to get ideas for characters. I know some authors do.'

I was stunned at first, not quite sure of where I stood. 'You want me to interview him for a book?'

'Yes,' replied DI Forbes.

I thought about it, about how I'd approach an interview, what I'd have to say, how it would be received. And then I began to warm to the idea. I must admit, I was beginning to find the whole thing rather intriguing. Although I didn't see how it would do any good. And I didn't see why they thought it was him. I decided they were clutching at straws. Narrow straws.

'Just because someone splashes his cash around doesn't mean he's a thief,' I said. 'I mean, his dad's probably rolling in it.'

'It's not just that. He's been done for drugs – for carrying,' replied DI Forbes.

I shrugged dismissively. 'Oh well, that makes him a thief then.'

'And his father's not the most honest when it comes to selling cars,' she insisted.

'The police just have a feeling about this one,' Sean said. 'But if you're not sure about it ...'

'No,' I said. 'It's okay. I'll do it. Do you want me to arrange it all?'

'That would be best,' she said.

'What do you want me to find out, exactly?'

'We need general characteristics, what kind of person he really is when he's not being questioned by police. He comes across as pretty arsey most of the time. Here, we've made a list of details,' she said, opening the folder and passing me a sheet of lined A4.

It gave Toby's name, address, date of birth and occupation. It also provided details of his girlfriend, a Rachel Brunwin, with whom he'd had a baby the previous year. Now her address interested me - she lived just after the bend on Jaggers Lane. Alarm bells began to ring.

I turned to Sean. 'You know, I think I may have seen him. You know that night I babysat for Toni, when you went to the theatre?'

'Yes?'

'I mean, I may be wrong – it's just a feeling. But I saw this chap hanging around, behind the post office. And then, on the way home, I heard someone following me.'

'When you ran back to Toni's?'

'Yes.

He nodded. 'She told me.'

'I suppose it might *not* be him,' I decided.

DI Forbes studied me carefully. 'If you'd rather not do this, April ...'

'No. I'm fine. Honestly. What harm can it do?'

'Okay, if you're sure.'

'I'm sure.'

'That house near your mum's, by the way, we've got plain clothes going out there this afternoon.'

'Good, that's great. Let me know what happens?'

'Of course we will. Now then, we need to get down to business. Firstly, there's a list here of all the incidents so far, times, dates, modus operandi, and so on.'

*

We sauntered back through the sunshine. The market stalls were being packed away, the stall-holders chitchatting to one another, laughing and joking and calling out as we passed. Just then, however, one particular stall caught my eye. It had beautiful bone china. Intrigued, I pulled at Sean's arm and wandered across. I picked up a small white plate. Its delicate blue flowers, as faded as a whisper, looked as if they had been drawn on. I'd never seen anything like it.

'What do you think?' I said Sean.

'Very pretty. But it's up to you – it's your house.'

I shook my head. 'It's for Toni. To help replace the stuff that was smashed.'

'That's a kind thought.'

I grinned. 'I'm full of them.'

'You think she'll like it?'

'She'll love it. It's just her.'

'Okay.'

'Besides, it's a present from me,' I grinned.

'I'll help carry.'

'Is it dishwasher-proof?' I asked the stallholder, a woman wrapped in numerous jumpers, three scarves and a pair of woollen gloves, despite the sunny August day.

She peered at me in disdain. 'It's real bone china, that. Ex Fortnum and Mason's, it is.'

And the price reflected it. But I was happy. It really was beautiful. I bought six of everything – cups and saucers, mugs, tea plates, dinner plates, soup plates, cereal bowls, and the teapot, sugar bowl and milk jug.

'Do you think she'll have enough there?' asked Sean, dryly.

I laughed. 'I love it.'

*

I called in at Rita's again on the way home. The café was closed, but I knew she lived in the flat above, so rang the bell, praying she was home.

Instead, an attractive thirty-something opened the door. 'Yes?'

The bright red lips gave the game away. So Rita's daughter wasn't such a 'young thing' after all.

'Rita's daughter?' I asked.

'Yes?' She looked at me quizzically.

I offered my hand. 'Hi. I'm April, Judy Hutton's daughter. She's a friend of Rita's.'

'She's just making tea. Come on in.'

The flat I walked into wasn't quite what I'd been expecting. The exterior of the building was old, dirty red brick, and the café itself traditional, slightly worn, with the familiar glass cabinet of cakes, small round tables, and faded pictures upon the wall. The flat, however, was modern, clean, one big room with doors leading off to bedrooms and bathrooms. A black wrought-iron spiral staircase led upwards to yet another room. The main room contained a white leather sofa, white dining chairs and an open-plan kitchen with white units, a washing machine and a fridge. Everything else was teak. There were a few toys on the cream carpet and knick-knacks on the mantelpiece, but other than that you'd have thought they'd been expecting me. Rita was obviously very houseproud; the place was immaculate.

Rita, who'd been washing up at the sink, turned, frowning, concern etched into her eyes.

'Hullo. April, isn't it? Is your mum okay?'

I smiled. 'She's fine. I just – I'm sorry to barge in like this.'

'It's no problem. She's very proud of you, your mum is.'

'Thank you.'

Drying her hands on a towel, she waved me in. 'Come on, come in, we're just about to have something to eat. Would you like to join us?'

I was embarrassed. What had I been thinking of, arriving at this time? Of course they'd be eating their tea; Rita wouldn't have been able to shut the café until half past five. But suddenly a small girl ran down the staircase, taking our attention. She was adoringly beautiful, with dark, golden skin and huge brown eyes, and a doll tucked under one arm.

'Teru!' her mother chided. 'Do not run down those stairs. How many times?'

'Three hundred,' she replied cheekily, giggling and running into her mother's arms.

She really was adorable. I couldn't help but laugh.

Rita motioned for me to sit down. 'Forgive my grandchild. She is very cheeky to her mother. Now, would you like some tea with us?'

I shook my head. 'No, it's very kind of you, but I've just eaten, thank you.'

'A cup of tea, then?'

'That would be lovely. I won't be long. I just wondered whether you could help me out.'

'Of course. I'm just steaming the couscous, so no need to rush.' Filling the kettle, she made tea, chatting continuously. 'Teru here is three years old. She is very beautiful, but very impudent sometimes. Her mother is Sofia, also very beautiful. She became a wonderful photographic model, then got herself into trouble. So she had to give it all up.'

Sofia smiled at me. 'She was worth it, though.'

Teru was now hiding behind the sofa.

'I have to agree,' I replied. 'She's beautiful.'

Rita handed me a mug of milky tea. 'So, what is it I can do for you?'

'Well, I – I just wondered whether you happened to know of anyone in the area who does cleaning, and maybe a bit of ironing? It's just – Mum has someone

214

from Help the Aged to help out, but she could really do with someone older, more mature, someone she can talk to, who will chat to her, keep her company for a while. And I just thought you might know of someone who lives locally.'

Teru crawled from behind the sofa on her hands and knees, a cheeky expression on her face.

'Mummy likes cleaning. Mummy's always cleaning.'

*

Toni was in the dining room, on the phone to her mum, when I reached the house. It was Jack who let me in.

I waved to her from the hallway. Beckoning me in, she finished her call.

'Hi, April. How are you?'

'Fine, thanks. But I'm just on my way home, so I won't keep you.'

'Okay. You don't fancy a cuppa or anything?'

'No - thank you. I'm fine.'

She tipped her head quizzically as if to say, *why are you here then?*

'I've brought you a present. I hope you like it.'

She smiled. 'What is it?'

'It's in the car. I've managed to park just outside. Could you help me carry it in, please?'

'What is it, April? I hope you've not spent money.'

215

I was leading her out, through the kitchen door, beneath the weeping willow, and round to the gate.

'I just thought I'd help out a bit, that's all.'

Opening the car-boot, I lifted the lid of the box nearest to me and prayed she would like it.

'Oh, I love it,' she screamed, jumping up and down and throwing her arms around me. 'April, it's beautiful. Thank you.'

She turned to pick out one of the dinner plates, holding it carefully with both hands. 'It must have cost a fortune. You really shouldn't have, but I love it.'

*

I arrived home to find Emilisa had posted a script through my door, asking me to play the part of Miss Forsyth, a middle-aged spinster. No typecasting there, then.

I spent some time hanging my new rug above the bed. My bedroom was quite a simple affair. Pine king-sized bed with white cotton sheets, a chest of drawers, a large wardrobe and a cheval mirror, all to match. The walls were papered in Laura Ashley, pale ivory with a lovely sheen that caught the light. So the rug looked amazing, with the azure blue set against the ivory and the wise old elephant smiling down on me.

Happy with my day's work, I rang Mum.

'I was just sitting down with a nice cup of tea,' she complained. 'Dashing all over the place makes me so tired.'

'Why, what have you been doing?'

'You. Dragging me all over the place.'

Slightly alarmed, I said, 'But Mum, that was yesterday.'

'I know that, April. I'm not stupid, you know. It's just, it takes me a few days to recover, that's all.'

'Oh. Well, that's alright then,' I sighed, relieved.

'Anyway, I was just going to watch my programme.'

And there I was, worrying about her being all on her own.

'I won't keep you long. I just wanted to let you know about Rita. I called round to see her today.'

'Oh. What for?'

'Just to see if she knew of any cleaners in the area. Sofia's offered to come and clean for you. Would that be okay, Mum?'

'But what about Caroline? And what about the young girl they've been sending? Won't she lose her job?'

'No, Mum. Caroline will be working at someone else's house by now. And they'll give the young girl other work to do. No-one will lose their job. I'll ring Help the Aged in the morning and let them know you've found another cleaner. I'll just say Sofia's a friend, which is kind of the truth, isn't it?'

There was a long pause while she thought about it, and while I panicked.

'Okay,' she mumbled. 'When's she coming, then?'

14

I'D arranged to meet Toby Wilkinson, the suspect, that Friday, at eleven o'clock. I had wanted to meet up at the Flying Toad. A nice, relaxed atmosphere, I thought, on neutral territory. But he didn't want anyone to see us. People talk, he said, questions would be asked, and two and two becomes six.

He was definitely the young man I'd seen outside the post office, and possibly the one I'd seen standing beside the seat on Coggers Lane. But by the end of my interview, I didn't think he was the thief.

He appeared a personable young chap, and I could see how he'd earned his reputation as *a bit of a lad*. We met at his home, a modern stone-clad house next door to the motor repair shop. His mother greeted me, beaming as she showed me into the sitting room.

'Come on in, Miss Stanislavski. It's nice to see you again. Would you like a cup of tea or anything?'

Sarah Wilkinson was in her late forties or early fifties; I could never really tell because of the clothes she wore. Today, she was shrouded in a grey cardigan, black woollen skirt and thick stockings. Admittedly, the house was cold, despite the weak sunshine outside, so maybe there was justification for her warm clothing. But I always felt a little sorry for her. Whenever I took my car in, she was always very chatty, handing me my bill, taking my money; a kind gentle woman. But she never ever wore makeup or jewellery, apart from a plain wedding ring.

'Tea would be lovely, thank you,' I replied, walking into the room.

Toby was already seated, his legs stretched out, his back a careless C shape on the sofa. I sat down onto the other sofa, set into the bay window. Both sofas were blood-red to match the curtains, the cushions lumpy and worn. The room itself was clean, and would have been expensive to furnish in its time, but there was an *I really can't be bothered* look about it, like a beautiful ball-gown that's seen better days. Not quite in keeping with the black two-year-old Jaguar XJ6 I'd seen parked on the drive.

'Hi, Toby,' I smiled. 'Thanks for agreeing to meet up with me.'

Sitting up a little, he crossed one leg over the other. I took notice of the size of his feet. Quite small, maybe a seven or an eight.

'It's okay,' he replied. 'Mum, like, reads all your books.'

'Brilliant,' I smiled. 'That's what I like to hear.'

He grinned good-naturedly. 'So – what is it you're wanting?'

Pulling a pen and writing pad from my handbag, I studied my notes carefully.

'I'm writing about a young man in his early twenties, plenty of money ...'

He smiled again at that, which was the intention.

'He's just left his job and is going out into the big wide world,' I continued. 'I want to know what kind of thing he'd like to do with his life, what kind of person he is, what turns him on. You know the kind of thing.'

Mrs Wilkinson arrived then, with tea and a plate of chocolate biscuits.

'Here you go, Miss Stanislavski.'

'April – please.'

She blushed, her eyes shining with admiration. She would have looked quite pretty with the right clothes and makeup. Placing the tray onto the small, dark coffee table, she turned and left.

'Thank you,' I called.

Toby picked up a biscuit, biting into it carefully. 'So, you want to know what makes, like, a twenty-three year old man tick?'

'Yes.'

'Okay.' His brown eyes gleamed, obviously seeing this as a challenge. 'Well, if I'd just packed in my job, what I'd do is I'd go around the world, travel, like.'

'Okay.' I scribbled. 'If we're speaking realistically, though, how would you earn your money?'

He studied the remainder of his biscuit carefully. 'You said I'd have plenty of money.'

'What I meant was - his parents, his family, would have money. Obviously he's expected to earn his own if he's going to travel.'

'Okay.'

I waited patiently, studying him, analysing, surveying. He seemed a bit full of himself, but then I assumed kids (I did think of him as a kid, still living at home with his parents) his age probably were, on the whole. Life hadn't knocked them back yet.

He finished his biscuit. 'Well, I suppose I'd like, make sure I didn't get my girl pregnant.'

I took notes. 'Yes?'

'I'd try and make loads of money, as quickly as possible, so I didn't miss out on anything.'

'How do you mean, miss out on anything?'

222

'Well, I'd try and fit everything in before I got too old, before I had to settle down with a wife and all that.'

'Okay.' I looked up. 'Is that why you're not living with the mother of your baby? So you can have a good time before you're too old?'

His face turned scarlet. 'What? You've got a fucking nerve …'

Actually, I thought – he's right.

'Sorry, Toby, that's really none of my business. I do apologise.' I sighed deeply, allowing time, trying to diffuse the situation. 'But it can't be easy for her, can it - being a single mother, living with her parents, having them support her? And you must still love her, or else you wouldn't go and see her.'

'How do you know that?'

'What, that you go and see her?'

'Yeah.' He was studying me carefully.

'Wasn't that you waiting outside the post office three weeks ago? Staring at the window of the house behind it, with me at the window?'

Looking away, he smiled. 'Sorry.'

'Why, Toby?'

'I was waiting for Rachel. She was coming to stay here after getting off the bus – she'd been out with some friends. But then she texted to say she was staying out. And I recognised you, thought it would be funny to follow you,' he smirked.

'And was it? Was it funny?'

He shook his head slowly. 'No. Not really.'

'Well, at least we agree on something.'

'Is that why you're here? Because of that?'

'No, it isn't. But now I am here, I do think you need talking to. A good-looking young man like you, leaving a girl to take care of his baby while he splashes the cash on the good life?'

He blushed. So he has some sense of decency, I thought.

'Are you going to do this fucking interview thing or not?'

I nodded. 'Sorry.' I sipped my tea, watching him over the rim of the cup.

'Go on, then. Interview me.'

'Okay. So, your family has money, but you need to make your own, and within a short space of time. How would you do it?'

He shrugged. 'I don't know. Maybe, like, buy cars, and sell them on?'

'What, in this day and age? It will have taken your dad years to get this business going.'

'You asked what I'd do, so I'm telling you.'

'Okay. Sorry. I'm just playing Devil's Advocate here, trying to be realistic.'

'Yeah. Right.'

'No, really. I need to create a character who's believable. You ask your mum. She wouldn't want to be reading about someone who's made up, who's not for real, would she?'

He shook his head. 'No.'

'For instance, imagine this person wanted to see the world while he was still young, but didn't have enough money, and couldn't sell cars. Say he had no scruples, say he was dishonest, what could he do in order to earn it?'

'Steal it?'

He was looking straight at me, hadn't flinched a bit. I nodded thoughtfully.

'Could do. Anything else?'

'Set up in business on Ebay?'

I wrote my notes. 'Yes?'

'Sell drugs, I suppose. If he was, like, that kind of person.'

He wasn't looking straight at me now.

'Do you know people who do that, Toby?'

Outraged, he stood up, knocking his knee on the edge of the coffee table.

'Is that what all this is about? I'm not fucking thick, you know. I knew there was something going on.'

'No! No, Toby, it's not that. It's just …'

But he'd already stormed out.

*

I spent the afternoon researching for my next book, the two-parter, the historical romance I'd discussed with Sandy. But, even though I wasted precious time googling *Bartholomew Ashington* and *Edge Green School*, there was little information online. The local library would have to do. But I was able to google the history of the period, the clothing, the lifestyle, the social classes, and so on.

Bartholomew was to be a wealthy landowner who would buy land for the people of the village, arrange for a school to be built on it, and name it Edge Green School. It would consist of a schoolroom with two small rooms at one end. There'd be plenty of land left over for the children to play on, fencing, and a big green gate. I wanted him to fall in love with the first schoolmistress he interviewed. He would already be married, however, so their love would have to be clandestine, needy, ultimately flawed. I hadn't yet worked out how it would end. These things tend to have minds of their own, anyway.

*

It was the middle of August, but you'd never have thought it. The weather that evening was cold, with violent rain crashing against the windows and a screeching wind fighting for space in the sky. Low-flying plastic bags and scraps of paper scudded along the ground, hurling themselves through the air to become caught in the branches of the nearest tree. There was the occasional roar of thunder, but thankfully no lightning. An umbrella was impossible, so I pulled a waterproof jacket over my

226

woollen hoodie and brand new jeans. Placing my script safely inside a carrier bag, I made my way to the Flying Toad.

George welcomed me in. 'How ya doing? You heard about the death yet? Lady Barnstaple?'

I nodded grimly. 'I have.'

'Who'd have believed it? In a place like this? Guinness?' He pulled out a glass in anticipation.

'Thanks, George. I'm off to the back room.'

'Yep. They're waiting for you.'

I watched as Guinness poured smoothly from the tap, dark and luxurious. Then I had a sudden thought.

'George …'

'Yes?' He placed my drink onto the bar with a flourish.

Lowering my voice, I leaned towards him. 'Working here - you know everything about everything, don't you?'

'I suppose you could say that. But if you're thinking what I think you're thinking – no, I don't know who the bloody killer is.' He held out his hand. 'Two eighty-five, please.'

I fished inside my purse, handing him a five pound note.

'And if I did, I'd have said something, wouldn't I?' He gave me my change.

'I know, George, I know.'

I wandered through to the back room, to the loud murmur of people around the table gossiping, cajoling, laughing.

Alfie hugged me before I even had chance to sit down.

'April – darling. What awfully horrendous weather.'

Alfie had that easy-to-read kind of face. Probably why he became an actor. So today I knew something was not quite right, even before I'd asked the words.

'How are you, Alfie?'

'Dreadful, darling. Just dreadful. Emilisa's pulled out of the production. Can you believe? She rang me last night. Didn't have the decency to call at the house, just said she'd changed her mind. It's her mother – she's very ill, you know. And Emilisa has to go and look after her. But she's been ill for ages, so she should've thought about that before volunteering, shouldn't she?'

Stunned, I sat down. I'd always thought Emilisa liked being in the limelight, was looking forward to bossing everyone about.

'I'm really sorry about that, Alfie.'

He shook his head sadly, looking a little like Mr Toad when he's been arrested for driving too fast. 'Out of the blue, it was.'

'So what's happening, Alfie? Are we still going ahead or what?'

He patted my hand gently. 'But of course, of course. The show shall go on. I shall be directing. But a bit of new blood in the arena would have been good, don't you think?'

I nodded, secretly relieved. 'But I love having you direct, Alfie, you know that.'

'I love you, too, my darling.'

Wasting no more time, he stood up and clapped his hands for attention. I smiled. Life was back to normal.

'Ladies and gentlemen, welcome, welcome,' he began.

The hush was immediate.

'Now, as you may or may not have heard, Emilisa has decided not to go ahead with directing our new play. Her mother is ill, and even though she was really looking forward to joining us again, she's realised she just doesn't have the time. We shall obviously miss her, but, as they say in the best of circles, the show must go on.'

Frowning prettily, Gemma brushed back the damp hair from her face. 'So what happens to the play? Are you doing it, Alfie?'

Alfie bowed his head dramatically. 'I am.'

There was a surge of applause from the entire table. Maybe no-one liked Emilisa Meadows-Whitworth.

'Thank you, my darlings. You are too, too kind. But I know you shall all do this play the justice it deserves, so my role will be a pleasure, even an honour. Now then, to begin with, may I introduce you to Mrs Diane Downing of the Women's Institute?

He waved towards an elderly woman in a navy blouse, seated at the other end of the table. I'd noticed her as I walked in, talking quietly to Laura.

'Diane just wants to discuss the details of the Grand Auction for ten minutes or so, and then we shall begin our rehearsal. Please make her very welcome – she is such a sweetheart.'

And he wasn't exaggerating; Diane Downing *was* a sweetheart. She told us how she spent her time supporting various charities, both local and national. The swimming pool was obviously the one closest to her heart; she swam there every morning, come rain or shine. Many retirees in the village did the same. You could see them, driving along in their dressing gowns, taking their morning swim before driving home for breakfast. It was therefore really important we helped keep the pool open; the health of the entire village depended upon it.

Diane took us through the plan she had in mind. She and her team would contact local companies for donations. These could be as small as a basket of fruit from the greengrocers, or as large as a pine chest from Rick Jenkins, the joiner. The Grand Auction had a ready audience after the play, but other people could be admitted for a small fee. The players would remain in costume, serving drinks and canapés to the punters.

I thought it a wonderful idea.

'How much are we hoping to raise?' I asked.

'Over two thousand, we hope. That's including ticket sales from the play.'

I nodded approvingly. 'Great. And who's to be the auctioneer, do we know?'

'We're thinking about asking a local dignitary of some kind.'

Laura looked up tearfully from her sewing.. 'There would have been Lady Barnstaple.'

'I know. Very sad,' replied Diane. 'I suppose we really need someone who's used to public speaking, someone who can hold an audience.'

'Alfie,' shouted Gemma.

Diane looked across to Alfie. 'That would be lovely, and very appropriate, but Alfie will probably have had enough once the play's run for a week.'

Alfie raised his hand in mock salute. 'If you have difficulty finding someone …'

Ginnie Thomson, a twenty-something with short red hair and denim dungarees, piped up. 'There's always Jim Allsop. He'd be good at that kind of thing.'

Jim Allsop, the ageing songwriter who paid Josie to do his gardening. He liked his privacy too much, so I wasn't sure he'd want to do something like this.

But Diane was smiling. 'That's a very good idea, Ginnie. I'll give him a ring. Thank you.'

Alfie stood up then, clapping his hands once more. He hated having to shout to gain our attention, said it ruined his voice.

'Thank you so much, Diane. You really are a sweetheart. If you need help with anything, anything at all, my darling, you just ask. Okay?'

She nodded, picking up her bag. 'Thank you, everyone. I'll be getting home, then.'

'No, no, you're welcome to stay,' replied Alfie.

'It's not really my thing. And I'm sure you'll all want to be getting on.'

I held up my hand. 'Diane, I'd like to get involved in helping collect prizes and stuff. You know, around the village. If that's alright?'

She beamed. 'Thanks, that'd be brilliant. If you give me your number, I'll be in touch.'

Scribbling it down on a scrap of card, I handed it to her.

15

SATURDAY morning. The rain had stopped and the sun was out. Mist was rising from the hills, settling in the valley like clouds of cotton wool. So there was a definite sparkle in the air as I opened the door to Colin at eight o'clock.

'Come on you. Back to bed,' he whispered, kissing me and taking me upstairs.

We came downstairs much later, for coffee and a leisurely brunch of cereal and eggs on toast. Colin walked to the newsagent's for papers while I showered and dressed. I thought maybe Levi's and a white t-shirt, with a favourite pink cardigan slung across my shoulders. Which worked. So I packed a few things and we drove to Colin's apartment for the weekend.

His apartment was part of an old detached house in Whirlow, a small district south east of Sheffield. Very suburban. Very nice. Built in 1910, the kitchen and bedrooms were quite small, but the lounge-diner was enormous, overlooking a wonderful avenue of matured oaks and the old brick walls of salubrious housing. I unpacked while Colin busied himself in the kitchen, tidying up.

Afterwards, I wandered through to the kitchen, leaned against the sink, and smiled.

'What?' Colin asked, suspiciously.

'Nothing. Just thinking how nice it is, spending the weekends with you. You're very relaxing to be around.'

'Thank you. Is this some kind of bribe, so I give you my chocolate biscuits?'

I shook my head. 'No. I'm being serious.'

'Wow. I like it.' He placed his arms around me. 'Actually, April, there's something I need to tell you.'

His tone set my heart pounding. 'What?'

'My contract's finishing at the end of this month.'

Stepping back, I stared up at him. 'Oh. So what will you do?'

'Brussels. A six month contract.'

Disappointment echoed through my words. 'Brussels?'

'It'll be fine. You can come and visit.'

'But what about our lovely weekends?'

'It's an hour and twenty from Manchester Airport. You could get there Friday and leave on Sunday.'

'Or you could get here Friday and leave on Sunday,' I retorted.

He nodded. 'Okay, not a problem. We could take it in turns.'

'It won't be quite the same, though.'

He kissed me, trying to worm his way into my good books. But I pulled away.

'No.'

'You're just a home bird at heart, aren't you?'

I shook my head. 'No.'

'Yes, you are. Even though you like gadding about – Paris, London, Edinburgh – you just can't wait to get home and sit in front of your desk.'

'I can. I just have work I need to do.'

'Okay.' He dropped his arms. 'I won't argue. And I'm sorry if I've upset you.'

'It's okay. You can't help it. I suppose you have to go where the work is.'

He filled the kettle noisily. 'You know what? It'll be fun. And just the two of us, no interruptions. I'll find us a gorgeous apartment on the Avenue Louise - it's where the Gestapo set up camp in the Second World War.'

I scowled. 'Lovely.'

He laughed. 'I've already started looking. You can come with me if you like, and help choose.'

'When is it? When will you go?'

'They want me to start the beginning of September. So not much time, really.'

September. The very time I was planning to take Mum on holiday.

'Colin?' I said.

'Mm?'

'Talking of going abroad …'

'Mm?' Switching off the tap, he stood there, holding the kettle, his back to me.

'You know your apartment in St Raphael?'

'Mm?' He carried on standing there.

Laughing, I took the kettle from him, placed it onto its stand, switched it on, and pulled him round to face me.

'Talk to me. Properly!'

He grinned. 'Okay. What would you like to know?'

'Your apartment in St Raphael …'

'My apartment in St Raphael. If you're asking whether I rent it out, then no, I don't. Why?'

'Oh.'

I was disappointed. Visions of Mum walking along the sandy beach, wandering through scented markets, eating in lavish restaurants, all vanished from my mind like snowflakes in the sunshine. I'd just have to think of somewhere else.

Suddenly, however, Colin was pulling me into the lounge and onto the sofa, a chunky brown leather affair.

'You want to rent my apartment?' he asked.

'Not if you want to keep it all to yourself.'

'What, is this for research or something?'

'No.'

He kissed me softly on the nose. 'You have another lover?'

I laughed, pushing him away. 'Be serious. No, I want to take Mum on holiday, and I just thought …'

'Okay, it's fine. No problem.' He was pulling me back again, gently, seductively. 'So, how are you going to pay me?'

I laughed. 'Euros?'

'Not worth a penny.' We kissed slowly, his hands reaching for me.

'Dollars, then?'

'No.' He was undressing me slowly.

I heard the kettle click off. 'Colin, the kettle's boiling.'

'I know.' He carried me into the bedroom, the great king-sized bed still unmade from his mad dash to my house.

'Colin …'

Our kissing became hard and fast. Furious. We made love again, eagerly, bright sunshine filling the room through pure white curtains, his green eyes taking on a brilliance I can only describe as breathtaking. I wanted him more than I'd ever wanted any man.

Half an hour later, we were fast asleep.

*

We had a late lunch in a tiny bistro on Ecclesall Road, where tall, hunky Italian waiters filled our every need. But shopping was next on the list, obviously, and I bought a soft pale grey cashmere sweater at knockdown price. Okay, knockdown price compared to London. Colin shopped for shoes, but couldn't find any he liked.

'I'll have a think about it. Come on, I'm thirsty - let's get coffee,' he said, pulling my arm.

'Coffee? When you're thirsty?'

'I'll drink water with it. Like the Parisians.'

We'd reached an area of the city called Hunter's Bar. It being a Saturday afternoon, the place was swarming with people, and I spotted Steve Yates and a couple of his mates hanging around outside the framing shop, until he spotted me and they moved on. But I was kind of glad to have seen him; I'd always thought of him as a loner, somehow.

Colin and I decided on an arty, dressed-up coffee shop. It was only the scent of roast coffee that drew us in, but we were not disappointed. The place was deliciously over the top, with rococo furniture and pink silk roses everywhere. Nicely relaxed after our mid-morning sleep, we chatted over coffee and chocolate cigarellos, about our childhoods, our hopes and our dreams.

Colin's childhood had been pretty much working class. His dad was a builder in Leeds, working on the high-rise flats and shopping centres of the sixties and seventies, his mum a stay-at-home mum, the kind who always had the kettle on and toast ready when you walked through the door from school. I never had that, because my mum always worked. Not that I minded. What you've never had, you don't miss. Although it does sound nice; kind of gives you a warm, cosy feeling inside.

'Do you wish you'd had children?' I asked.

He shook his head. 'When I first got married, maybe. Tasha and I tried for a baby for years, but it just never happened. I'm glad it didn't now. That's the worst thing about divorce, seeing the kids suffer. I know, I've seen the results in friends of mine. They go off the rails. Shoplifting, teenage pregnancies, even drugs. It just ain't worth it.'

'But that might not have happened. You might have been alright together if you'd had kids.'

'And that we shall never know.' He stared at me over his coffee. 'What about you? Did you want kids?'

'No. Not really. I don't think so.'

I hesitated, unsure, suddenly doubting my own feelings. And there lay the problem. There lay the reason I was still single, still childless. I smiled.

'I just wanted a career, really. Maybe if I'd met the right man ...'

'That is a shame.'

'Maybe. Maybe not.' I shrugged.

'You've got your babies, anyway.'

'My stories. Yes, I can make as many babies as I like.'

'Come on, let's get outta here. I'm exhausted. All this sex and shopping ...'

*

We decided to eat out that evening, at the little Italian where we first met.

'Appropriate name, don't you think?' asked Colin.

I rolled the name around my tongue. 'La Romantica. I suppose so.'

'I wonder how many people begin their love affairs here.'

'Is that what this is – a love affair?' I asked.

He took my hand. 'Is that what you want it to be?'

'I suppose so.'

'Just how long have we known each other?'

I had to think about it, admittedly. 'February?'

He nodded. 'Since February.'

I panicked suddenly. Not another proposal.

'And we've been lovers for exactly three weeks,' he said.

'You've been keeping count,' I joked.

'I have.' Picking up his wine glass, he saluted me. 'And I just want to say, I think you are the most adorable woman I have ever met.'

I smiled, all the while wondering if I would accept his proposal. Where would we live, for instance – his place or mine? How would I manage work if I had to look after someone else; I can sometimes write well into the night? And anyway, was I ready for another marriage? Had I ever really got over the disappointment of the first? Not yet, no. Definitely not. But, picking up my glass, I saluted him.

'I thank you, kind sir.'

But he must have seen the terrified look in my eyes, sensed the clutch of fear in my stomach.

'Don't worry, darling, this is not a proposal. I'm not doing an Ed. I know you value your independence. And anyway, it wouldn't work, not with me working away so much.'

Despite myself, I grinned. 'But you're so wrong. That's the way it would work. If ever …'

'If ever you did want to get married.'

'Yes.'

'But you don't.'

'No.'

'Okay.'

'Not just yet.'

*

Sunday morning was spent back in the Peak District, trawling Bakewell's antique shops. Some of them had expensive pieces, but they were genuine. Some had cheap reproduction, and others very pricey reproduction. But my favourite shop was a tiny place

240

at the end of a walkway, full of old records and silly bric-a-brac with enamel kitchen utensils and lace gloves. I bought myself a pair in black lace.

'They might come in handy for a play,' I murmured to Colin, handing over my pound coin and walking out of the shop.

He grinned. 'You should have bought suspenders to match.'

'Cheeky.'

It was then I noticed Toby Wilkinson walking idly along through the marketplace. He was pushing a pram, a tall girl with long dark hair by his side. She kept pausing to pick up items from stalls, discussing them, and replacing them. They looked really happy together. A shame they were still living apart, I thought.

We passed the WI table, littered with home-made produce. I looked out for Emilisa, but she wasn't there. I bought some jam, asking after her.

'She has to go and visit her mother in London. She's in a home, you know, not very well at all, by the sound of it.'

I thanked the woman, a well-heeled horsey type, and we moved on.

*

That evening, after Colin had gone home to pack for Dunfermline, I set about learning my lines for the play we were rehearsing. We'd gone through our moves briefly, although there wasn't much to it; the scene was set in the drawing room, just after dinner. The action was in the script, the tension shown through body language and facial expression. The play doesn't actually name the culprit, so I thought about how the audience would work it out. How would you decide for certain? What little nuances should you detect in the characters' voices, their actions, their responses?

I confess, as I sat there in my study, to the beginnings of an itch. How would I have ended the play, and what kind of experiments would my host perform in order to determine the murderer? Pulling my laptop toward me, I began to write. But my words stuttered on the very first page. I'd begun to describe Lady Isabella's distress at the loss of her diamond necklace when suddenly a vision of Toni, of her pulling out that necklace, of her trying to hide it from me, filled my head. Why had she done that? Why hide something you've found on the floor after a burglary?

Was Toni the burglar? Could she have burgled herself to put us all off the scent? Had she really been at her mother's that night?

Or was my writer's imagination making something out of nothing?

*

I hardly slept. I tossed and turned for hours. Eventually, hot and sticky, I climbed out of bed. It was ten past three in the morning, but the house was still warm from the evening sun. I padded down to the kitchen, made soothing camomile tea, and carried it through to my study. Soft moonlight filtered through the curtains as I wrapped my big cardigan around me and began to write. Reams and reams and reams. Bartholomew Ashington, Esquire, and Edge Green School were materialising before my very eyes. The schoolmistress would be called Mary

Tubney and she'd be very petite with fair hair and hazel eyes. The builders would be completely windswept whilst building the school (the land being very exposed), with sand and soil blowing everywhere. Old yew trees would be felled because of their poisonous leaves, and oak trees planted instead. Bartholomew would be tall, dark and handsome. Of course. But a cad, nevertheless. His wife Isabel, having nearly died giving birth to their first child (think *Call the Midwife*), would be mindful of his attentions, not wanting another pregnancy so soon. Thus his affair with Mary.

*

It was six thirty when I crawled up to bed. Exhausted, brimming with satisfaction, I switched off my alarm clock and slept the sleep of the dead for three whole hours. It was only as I awoke that I realised I'd made up my mind about something; I would no longer help Sean in his pursuit of the thief. It could very well be Toni.

16

BOB Prendergast, his kind face a smiling sun, tapped my brand new mahogany door with weather-beaten hands.

'There you go, love. That'll keep the sods out.'

Picking up his empty coffee cup from the kitchen floor, I returned the smile.

'I hope so. Thanks, Bob. I really appreciate you coming out last minute.'

'No problem. Now, I know it's none of my business, but have you thought about a burglar alarm? This door'll do the job for a while, but if the little bastards are determined enough ...'

My fingers were digging into the cup of their own accord.

'They're coming out later. That's why I rang you. Seems a bit pointless paying out for a burglar alarm when the back door looks so inviting.'

'You're not wrong there, love. Now, is there anything else I can help with?'

I shook my head. 'I'm fine, thanks, Bob. The bathroom door still needs some attention, but I'm thinking about a new suite anyway, to be honest.'

'Okay. Well, let me know then.' He began collecting his tools together. 'How's the play coming on, by the way? I heard you got a good part.'

'We had our first rehearsal on Friday. Although there was a bit of a hiccup.'

He grinned. 'Isn't there always?'

Bob had been a member of the Players for years, helping with the set, scenery, lighting, everything. But that was before his wife became ill.

'Emilisa came back, you know. She was producing. But then she decided to quit, only last week.'

'You're joking. She pulled out?' Using an old dustpan and brush, he swept sawdust and tendrils of wood from the doorstep. 'Mind you, she's got her own share of problems, hasn't she?'

'Really? Well, I know about her mum, but I thought the world was her oyster, marrying a rich man and all that. I mean, it's a beautiful old house they've got.'

Emilisa lived just outside the village, on the main road to Castleton. I'd been inside the house only once, when she'd held a rehearsal there. It was amazing, an Edwardian lodge, five bedrooms and a beautiful lounge with long velvet sofas in silver. We'd actually rehearsed in the conservatory, the house was that spacious.

Pausing, he looked up at me. 'The problem is, although I'm sorry to say it, that son of theirs, Sebastiano. He's a junkie. Heroin. Our Chris was friends with him for a while, that's how I know. She keeps it quiet. Even his own father's disowned him, doesn't want to know. How you can do that to your own son beats me. I just thank the Lord our Chris got away from it all when he went off to uni.'

Bob was very proud of his son, always talking about him. He was studying for a Law degree, a very bright boy.

'Sorry. I didn't know about that,' I replied sympathetically. 'The poor woman.'

'We all have our crosses to bear.'

'How *is* Linda?' His wife suffered from MS and had been in a wheelchair for the past year.

'Oh, she doesn't complain, you know.'

I really wanted to help. 'Tell you what, Bob, while you're here, how about measuring up the bathroom, giving me a quote for fitting, and a new door? I've not picked a suite yet, but …'

DI Forbes had left a message while I'd been chatting to Bob, so I returned her call once he'd left. It was like trying to get through to President Obama during a nuclear war, but eventually her melodic tones greeted me.

'April. Sorry to keep you hanging on.'

'It's okay.'

'Thanks for ringing back. I really needed to speak to you before I left as I've got a damned meeting to attend. I just wondered how it went on Friday with Tobias Wilkinson.'

'Well, to be honest, and I know you'll be disappointed, but I really don't think he's the culprit. He's not the most honest of characters ...'

'You can say that again .'

'But he was actually quite open about everything – money, girlfriend, drug conviction. I asked him whether he'd ever consider stealing for a living, and he didn't flinch an eyelid. Unless I'm just not very good at interviewing people. I mean, he guessed why I was really there in the end.'

'Okay. Well, we've tried our best. We will keep an eye on him, of course.'

'I really don't think it was him.'

'Thanks, anyway, for giving it a go. I do have another trick up my sleeve, but I'll ring Sean when I'm out of this meeting.'

*

I'd planned on starting the next chapter of my Bartholomew Ashington story before the alarm company arrived at three thirty. The plot was developing quite nicely, I thought. I'd introduced the main characters, begun building the school, and was hoping to write a scene set in the village, children playing and women gossiping. But it was not to be.

Toni rang.

'I'm thinking about having a garden party, in aid of the swimming pool fund.'

Pushing aside my vague doubts about her burglary, I enthused wildly.

'That's a wonderful idea, Toni. In your garden?' I was surprised; it wasn't really that huge a space.

'It is actually big enough. Just. Jayne at the Village Hall is lending me some tables for the day, so we've measured up. I've got it all arranged. I'm selling cake and teas and coffees. And I'm hoping the kids at school will make some goodies, too – you know, from papier-mâché and stuff. They're the ones who'll benefit most, don't you think? So I'll get a couple of teachers on board. I just thought it would be nice.'

'It's a brilliant idea, Toni. Well done. So how much are you trying to raise?'

'As much as it takes, I suppose. Every little helps.'

'When is it?'

'The second Saturday in September. Why?'

248

'Josie and I are taking Mum to France, that's all. But we're setting off the weekend after that, so it's fine. I can help out.'

'Wow, she'll love that. But yes, if you could help, that'd be brilliant. All hands to the deck and all that.'

'I'll see if I can't donate a few books to sell, too. I could sign them for people, if you like?'

'That'd be fantastic, April. Thank you.'

'Let me have a word with my agent first.'

'Talking of holidays, I've just got to tell you – I've booked two weeks in Greece for next year. And a week in Rome for spring half-term. Mum's coming with us. I'm just so excited.'

My stomach churned suddenly. Toni didn't usually have two beans to rub together.

'Wow. Toni.' I swallowed hard, not quite knowing what to say. 'Has your mum come into money or something?'

'No. It's an endowment policy Mike took out for me years ago. I'd forgotten all about it. But I got a letter telling me it matures at the end of this month. Five thousand pounds.'

'Fantastic, Toni, that's just fantastic. Doesn't Mike mind you spending it all on yourself?'

'I rang him yesterday. He says we can have it, as long as I spend it wisely.'

'Going on holiday is spending it wisely, then?'

Despite my misgivings, I grinned at the phone; her excitement was infectious.

'Yes. Yes, it is. Going on holiday with the kids is. They'll have a wonderful time. And Rome is very cultural, don't you think?'

'I suppose.'

'Oh, April, I'm just so excited.'

*

To be honest, the chap from the alarm company looked a bit dodgy. Tall, with long dark hair and a constant sniffing action, I wondered whether he was on drugs. But maybe that's just me, and maybe Bob Prendergast's revelation had set me off. But if the chap was capable of setting my alarm, what was to stop him unsetting it if he wanted? He knew the code, knew where everything was. But that was me being paranoid again, I decided. He was only there a couple of hours, so I made cups of tea and learned new words such as PCU and PIR. It all looked very nice. I had the premises control unit placed just behind the front door and chose a code I would remember.

But I was still slightly worried I might be locking out Toni, my friend.

*

Sean called round that evening. I didn't mention my conversation with Toni, though. I needed to think about it, process it, first. After all, I'd known her for years. Why would she suddenly start stealing? And why had I suddenly begun to question her motives, her burglary? Maybe I was becoming too involved, too willing to see the dark side in people.

Anyway, we really needed to get down to consolidating what we'd learned so far.

Sean had been to see the Roystons while I was on holiday. He brought his notes along, inside a blue plastic folder, the kind that makes you cringe when you rub your nail against it. He'd also copied down details of DI Forbes' notes on the other burglaries. Including my own.

'What does it say about me, then?' I asked, grabbing hold of the folder.

He pulled it away. 'No. Confidential information.'

'But Sean, you said I could see it. I'm here to help, aren't I?'

He waved it around, laughing. 'It says 'April Stanislavski, aka April Clouseau, a well-known author turned junior crime reporter, had her bag stolen whilst rehearsing for the part of Miss Gossage, a lovesick ...'

'She wasn't lovesick,' I protested, finally pulling it away from him and reading it in front of the kitchen window.

I read it all, the detailed description of my theft, the layout of the village hall, a precise list of the stolen items. Inexplicably, I began to tremble.

Sean pulled me to the table. 'Come on, sit down. Are you okay?'

'I'm fine.'

'Right. Where are the teabags kept?'

He quickly made tea in two mugs, and we sat there, studying his notes.

I held my mug in both hands, the warmth comforting and soothing. 'I'm still a bit shaken, I think.'

'It takes a while to get over something like that. It's a shock to the system.' He nodded at my tea. 'You want something stronger?'

'No. Really. I'm fine, thank you.'

'If you're sure. Sorry I upset you.'

'It wasn't you.'

'Sorry, anyway.'

I stood up suddenly. 'Actually, I will have something stronger. Fancy a glass of wine?'

'Half a glass. I'm driving.'

'Half a glass it is.' I pulled a Beaujolais from the wine rack.

Sean read the label. 'A lively bouquet of mulberries and cherry. Sounds good.'

'It is. I bought a case of six. Look, two left.'

'I never realised you were such an alcoholic.'

I grinned. 'I bought it last year. Actually. I think it's done quite well.'

Collecting two glasses from the cupboard, I shuffled around in the cutlery drawer for the corkscrew.

'Come here, I'll do it. You sit down,' he said.

Tired suddenly, dispirited, I obeyed without a word.

'Here you go,' he murmured, passing me a full glass.

'Thanks, Sean.'

I drank some, licking my lips.

Sean lifted his glass. 'Here's to a good piece of detective work. And if *we* don't find the bastard, no-one will.'

'Let's hope so. Cheers.

'DI Forbes rang earlier,' Sean continued. 'Apparently, Toby Wilkinson is a no-goer. You're sure about that one?'

I nodded. 'Definitely. I got this feeling as soon as I met him. He's not the nicest of characters, admittedly, but I don't think he's our thief. Anyway, he doesn't need the money. They've got pots. And I think this person needs money. They seem kind of desperate, somehow.'

'Okay. So, back to the drawing board. DI Forbes has another idea in the pipeline, but we'll read through her notes before we jump to conclusions, I think.'

He had a whole list of names in his folder. Couples, people living on their own, families, even the old folks' home. There was my theft, the Jones's burglary, Toni's, Dr Jani's, the Roystons. The Royston family had only left a purse on the side in the kitchen – someone had sneaked in and taken it while they were watching the telly.

I sighed. 'He's got a nerve, this chap.'

'You're not kidding. In the middle of the afternoon as well. Just walked in there and took it. Mrs Royston was beside herself. She'd left the baby in its pram, out in the garden. You do wonder if this chap's invisible.'

'I'd say the opposite. I'd say he's able to mingle in, walks around unnoticed, fits in with the furniture. But the old folks' home? I mean, how do you go unnoticed in there?'

'They employ casual staff from the village, anyone who's willing to go in and help serve tea and biscuits. They do CRB checks, of course, but other than that it could be anybody. I've got a list here of staff from the past two years.'

Working my way down the names, I followed my finger carefully. I recognised a couple of names near the top, but dismissed them as they were both quite elderly themselves. Then, further down, there was one that suddenly made sense.

'Steven Yates. He's with the Village Players, does the lighting.'

'Does he now?' Sean had never looked more serious. Or more excited. 'So he was there the night …'

'The night my bag was pinched.' Sudden tears filled my eyes. 'Do you think he'll still have everything? My jewellery and everything?'

Sean shook his head. 'I doubt it. Sorry, April. They fence stuff, get rid of it, as soon as they can.'

'You mean as soon as some idiot's willing to pay a fiver for something that's actually very precious.'

He took my hand. 'I know.'

'Sorry,' I murmured. 'It's only a bit of jewellery.'

'No. I understand. It meant a lot to you. But we'll catch him, don't you worry.'

'But how? How do we prove anything?'

He winked audaciously. 'Ways and means, April. Ways and means.'

'We could set a trap. We could leave a bag somewhere, or a purse.'

'When's the next time you all meet up?'

'This Friday. But it's just a rehearsal, so he might not be there.'

'That's a pity. Well then, we'll just have to wait until he is.'

17

THE week was filled with work, rainy walks, visits to Mum's, and phone calls. Josie, Joe and the kids had returned from their holiday in Majorca, beautifully tanned and lazily energetic. Sean had rung to say DI Forbes had pulled Steve Yates in for questioning, and he had alibis for most of the burglaries. But they were still checking through them, step by step, a laborious process. They were also investigating other casual staff who'd worked at the old folks' home, and had a few leads that looked hopeful.

I spent one rainy day looking at bathroom suites, my new back door having inspired me to sort out the rest of the house. My house was not quite the type of residence I'd have envisaged living in. I'd always seen myself in an old Victorian property, with a large open hall, spacious farmhouse kitchen, and French doors leading out to a tree-filled garden, possibly overlooking the sea. No, the house I lived in was circa 1950's, stone-built, with a south-facing veranda looking out over the valley below. The garden was fairly simple and easy to look after, Jo having had a hand in the design, but if you stood at the front door you had the most glorious view. Green hills dotted with tiny sheep, leading right up to the sky. The front door led to a hallway that was central to the house. There was a study and small cloakroom to the right, a sitting room to the left, and a large, deep dining kitchen at the end. Stairs led up to three bedrooms and a bathroom.

But I loved it, even though it wasn't Victorian and it didn't overlook the sea. The bathroom, however, was looking a little shoddy, and I'd had my eye on a roll-top bath for a while. So I took advantage of the rain, a sniffly summer cold, the fact that Sandy had just credited my account with a nice fat salary, and bought the most amazing bathroom suite you've ever seen. Okay, slight exaggeration there. But think white, curvy, ceramic with old-fashioned silver taps, and you've got it. My roll-top bath had white claw feet, and I intended asking Bob Prendergast to paint the exterior a bright sunshine yellow, in matt *Farrow and Ball*. I wanted white tiling on the walls and grey limestone tiles on the floor. I could not wait to see it finished.

My weekend was spent with Colin. We'd spent Saturday morning walking the moors, finishing with a pub lunch at the Castle, a small friendly pub in Leasdale I'd visited before. A log fire burned, even though it was August, so we spread our wet coats out to dry before walking home again. The following day, the Sunday, was quite uneventful, really. We just pottered around at home, conscious of time slipping away before he'd be off to his new job in Brussels.

*

The following Wednesday, however, the rain had stopped and the temperature hit a muggy twenty-one degrees. No sunshine, just mist and a sad, grey landscape.

Mum was up and dressed by nine thirty. I knew it for a fact because that's when I rang the doorbell. She opened the door promptly, no shuffling around, no prevaricating. No winceyette nightie or unwashed hair. In fact, she looked good, in neat grey trousers and a white shirt.

I hugged her. 'Morning, you. You look well today.'

'I thought I'd make an effort, seeing as Rita's daughter's going to come visiting.'

'Oh, I see.' I smiled.

'What's her name again? I never can remember.'

'Sofia. Think of Sophia Loren.' I followed her into the kitchen, Lottie running up for me to stroke. 'And her little girl's called Teru.'

'Now that is a pretty name.'

I switched on the radio and music filled the room. I think it was Brahms, but don't hold me to that. Mum was messing with cups.

'I've tidied up the sitting room, so she won't have to do too much.'

'But Mum, that's her job.'

'I know, I know. But I don't want her thinking I'm a complete scruff, do I?'

'Okay. But she's here to help, remember.'

'I know. And I could do with it. That whatever her name is from Help the Aged – she was useless.'

'Exactly. That's why I arranged for Sofia.'

She spooned coffee into mugs. One of them was a Smarties mug she'd bought me as a teenager. Made at Hornsea Potteries, it had contained an Easter egg. A long time ago.

'You could have asked me first, mind,' she said.

'You'd only have fussed, wouldn't you? Then, once you'd said no, it would have taken ages to talk you round.'

She nodded wearily. 'I know.'

'How are you feeling, anyway, Mum? Are those tablets doing the trick, do you think?'

She passed me a mug. 'Dr Whitby said to give it three months, see if they lift my spirits.'

'Okay. Fair enough.' I smiled. 'But I know something that *will* lift your spirits.'

'What's that, then? A holiday in the Bahamas?'

'Not quite.'

'What then?'

'The South of France. With me and Josie for company. Joe will look after Lottie for you.'

'Just you and Josie?' Her eyes widened in shock and disbelief.

'Just me and Josie.'

Soft tears appeared. 'Oh, that would be lovely.'

I hugged her. 'Don't cry, Mum.'

'Sorry,' she sobbed. 'It's just, I don't know where I'd be without you two.'

'It works both ways. You're always there for us.'

Suddenly, the doorbell rang and I rushed to answer it.

'Hi, Sofia.'

But Teru, as nimble and as fast as a field mouse, shot past me, running headlong towards the kitchen, then stopping suddenly to stare at the huge print in the hallway.

'Mummy – look,' she called.

It was a picture of Beachy Head lighthouse with its iconic red and white stripes. Mum always did love the seaside.

Walking in, Sofia shrugged good-naturedly. 'Sorry, April, she's a little hyperactive today.'

'It's okay,' I said. 'She has good taste. That's a real lighthouse, Teru. It's over a hundred years old, but they paint it regularly, so it's always nice and shiny.'

Teru didn't say a word, merely glanced up at me, her eyes big and round.

'Come on, let's see the kitchen, shall we? I said.

I turned to Sofia. 'Would you like a coffee or anything before you begin?'

'That'd be nice, thank you. But I'll drink it while I work, if that's alright.'

Mum greeted Sofia like a long-lost friend, showing her where everything was – cloths, dusters, hoover, mop, bucket. Teru made friends with Lottie, then followed Mum and Sofia round, the fluffy terrier at her heels.

'You have a lovely house, Mrs Hutton,' said Sofia.

'Call me Judy. Please.'

Seizing her chance, Teru pulled suddenly on Mum's hand. 'Judy - are there any toys?'

Mum looked embarrassed, but Sofia nodded calmly.

'It's okay. You'll get used to her. She's used to Mum, that's all.'

Mum's face suddenly softened, and I saw my old mum there. Warm. Intelligent. Kind and caring. She looked down at the child.

'Do you know what? I think we may have. There's some stuff in the spare room, in the cupboard. Come on, I'll show you.'

As Mum, Teru and Lottie meandered upstairs, I smiled. Sofia was already cleaning the kitchen sink, the taps shiny, the surfaces littered with white bubbles.

'Thank you,' I said.

She turned. 'That's okay. Just doing my job.'

'No. Thank you for Teru. She's just what Mum needs.'

'Oh, she's a cheeky one, that.'

I switched on the kettle. 'She's lovely. Will you bring her every week?'

'I have to. Mum's in the café, so there's no-one to look after her.'

'No, that's fine. Mum loves her being here, you can tell.'

'Do you have kids?' she asked, rinsing her cloth.

I shook my head. 'No. I got divorced years ago. Never remarried, and now it's too late.'

'That's a pity.'

'Mum does have grandchildren. My sister Josie has three girls. They're lovely kids, but they're all at school now, so she doesn't see much of them.'

'That's a shame. Teru goes to school next year as well. I'll miss her.'

The sharp sting of bleach hit my nostrils as she poured it into the sink.

'Why did you not marry Teru's father?' I asked. 'Or am I being a bit forward?'

Turning to me, she grinned. She really was very beautiful, her face angular but feminine.

'It's okay, I don't mind.' Taking a deep breath, she told her story. 'I was a model. For the catwalk, for magazines. I travelled all over the world. Then I met this chap, and I fell in love. But we were far from home. I had no idea of his background, that he was married, already had two children. He was a photographer, white, from London. He was confident, tall, dark and handsome. I was a fool.'

I smiled. 'These things happen.'

'I know.' She moved around the kitchen with her cloth, scrubbing furiously.

'I'm sorry.'

'It's okay.'

'And you do have a very beautiful daughter.'

'Thank you. You are very kind. I'm trying to teach her not to fall into the same trap.'

'None of us can stop ourselves from falling in love, even if it's with the wrong person,' I replied, knowingly.

'This is true.'

*

We had tea and cake in Debenhams, me and Mum.

'This is lovely, April,' Mum said. 'I never thought coming to town was very exciting, but it is.'

'But you used to, Mum. You used to love going shopping. What's happened?'

'Oh, I don't know. What's the point? Really?'

'What do you mean?'

'Well, when I try something on, it never looks right. I'm just a little old lady trying to look young again. So what's the point?'

'The point is, Mum, you're a lovely person. You're still attractive when you make the effort. And why shouldn't you enjoy buying new clothes? Who says it's just for the young?'

'Oh, you'll understand one day, love. When you get to my age.'

'Mum, don't. This isn't like you. I want you to have a lovely afternoon, buy yourself some new clothes, and then we're going to go away and have a wonderful holiday. Okay?'

She nodded, soft tears rolling down her cheeks. 'I know, love. Sorry. I know you're only trying to help.'

It was while we were surveying the contents of John Lewis's window that she finally gained some of her old enthusiasm, a soft gleam in her eye.

'This one, this one over here. Look.'

She pointed enthusiastically to a long skirt, worn by a six foot mannequin with legs the width of pine twigs. Subtle stripes of black and gold flowed down to a single crimson flower at the hem.

'That would look lovely against a suntan,' she said.

I swear she looked twenty-one again, her eyes sparkling, her dimples dancing.

'Come on, then. Let's have a look.'

The skirt was nearly seventy pounds, but Mum thought it was too expensive. So when she visited the Ladies I dashed off and bought it myself. Well, if I can't treat my own mum, who can I treat?

We bought new sandals, flip flops and a couple of strappy tops each. I knew St Raphael wouldn't be scorching hot the third week in September, but it would be warm enough, even for the likes of me. And was I beginning to get excited.

*

I'd finally made up my mind.

I rang Sean that evening, my stomach churning, my nails digging into my hands.

'Are you busy, Sean?'

'I'm just about to go out, but I can spare two minutes for my favourite junior crime reporter.'

'Sorry. It's just ...'

For once, I was lost for words, didn't know how to begin the conversation.

'What's wrong?' He sounded upset already, and I hadn't even said anything.

The phone was suddenly a hot coal in my hand. 'It's just, would you mind very much if I didn't help with the investigation anymore?'

'What?'

'Sorry, Sean.'

'Why?'

'It's just, I'm really busy at the moment. Lots of eggs being juggled, so to speak.'

'Come on, April, this isn't like you. What is it, really?'

'I just don't have the time any more. Sorry.'

'Do you fancy meeting up?'

'Why?'

'To discuss it.'

He always could talk me into anything.

*

I rang Josie after tea. She answered the phone within three rings, which was pretty good for her, especially at that time of day. Between the hours of five and eight, and especially during term-time, their house was insane. Josie had three lots of homework to help with, tea to make, washing up to do, tidying up to do, and Daisy to get through the bath and into bed. I constantly took my hat off to her.

'Are you okay to talk?' I asked.

'No probs. Joe's putting the kids to bed. We've been gardening all day. Talk about a busman's holiday. But they're exhausted, bless them.'

'At least they'll sleep well. I'm really just checking everything's still okay for us to go to St Raphael.'

'How do you mean?'

'I mean, have you discussed it with Joe yet?'

'Of course. It's fine. Well, I knew it would be.'

'You mean he doesn't mind looking after three kids and two dogs, as well as holding down a full-time, very responsible job, while you go gallivanting to the South of France, doing God knows what?'

She laughed. 'Well, you know Joe. He actually thinks it's a very good idea and will give me a much needed break. So there.'

'Excellent. Right. Second question.'

'What?'

'My friend Toni is having a garden party on the tenth of September, and I just wondered if you'd do us a favour.'

'Is it a biggie?

'Kind of.'

'Go on then. What?'

'I just thought a few touches - you know, creative stuff - from my wonderful gardening sister?'

She sighed. 'Okay.'

'It is in aid of the swimming pool fund.'

'No, it's fine, really. What time does it start?'

'Two o'clock. Would that be okay?'

'I'll be there.'

18

THE last Friday of August. The forecast for that day and the weekend was amazing. It was going to be a scorcher, a sizzler. So I got up early and walked before the heat set in. The birds were singing, the hedges buzzing, and all was well with the world. I'd even arranged for Bob Prendergast to come and fit my bathroom during my intended holiday to France.

But all through my walk, I was thinking about Sean. How would I face him? Would I tell him the truth? Would I really tell him I suspected Toni? I was dreading it.

But I also needed to convince myself. I still wasn't one hundred per cent completely, utterly, sure. Maybe it wasn't Toni. Maybe she'd tried hiding the necklace for another reason, not because she'd stolen it. After all, if she was that desperate for money all she had to do was ask her mum, or even the ex-husband. But, you had to admit, it was all very strange. She was definitely hiding something. And I didn't want to be the one to find out what it was.

*

We met in the Library Café. Sean bought the cappuccinos this time.

I wore white cropped trousers and pumps with a silver jacket, a little number I found in Paris many years ago, the buttons reminiscent of Sergeant Pepper. It seemed to go with the orange and black décor, somehow.

But as Sean greeted me I felt terrible. How could I let him down like this? How could I tell him I thought his lady friend and lover (I assumed) might be the culprit? After all, I was no detective. I was probably using my overactive imagination and making forty-five out of two plus two.

'Come on then, spill the beans. And excuse the pun,' he joked, indicating his cappuccino.

But I couldn't smile, couldn't even look at him. Instead, I played with my coffee.

'April? What is it?' he pleaded. 'Come on. There's nothing wrong, is there?'

I shook my head. 'No.'

Reaching across, he touched my hand gently. 'April, we're friends, aren't we? You can tell me anything and I promise not to judge you.'

I pulled away. 'I know. But Sean, you're going to hate me for this.'

'We go back a long way, I could never hate you. You must know that.'

My stomach churning, I took a deep breath. 'Okay, then, here goes. I don't want to continue with the investigations because the thief may be a friend of mine.'

'You mean Steve Yates?'

'No. He's not really a friend, anyway. As such.'

'Who, then?'

I shook my head, tears threatening. 'Sorry, Sean, I just ...'

But his eyes narrowed, the colour draining from his face. 'Who is it?'

I shook my head emphatically, wishing I'd not come, wishing I'd carried on as if nothing had happened.

'I can't say.'

'Why not?' He smiled gently. 'You don't think it's me, do you?'

'No.'

'Then who? Someone from the Village Players?'

'No, Sean.'

I stood up to leave, but he grabbed hold of my arm.

'You have to tell me, April. If you want to back out, that's fine. Well, it's not, not really. But you have to tell me.'

There was no other way of saying it. 'Toni.'

'What?' he exploded, jolting out of his seat.

Tears filled my eyes. 'Sorry.'

Giving himself time to deliberate, he sat down. 'Toni?'

I merely nodded.

'You are joking, right?'

'Sorry.'

'You must be joking. I mean, what do you have on her? What evidence? She's just a little thing. There's no way she'd be able to lift the Jones's safe, or break into Dr Jani's house.'

Tearfully, I sat down and told him everything. The necklace, the money, the holidays.

'But, it's the proceeds of an endowment policy. She told me that herself.'

'So why has she never mentioned it before? She's always crying poor, never has two pennies to rub together. Usually.'

'Maybe she thought Mike would keep the money when it matured. I don't know. But she's not a thief,

April. I mean, she's one of the victims, for Christ's sake.'

'But if there'd been an endowment policy coming up for maturity, surely she'd have known about it already, been talking about it. Wouldn't she?'

'Possibly. I don't know, April. There's obviously a good explanation for all of this. Have you asked her?'

I wiped away my tears. 'No. But what about that necklace? Why did she hide it when I walked in?'

'Maybe you startled her. She'd just bloody well been burgled, damn it.'

He was gritting his teeth in anger. I'd never seen him like this before.

'Sorry, Sean.'

'Come on, April, think about it.'

'You could be right. Maybe all this is getting to me. I'm a bag of nerves just lately, and especially since Lady Barnstaple ...'

'I know. I'm sorry. I dragged you into all this.' Avoiding my eyes, he played with the spoon on his saucer.

'Don't be,' I said. 'It was actually quite fun at first. But maybe it's better if I back out now?'

'If that's what you want, okay.'

'Sorry.'

He looked up, suddenly thoughtful.

'Don't you think it funny? They've all stopped since Lady Barnstaple.'

'What?'

'The burglaries. They've all stopped.'

I sat upright. 'They have, haven't they?'

'Guilty conscience, do you think? Now someone's died?'

'Could be.'

My mind was veering all the way back to Toni again. She'd be awfully, terribly upset if she killed someone by accident.

But Sean had read my mind. 'It's not Toni, April. Don't even go there.'

'Sorry, Sean. No, really, I am. I said you'd hate me.'

I felt dreadful. How could I suspect my friend? How could I even think for one second it might be her?

'I think it is better you don't continue with the investigations. I can manage on my own from here, anyway.'

*

George was ready with my Guinness as I walked through the door. And I needed it. It was ice cold, delicious, condensation dripping down the glass like a deep mist.

He smiled. 'They're waiting for you, love. Laura's been carrying the costumes through. Very nice they are, too.'

I paid for my drink. 'Thanks, George.'

It was Monday night; the bar was empty. I walked straight through to the back room, to the rumble of murmured lines being read.

Alfie welcomed me, as always. 'April, darling, lovely to see you. Come sit. We're just blocking the second page, Act One.'

'There is only Act One,' I retorted.

'Oo-ooh. Someone's touchy today.'

'Sorry, Alfie. Bad day.' Sitting beside him, I found my page quickly, then looked up. 'Hi, everyone ...'

There was a mumble of greetings from around the table, heads engrossed in scripts. I noticed Steve Yates at the far end. He was chatting to Daniel Oxley, both studying something on his laptop; the lighting plan, I suspected. An ineffectual-looking, slightly unsavoury character, with fair hair, he had small eyes that were always slightly pink. Unlike Daniel Oxley, a barrister from Sheffield, who was gorgeous. Greying hair, deep brown eyes. Happily married. He had the lead part, Sir Hugh Tompkinson's brother.

'Okay,' called Alfie. 'Back to work, everyone, please.'

We read the first twenty pages, deciding where to move and when to move. There being only the one scene, it could have become quite stilted, but Alfie managed to bring the whole thing to life with his characterisation. As always.

During our break, I bought myself a tomato juice and Alfie a white wine. We chatted for a while about costumes and holidays, the usual. But then I excused myself to visit the Ladies. Furtively, I left my handbag on the table beside Alfie, the zip undone, my purse peeking out. Upon my return, Steve Yates was nearby, chatting to Daniel and Alfie about ordering new gels for the lights. I checked my handbag. Untouched, my purse just where I'd left it. I felt quite disappointed.

Our rehearsal continued, beginning again from page one.

'Right,' called Alfie. 'I want Lady Isabella stage right this time. It didn't look quite right, my darling.'

'Okay, Alfie,' murmured Gemma, moving across the room.

'And Sir William, a touch more mystery, please. We need to suspect your ulterior motive right from the beginning. Thank you.'

Daniel grinned. 'Don't worry, Alfie, I'll get there.'

'I know, my darling, I know. But we need to crack this thing as soon as.'

At nine o'clock we stopped for costume fittings, men in the toilets, ladies in the main room. Laura had been busy adding finishing touches while we rehearsed. With her wonderful eye for detail, Alfie relied on her one hundred and ten per cent.

'Okay,' she murmured, her hands pulling at the shoulders of my dress. 'It needs pulling up and back, or there's too much cleavage.'

I wriggled at the scratchy fabric as she pinned the seams together. 'I thought they showed their cleavage in those days,' I replied.

'Miss Forsyth wouldn't have done. Not much, anyway. She'd been Sir Hugh's secretary, remember, all prim and proper.'

'Despite having a mad, passionate *affaire* with him,' I murmured.

The dress was long and slender with an outer layer of chiffon in a kind of drab coconut colour. But it suited my character down to the ground. I loved it.

'Where did you get this material, Laura?'

'Oh, I didn't make it. It's a little something I found on Ebay and altered to suit.'

'It's beautiful. You are clever.'

*

I walked home slowly, wondering at the bright orange sky bordering the hills, the sun's rays fading in the distance. It was stunning, beautiful.

My phone bleeped suddenly, so I pulled it from my bag. Colin had texted.

So looking forward to seeing you in the morning. And stop worrying about Brussels. Love always. xxx

I replied as I walked.

Looking forward to seeing you too. This is my smiley face ☺ xxx

It was nice to walk into the house and hear the bleep-bleep-bleeping of the alarm. Rushing to unset it, I felt safe, my home my fortress, my shelter, strong and secure.

Diane Downing had also left me a message, on the landline, asking me to ring upon my return from rehearsal. I rang.

'Thanks for ringing back, April. I thought we could arrange to meet up and organise things for the auction. But I'm a bit pushed for time, so if it could be either Wednesday or Thursday next week, I'd appreciate it.'

'That's fine, no problem. Either day is okay for me.'

'Shall we make it Wednesday? Half seven at the Flying Toad? And Jim Allsop will be there. I hope that's okay.'

*

Tired and slightly dispirited, I made soothing camomile tea and carried it out to the garden. It was still warm and musky at eleven o'clock, a Mediterranean kind of evening, and I was just in the mood for hearing crickets, but sadly there were none to hear. So, sitting there, my blue writing cardigan wrapped around my shoulders, I pondered over Toni, debated whether or not to continue with Sean's investigations, and worried over Colin working abroad. Despite his text.

But at midnight my bath called me inside, complete with strawberry-scented bubbles, and I eventually relaxed into a solid, deep sleep.

19

MONDAY morning. But we'd had the most amazing weekend. Colin and I had taken swimsuits and towels to the pool, complete with white wine in a flask (it's not actually allowed, but people do it anyway) and a picnic with fresh succulent strawberries for pudding. The air had echoed with the scent of wet chlorine and suntan lotion as we stretched out on the lawn, eating and drinking, reading the paper, and generally enjoying the warm fingers of sunshine on our backs. This would be the final hot weekend of the summer, we knew, and we determined to make the most of it. It was also our final weekend before Colin flew out to Brussels.

Saturday evening had been spent at my house, eating, drinking, and making love. In fact, I *was* in love, I can't deny it. Truly and madly. Colin was everything I could have wished for in a man.

Despite this, I had the awful feeling it was all too good to be true, that our days together were numbered. Pessimist or what?

Colin returned home Sunday evening to pack, ready to fly to Belgium. He'd arranged a letting agency to look after the apartment for six months, and we'd spent time checking flight times from Manchester for our weekend visits. I was so happy with Colin, yet this job in Brussels was stirring at me like the spoon of a witch's cauldron. You see, he'd just told me his ex was currently working over there. They were in exactly the same business, IT contracting. In fact, that's how they met.

Apparently, she was still unattached, still beautiful, and still not over him. Ouch. Colin had merely brushed it to one side, as if it was nothing.

But it was everything.

*

So, after such a bittersweet weekend, it was back to business. I had my usual walk, but in tee shirt and shorts, a big smile on my face, the birds singing, the sky lifting its head to the sun.

Upon my return, I rang Sean. I needed to let him know Steve Yates was off the hook.

'Thanks for letting me know, April. But he's not really off the hook as such. He just didn't steal your purse. I mean, he just may not have had the opportunity, with a roomful of people and all that.'

'I know. I just thought you should know I tried to tempt him, but he didn't bite.'

'Actually, it's funny you should ring me – I was on the point of ringing you. I had DI Forbes on the phone after I saw you on Friday.'

'Oh?'

'You know they've been watching the house next door to your mum's?'

'Oh. God,' I murmured.

'No, it's alright. Well, kind of.'

'What then?'

'They're on the trail of the people who live there. Well, they don't actually live there, but they hang out there and they get plenty of visitors.'

'Really?'

'Yep.'

'What, to buy drugs?'

'Yep.'

'Crikey.'

'Clever girl, April. You could just have cracked the biggest drugs ring this side of Manchester.'

'I only helped out so I could get the chap who stole my bag,' I moaned, not quite sure I deserved the compliment.

'Well, at least you've achieved something - something much more momentous. Well done.'

'Do you think Mum will be okay? I mean, living next door to all that? Should I get her to come and stay with me for a while?'

'I think she'll be okay. It depends whether they're raided or not. But even then she shouldn't really be affected.'

'It's not like she's attached, and there is a bit of distance between the houses. And I suppose I'd upset her if I told her,' I decided.

'She'll be fine. Don't go worrying about it. If DI Forbes is on the case ...'

'She's not doing too well with the Millerstone burglar,' I retorted.

'Sometimes these things take time.'

*

I went round to see Mum late that afternoon. She was fine, nearly back to her usual self, fussing round me like an old mother hen.

'Come on, April. Let's dig out our old holiday snaps and get in the mood for France. What's the name of the place you're taking us to?'

'St Raphael, Mum. It's in the South of France, Provence.'

'That's it. Come on then, let's have a look.'

We rummaged through photo albums in the spare room upstairs. The room smelt fusty, as if it belonged in the past, the photo albums too.

But we brought them downstairs, dusted them off, and brought them to life again.

'This one here,' said Mum. 'Now this one's me and Dad in Blackpool. Just started courting, we had.'

It was Mum and Dad in typical seaside attire. For those days. Mum in a white dress, billowing out around the knees, Dad with his trousers rolled up, a spade and bucket in one hand. The year was 1960, the photo shiny in black and white. Mum would have been nineteen, so Dad was twenty-one. She looked so beautiful with her dark hair and serious eyes. He looked more of a comic character – you could tell just from his expression. Poor Mum. How she must have missed him.

'Who took this photo, Mum?' I asked.

'A friend of ours - Deborah. We went there for the day. Her boyfriend had a car, a Ford I think it was. Quite a big thing in those days, owning a car. But he was a student doctor at Chesterfield Royal, so a bit older than her. Plenty of money. I remember him offering to buy the fish and chips, but your dad would have none of it. Very proud, he was.'

'He was always willing to work for what he wanted, Mum.'

'He was. A true Yorkshireman, bless him. There's a picture of them somewhere.'

She turned the pages happily as faces from the past smiled up at us.

'Here it is, look. Debs and Andy. She only worked as an auxiliary, not quite up to his standard. But he was besotted with her.'

This photograph hadn't been taken in Blackpool. They were all dressed up, he in black tie, she in a beautiful dress and high heeled shoes.

'Where was this taken?' I asked.

'Chesterfield. They used to do a charity ball at the hospital. All the well-to-dos went. Black tie, posh frocks.'

'Did you ever go?'

'We went the once, your dad and I. The Christmas after this was taken, I think. It was all very glamorous. There was a photographer in the foyer of the Hotel – took everyone's photos as they arrived, then charged a fortune for the privilege. But it all went to charity, so it was for a good cause, I suppose.'

'Where's your picture, then?'

'Oh, we had it on the sitting room wall in the old house for years. I don't know where it is now.'

'I think I remember it.' I recalled the picture on the wall above the sofa, a simple black frame set against flowered wallpaper. 'I wonder where it got to, then?'

'It's probably still in a box somewhere. We never really finished the unpacking when we moved here. But oh, we always made a lovely couple. Everyone said so. I saved up for months for that dress – cherry red, it was. It pulled right in at the waist, then flared out when you danced. Loads of material. Gorgeous. And your dad hired a dinner suit. He did look smart.'

'We ought to go and look for it some time.'

'It'll be in the loft, I expect. But not now, April. Right now I need a nice hot cup of tea.'

So I made tea, stirring at the pot thoughtfully. The late afternoon sun was shining onto the glass doors of the kitchen cupboards, a warm oak. The kitchen units were old when Mum and Dad moved in, but Dad had sanded them down and re-waxed them so they looked like new. He never seemed to stop, my dad, not ever. Always doing something, always busy. Maybe he should have stopped sometimes. Maybe then he'd still be with us now.

I sighed, poured tea into mugs and carried them through to where Mum was sitting, her own thoughts chasing around her mind.

'Here we go,' I said.

She smiled. 'Shall we drink it in the garden? It's such a beautiful day, and Lottie can have a run around.'

'Come on then.'

The warm air chased away my sudden melancholy, and we sat there for an hour, chatting, cajoling, discussing Josie, her girls, my plans, and the holiday.

'So what's it like then, the South of France?' Mum asked.

'It's just beautiful, Mum.' I'd been to St Tropez once with Jeremy; a very long weekend in the first throes of our marriage. It had charm, panache, style and elegance. 'You'll absolutely love it, I promise. It's where all the Parisians go for the summer.'

'Will it be busy, then?'

'No. I expect they'll all have gone home by the time we get there. So we can relax, walk, sun ourselves on the beach.'

'Is it very hot?'

'Not in September. There's the *mistral* – that's what they call the wind at that time of year. It's a warm wind, not cold, so it cools things down a little. But it's just perfect. You'll see.'

*

Mum and I made tea together; potato salad, baby spinach and cherry tomatoes, Wensleydale for me, boiled ham for Mum. Followed by bananas and custard, one of Mum's favourites.

It was only as I left the house later, at about nine o'clock, that I noticed lights on in the house next door, the drugs house. So, instead of just driving off, I waited until Mum had waved goodbye and closed the door, then moved slowly forwards to pull up outside the small wooden gate. There was already a

286

car parked there, a dark Vauxhall Astra. I couldn't remember having seen it there before.

Switching off my lights, I sat there, debating what to do. Should I ring the police? Or Sean? But DI Forbes had already said they were keeping an eye on it. So what good would it do to interfere?

The debate, however, was suddenly and viciously taken from my hands.

The car door was wrenched open, and a deep, throaty voice whispered hoarsely.

'Get out the car. Now!'

I felt a rough pull at my arm. Angry, yet sick to the stomach, adrenaline filled my taste buds and I yanked it away.

'What are you doing? How dare you!'

'Keys ...' Grabbing my arm again, he pulled me from the car, and the key from the ignition.

I was livid. How could anyone even think of stealing my car, my beloved Mini Convertible?

'You leave my car alone,' I screamed, reaching out to scratch him. It was then, as my fingers touched his skin, that I saw his face in the lamplight. 'You!'

I recognised him. He was one of the guys I'd seen with Steve Yates, hanging around Hunter's Bar. His hair was distinctive. A pony tail dyed pink, the rest of his hair bleached blonde.

'What?' Staring at me in disbelief, his grip tightened. 'What d'you mean?'

'I recognise you,' I admitted.

But he pushed it aside. The way he was looking at me, he probably thought I was senile, anyway.

'What you doing here?' he grunted.

'I could ask you the very same thing,' I retorted, trying to wriggle away.

But his grip on my arm became harder. 'What you doing here, noseying around?'

Kicking the car door shut behind me, he pressed the key and there was a bleep-whoop sound as the doors locked.

'Get off me, you're hurting me,' I screamed. 'And get off my car.'

But he pushed me towards the gate and I stumbled, nearly falling, catching hold of the fencing. The posts were sharp and tears filled my eyes.

'Into the garden, go on,' he whispered. 'And less of the noise.'

'I'll make as much noise as I like,' I tried to shout, hoping Mum might hear. But my voice had become a tiny squeak in my throat.

Losing hope suddenly, wondering what it was all about, I groaned loudly.

'One more sound, and I'll knock you out.'

'What?'

'You heard. Not a sound.'

I felt suddenly sick. It was like a bad dream, a nightmare that wakes you up in a ball of sweat.

'I know you,' I said, bravely. 'I'm a friend of Steve's. I can identify you.'

'Steve? Steve who?' He pushed me along, down the side of the house towards the back garden.

'Steve Yates. I saw you together.'

'Did you now? Well, that don't prove nothing.'

'What I mean is, I can tell the police who you are.'

'*You're* the one who's been snooping round other people's property.'

'I wasn't. I was just parking my car.'

'Don't play the innocent with me. I saw you. Before.'

'What?'

I realised now, too late, that the house hadn't been empty when I'd been *snooping round*.

'It's about time we sorted you out.'

'We? Who's *we*, then?'

I'd reached a wooden shed, an old disused thing at the bottom of the garden, behind some kind of evergreen bush.

'Never you mind. None of your business. But I'm gonna teach you a lesson, that's for sure.'

I caught my foot on a twig and my ankle rolled over painfully. 'Ow. Stop. Please.'

'Don't try it on with me. Come on,' and he pulled me towards the open door of the shed.

'What makes you think you'll ever get away with this?' I hissed, my mouth dry, but my determination ice cold steel. 'I know your pal's name. I can go straight to the police in the morning.'

'What makes you think you'll be here in the mornin'?' he sneered, pushing me through the doorway.

The sickly sweet scent of cannabis hit me as I fell to the floor, but I was too scared to react. My legs had become sticks of jelly.

'Don't. Please,' I pleaded, sitting up straight. 'We can sort this out, surely.'

'Sort it out? Sort what? You're the one who should be sorting things out. You're the one what should've kept her nose out of things. Things that have nothing to do with you.'

'I'm sorry, okay? I apologise. But you shouldn't be growing cannabis ...' I was about to say right next door to my mum's house, but thought better of it. God knows what he'd have done.

'You see. You know everything. You've messed it all up now. We'll have to move, start again.'

'You shouldn't be involved in all this stuff. I saw you hanging around in Sheffield. You're a nice kid. Why do you do it?' Flattery will get you everywhere, I thought.

'Why d'you think? You think I make enough money working for my uncle, do you? Selling stuff for him? I work every hour I can, and for what?'

I stood up. 'To live? Eat?' I was getting ready to run.

But he guessed my intention, quickly pulling shut the door behind him and blocking my way.

'To give to the fucking landlord, to give to the fucking taxman. I eek out a living, and what's the point?'

I stared at him through the darkness. 'The point is,' I insisted, shivering and rubbing my arms, 'you do the same as everyone else. You get by. You do the best you can. You're young. You have time to start again, retrain, study, make the best of the talents God gave you.'

'God? You are joking me.'

Desperately, I tried again. 'Look, I can see you're not stupid. You must do a good job for your uncle, or else he wouldn't employ you. You could put that talent to good use elsewhere. Try and earn more money, if that's what you want.'

The walls of that awful shed felt as if they were closing in on me. I felt claustrophobic, paralysed, a tiny sardine trapped in a huge net. I wanted out. My mind began to chase its own tail, planning, planning, planning.

'It's all too late now, though, init? And it's all your fault,' he moaned.

'It's never too late. If you let me go now, I'll say nothing, I promise. If the police are onto you already, then you may only get done for possession. I mean, I don't know how involved you are in all of this.' I paused. 'How involved are you?'

'None of your business. And what d'you know about getting by? You don't know the meaning of it – of having to struggle for every penny. No money left to have a good time, get girls, nice cars, flash holidays.' He paused. 'You've got a nice car. What do you do to get money?'

'I write. But I work hard. It hasn't all come easy. I've made it work for me. It would have been easier to rob banks, yes, or grow cannabis, or prostitute myself by marrying a rich man. Much easier. But I didn't. I put in the hours. And it's hard work. But you could do the same, if you really wanted.'

'No. I'm done.'

I had the distinct feeling there was something he wasn't telling me.

'What is it? Who's pulling the strings here? Who are you working for?'

'If I told you that, I'd have to shoot you.'

I sensed him smile, as if he'd cracked a joke, and I recognised the quote from *Johnny English*. Even so, I felt a cold, dark icicle drip down my spine.

'Don't even joke about it. Please.'

'I'm not.' His tone was deadly serious.

'Right.'

'Enough of this talking. You can stay here the night, then in the morning we'll have decided what to do with you.'

White panic screamed through me. 'No! No! Please!'

'You'll be okay.' Pulling open the door, he turned to me. 'Look, it's a nice evening. There's a blanket in the corner.' He pointed at the floor behind me.

I turned to look, but as I did, he left, locking the door behind him.

'No ...!' I screamed.

Hammering my fists against the door, I rattled and pulled at the handle repeatedly, all the while screaming and screaming.

But there was no reply. Just the distant roar of traffic.

Everyday people going about their everyday business.

20

Sheffield, Yorkshire

IT was DI Forbes who opened the door. I blinked as light filled the space around me.

'You alright, April? Come on, up you get now.'

Taking my arm, she helped me to stand.

I'd spent hours pulling and yanking the wooden slats of the walls, banging at the door, shouting and screaming at whoever might be passing. All to no avail. The shed was much more solid than its age would have dictated. And if anyone had been walking by, they certainly wouldn't have heard me, stuck there in that putrid shed right at the bottom of the garden.

I must have fallen asleep around two o'clock. I had no watch, my phone was still in my handbag, and I had no idea where that might be. At first, I'd ignored the thick, fringed blanket in the corner; it smelled disgusting. But then I was so tired, so desperate to sleep, I'd needed it to sit on. I'd fallen asleep eventually, but still kept waking up, my mind whirring, straining, startling itself with thoughts of what would happen in the morning. After all, I'd seen his face. He wouldn't exactly have allowed me to go free, would he?

Thankfully, I was to be spared that most delightful occurrence.

I stood up quickly, brushing the dust from my clothes. Suddenly, Lottie came running at me, full pelt.

'Lottie,' I said. 'Where have you come from?' Picking her up, I hugged her tearfully as her warm tongue licked my face.

'She was sniffing round the door when we got here,' said DI Forbes. 'We guessed you'd be in here.'

'Ah, Lottie, you clever dog. She must have got through Mum's hedge.'

'Are you okay, April? Any injuries or anything?'

'No. Thanks. I'm fine.'

'Come on, let's get you home to a hot shower, then we can talk.'

'I need to take Lottie home. Mum'll be worried.'

'We can do that. I need to interview her, anyway, see if she saw anything.'

'No. Please don't,' I pleaded. 'Don't tell her what's happened, and nothing about this place. She'd never stay here, and she loves that house. And she won't have seen anything, anyway.'

'Well …' she hesitated.

'Please, I beg you, DI Forbes. If you could just say you found Lottie on the road or something?'

She nodded. 'Okay. For you, April.'

'Thank you.'

DI Forbes took Lottie from me while another plain clothes' chap checked the shed for evidence. A very young, extremely tall, uniformed policeman with acne led me back to my car. The traffic noise in the distance had stilled, to be replaced by the exquisite music of birds singing. My Mini was still there in one piece, my handbag on the back seat.

He unlocked the door for me, handing me the key. 'It was unlocked all night with the key still in the ignition, from what we can make out. Is that how you left it?'

'No, it was definitely locked. But the chap who accosted me - he had the key. He must have put it back again.'

'Who was it, do you know?'

'I don't know his name, but he's a friend of Steve Yates, lives in Millerstone. I know him.'

'Steve Yates. Do you know his address?' He pulled out a pencil and pad.

'No. I can get it, though. But how did you know where I was?'

'An old chap rang through. You're a lucky lady.'

I nodded in agreement, swallowing back the tears threatening to tumble out.

He smiled sympathetically. 'Don't you worry, we'll get him.'

'Thank you.'

Pulling my bag from the car, I quickly checked the contents. Everything was there.

'Good job it wasn't stolen,' he continued. 'But then, it's a nice neighbourhood round here.'

I didn't say anything. I was too tired, too upset, just wanted to get home to a hot bath and bed. A hot, strawberry-scented bath.

My bath, however, was somewhat delayed when Colin rang. But how good it was to hear his voice.

'How are you, darling? I tried ringing last night, but you must have left your mobile at home.'

'It was in my bag, in the car. I couldn't get to it because some idiot locked me in the shed at the bottom of their garden.'

'What?' he said, half laughing.

'I'm not joking, Colin. That house next door to Mum's - the one I told you about? I saw lights on …'

'You didn't go round there?'

'Yes.' The tears came flooding now, the horrors of the night finally sinking in.

'What? Why? I thought the police were watching it.'

'I know. I – I didn't actually go in. I was only sitting in the car, watching.'

'So what happened?'

'A friend of Steve Yates - I know him, he's in the Village Players - he saw me. He pulled me out of the car and locked me in the shed.'

'Are you okay, are you hurt?'

'No. Just a bit shaken, that's all.'

'He locked you in a shed?'

'Yes.'

'He must be crazy. What's the point of that?'

'I don't know. But yes, he must be. He must have known the police would catch up with him at some point.'

'Maybe he thought no-one would find you.'

A shiver, icy cold and calculating, seeped through me.

'I don't even want to think about that.'

'Sorry, darling.'

'How are you, anyway? How's your first day at work?'

'Everyone's very friendly, helpful. I just need a desk now.'

'What?'

'They need to set me up with a desk. Looks like it's going to be this afternoon now, so I've sneaked out for a quiet coffee. There's a Starbucks just round the corner. I'm looking out onto a small boulevard full of lovely old benches and gnarled old trees.'

'Sounds gorgeous.'

'You'll love it here, April. And the apartment's fantastic.'

Listening to his soothing voice, his calm, steady aura enveloping me, even down the line from Brussels, I smiled.

'I can't wait to come over.'

'I can't wait to see you.'

I yawned so deeply my jaw threatened to crack.

'Colin, I need to get a hot bath and go to bed – sorry.'

'Don't be. But if you need me just ring, okay? Any time.'

'Thanks.'

'I love you.'

'I love you, too.'

*

DI Forbes called at ten thirty the following morning, prompt. Rested and refreshed, I'd got up early, tidied the house, and made Colombian coffee. My writing could wait. I can never write when I'm upset, anyway. That thing about Writer's Pain has never applied to me. Thank goodness.

'How are you feeling?' she asked as I motioned for her to come in.

'Much better, thank you. But how on earth did you find me?'

'Didn't we tell you?'

'The young PC just said an old chap rang.'

I offered her a seat at the kitchen table and poured coffee.

'We thought it best to get you home and asleep,' she replied. 'The talking could wait. We've done what we needed to do. So how are you feeling?'

'A bit shaken, obviously. I think it's more a case of what could have happened, rather than what actually did happen.'

'Well, he's behind bars now.'

'Really?' I asked, surprised.

She nodded. 'It's been a busy twenty-four hours.'

'Fantastic.' Now I could smile. Now I could relax. 'So, come on then, tell me what's happened.'

'Okay.' She sighed deeply. 'We've arrested him and his two cronies, one of them being Steve Yates. The other one, the big chief by all accounts, was on his way to Holland. We caught up with him in Hull.'

'So, come on, how *did* you find me?'

'Your car. Big mistake on their part, leaving it there. A guy out walking his dog noticed the key in the ignition, then saw your bag on the seat. He thought they might get stolen, so he called 999. That was around five-thirty, yesterday morning.'

'That was nice of him. But it is a good neighbourhood. Usually.'

'So one of our coppers drove out there, radioed in to get your details, and we tried ringing you. When you didn't answer the phone or your doorbell, we grew suspicious. Then they saw the house was on our watch list, and I was notified. And Bob's your uncle.'

'I wonder why he put the key back.'

'Good question. Probably didn't know what else to do with it. Might have hoped someone would steal the car, then they'd get blamed for your disappearance. Who knows?'

'That's scary. What if you'd never found me?'

'Don't even think about that,' she warned.

'I take it he saw me at the house before, when I was 'noseying around', as he put it?'

'Apparently, he was in the shed when you called out, and he went to see who it was.'

'Oh.' Suddenly my highly fragrant, very wonderful Columbian coffee looked like mud.

'Yes. You need to be careful next time, my girl.'

'There won't be a next time.'

'We'll see.'

'What does that mean?' I retorted.

'It means, once you get bitten by the bug it can become addictive.'

'What bug?'

'Crime detection.'

I shook my head fervently. 'No. Never again.'

'Not even if Sean McGavin calls on you?'

'Not even then. He's Senior Crime Reporter for the Sheffield Star. I'm a lowly Mills and Boon-type writer. I have no idea what I'm supposed to be doing.'

'That's fine, then. Wouldn't want you in any more trouble, now would we?'

I grinned. 'Definitely not.'

'Good. That's settled then.'

'Right.'

We sat there chatting and sipping coffee, until curiosity got the better of me.

'What's his name?'

'Who, the creep who locked you up?'

'Yes.'

'Warren Craig. Parents divorced, into petty crime from the age of fourteen, now lives on his own. His uncle owns a spare parts shop the other side of Sheffield.'

'He did mention working for him. He doesn't get paid much, by all accounts.'

'Kids these days want it on a plate.'

'I suppose so, but it can't be easy for them.'

'My God, don't go feeling sorry for him. He deserves everything that's coming to him. Think of all the poor mites hooked on heroin due to the likes of him.'

'So, where exactly does Steve Yates fit into all of this?'

She looked at me carefully. 'The thing is, April, we think either Warren Craig or Steve Yates, or even both, may be the burglar.'

Talk about blood running cold. I'd just been locked in a shed overnight by a possible murderer.

'Lady Barnstaple's murderer?'

She nodded. 'Yes - possibly.'

'He did say he was always hard up, in need of cash. But what evidence do you have?'

'We've already interviewed Steve Yates about the burglaries, but he's denying everything. He's got alibis we're still looking into. But who's to say Warren Craig's not been in on it – the two of them together?'

'That's a possibility. I mean, one could act as a lookout or something, and that's why they never get caught.'

'Steve Yates was there when you had your bag stolen, he's worked at the old people's home, and the local Spar where Lady Barnstaple used to shop. She may easily have told him she was going away.'

I was horrified. 'No.'

'It's too much of a coincidence. He's a junkie, April, he needs the money to feed his habit. He helps

Warren Craig and their other pal, Neil Kennedy, sell the stuff. And one of their buyers, would you believe, is another friend of ours. Tobias Wilkinson.'

'Toby?'

'Yes. He only buys, though. Doesn't sell, doesn't get involved in the production.'

'You've been watching him, too?'

'We're keeping an eye on them all, and a few others to boot. Interesting work.'

'So, are you arresting them, Steve Yates and his pals?'

'Only for aiding and abetting the production of cannabis, and for dealing. Not for the burglaries, not yet. We need interviews, confessions.'

'What if they don't confess?'

'Then we need evidence. DNA. Something.'

'Let's hope they fess up then.'

'We've definitely got them for the weed house. DNA everywhere, it seems. We've a team there now, clearing it out. It won't be worth a penny by the time they've finished. They never are, these cannabis farms.'

I cringed. 'But what about Mum's house? Surely it will affect the price of her house, if ever she sells?'

'Oh, they're only renting the place. The owner will be made to sort it out, don't worry.'

But I was.

*

I rang Sean as soon as DI Forbes had gone.

'I have a confession to make,' I said. 'I feel terrible.'

'What is it?'

'It's not Toni.'

'What? You're telling me it's not Toni when I already knew it wasn't?'

'Sorry.'

'Right.'

'Has DI Forbes rung yet?' I asked.

'No? Why?'

'Okay. Then I have some really serious grovelling to do.'

'Now there's a first.'

He really *was* mad at me.

'Cut the crap, Sean. Please. I'm trying to be serious.'

'Okay. Carry on.'

'They think it's Steve Yates. And a pal of his.'

'How do they know?'

'It was DI Forbes who figured it out. His pal, Warren Craig, locked me in the shed at the drugs house, then left my Mini with the key in the ignition and my handbag on the ...'

'Whoa! Slow down, April. You're not making any sense.'

'Sorry.' Suddenly exhausted, I took a deep breath. 'Steve Yates is probably the burglar, although it could also be a friend of his, Warren Craig. Steve was at the dress rehearsal when my bag was stolen, he's worked at the old people's home, and he's worked at the local Spar, where Lady Barnstaple used to shop. And Warren Craig's just a nasty piece of work. Drug-dealing, kidnapping, the works.'

'So how did they work all that out? Not that I'm envious or anything.'

I grinned; same old Sean.

'That house next door to Mum's. They're involved in all of that. But there's some big chief as well.'

'Okay?'

'I was parked there on Monday night, outside the drugs house. I saw some lights on, so I just thought I'd see what was going on. Warren Craig pulled me out of the car and locked me in the shed. I was there all night.' I choked back my tears.

'Oh – April.'

'Some old chap out walking his dog saw the key in the ignition, and rang the police.'

'So DI Forbes put two and two together, did she?'

'They'd already been watching him.'

'Well, well, well. Good for her.'

'So what I want to say is, I'm sorry. I'm sorry I suspected Toni.'

'That's okay, April. I forgive you. Just never tell Toni.'

*

It was six o'clock as I drove to Mum's house that Wednesday evening. Simon Mayo was playing *Alright Now* on the radio, so I sang along. It seemed to fit my mood somehow. I was finally free. Free of the burglar. Free of the cannabis farm next door to Mum's. And free of the accusations I'd made against Toni. What a dreadful few weeks it had been. And what a tremendous relief, a weight lifted from my shoulders, to finally be rid of it all.

Mum was bright as a button. She never mentioned the police having been next door, or of Lottie having gone missing. I'd checked the drugs house as I drove past. There was just an old van parked outside, and a couple of guys in blue overalls carrying white plastic boxes out of the house. No sirens blaring, no flashing lights. Very low-key. Thank goodness. Mum really wouldn't have stayed there if she'd known.

However, fully dressed in navy trousers and cream blouse, makeup just so, orange nail varnish perfect, Mum looked incredible. I was taking her to meet Diane Downing and Jim Allsop at the Flying Toad. We were to be the team leaders of the Grand Auction committee. It was a good way of getting Mum out of the house and meeting people again. And I must admit, she'd gained a definite sparkle to her eye by the end of the evening.

The pub was buzzing as we walked in, despite it being mid-week. George greeted me as usual with my pint of Guinness, and welcomed Mum like a long-lost friend.

I introduced her. 'This is my mum, Judy. She's helping us with our fundraising. Mum, this is George.'

He smiled. 'Well, and what a lovely lady too. I don't know where she gets it from.'

'Flatterer.' I grinned.

'Welcome to our pub, Judy. What would you like to drink? On the house.'

'Well, I wouldn't mind a small white wine, please,' she replied, blushing at all the attention.

George poured her a glassful. 'Your wish is my command.'

'Thanks, George.' I winked at him, paid for my drink, and carried them both through. Jim and Diane were already in the back room, waiting for us.

'Hi, you two. This is my mum, Judy. Mum, this is Diane Downing from the WI, and Jim Allsop, songwriter extraordinaire.'

Diane extended her hand. 'Pleased to meet you, Judy. You must come along to one of our meetings some time. We could do with more helping hands.'

Mum shook her hand. 'Well, thank you for asking, but unfortunately I don't drive.'

'I could always give you a lift – you know that,' I said.

'Well, yes. But I don't like to bother you.'

'Oh, Mum.'

'Well, we'll see.'

But Jim, who was just as Josie had described him - a bit gnarled with shoulder-length silver hair and wrinkled, smiling brown eyes - interrupted.

'Judy, may I just say something here?'

Mum turned to him, eyes wide with astonishment at his use of her first name when she'd only just met him.

'Yes?'

'You saying you don't drive. What kind of answer is that? I realise you've had plenty of years in which to learn, and have never had the time, but what's stopping you now?'

She shook her head daintily. 'Oh, no. Not at my age. Come on now.'

'I do not believe you've just said that. Why not at your age? You've got a brain, haven't you? You've got two legs? You look like a very intelligent woman to me. So what's stopping you?'

Mum looked slightly uncomfortable, but said nothing.

I turned to Jim. 'Mum's been a little under the weather just lately, Jim. But it's a good idea, maybe something we can look at in the future. Yes, Mum?'

She nodded weakly. 'I suppose so.'

But he was insistent. 'No, we'll have none of this. You come round to my place and I'll teach you the basics. I have plenty of land, so you can practise there 'til you get more confident, then we can arrange a few lessons. And that'll be you, on your way.'

'But I haven't even got a car,' Mum said.

'We'll arrange that, too. Money's no object.'

'Oh, no. Thank you, but no,' replied my poor mum.

I smiled. 'It's a really generous offer, Jim, but we don't even know you. Not properly.'

Now it was his turn to look embarrassed. 'Sorry. It's just the thought of poor Judy here, sitting all on her own just because she can't drive. Sad, it is. Really sad.'

'Well, I'll see what we can do.' I turned to Mum. 'You could always get a taxi, I suppose.'

But Jim quickly fished a card from his wallet. 'Here's my address and phone number. Let me have yours and we'll arrange to meet up, for coffee or something. That's usually the best way of getting to know a person, to my mind.'

The rest of the evening was not quite so eventful, yet all the while I could see the hint of a sparkle between Mum and Jim. I was surprised, shocked even. I'd never pictured her with any man other than Dad. But there the picture was, well and truly framed, right before my eyes.

We made a list of shops, cafes, restaurants; anywhere really, that could provide us with something to auction. I offered signed copies of my books and Jim offered the promise of six guitar/songwriting lessons. He was a surprising phenomenon, Jim Allsop. Rumour has it he likes to keep himself to himself, but it became obvious that when he became truly involved in something, he became all encompassing, wouldn't take no for an answer.

'Right,' said Diane. 'We start as soon as possible. We need to visit each place in turn and ask for prizes or promises. I'll place an ad in the village magazine asking for promises. It could be something like ironing or childminding, or even washing cars, as long as we make money out of it.'

'Well, it's all for a good cause,' I replied. 'I don't know what we'd do without our swimming pool. It's such a wonderful thing for kids to grow up with.'

'Us oldies, too,' insisted Diane. 'It helps keep us fit as well, you know.'

'Did you know Toni Fitzgerald's having a garden party to raise money for the pool?'

'Oh? When's that?' she asked.

'The second week in September.'

'So soon? I've not seen it advertised anywhere.'

'Well, maybe that's something she needs a hand with. I'll give her a ring.'

'Will she need some help with stuff?' asked Mum. 'I'll bake if she likes.'

'Mum, that would be brilliant,' I enthused. *It's all coming together - she's trying to become involved.* 'I'll ask her, and I'll bring all the stuff over for you, if you like.'

'I'm sure I can get to the supermarket,' she replied, tartly. 'There's one just round the corner, you know.'

'Sorry, Mum,' I smiled. 'I didn't mean it like that.'

'The WI is always looking for excuses to bake. I'll get onto it first thing tomorrow,' said Diane.

'Thanks, that's great. I'll let Toni know.'

I caught Mum out of the corner of my eye, writing down her number for Jim and passing it along. Surreptitiously. Maybe she thought I'd mind her seeing another man.

*

I rang Toni as soon as I got home.

'Hi there. How's things?' she asked.

'Fine, thanks, fine. I'm just ringing about the garden party. How's it going? I mean, I've not seen any adverts or anything.'

'I know. It is all arranged, though. I've got tables and seats coming from the Memorial Hall, and tea urns and stuff. But I do need to get it out there.'

'I've just met up with Diane Downing from the Women's Institute. She's offered for the WI to do some baking. My mum, too. Is that okay?'

'The more the merrier. Thanks.'

'Good. So what are you doing about advertising, then?'

'The kids have both made posters at school, but they've forgotten to bring them home. Twice.'

'Oh.'

'I'm beginning to wonder if they're awful.'

'They won't be. Your Abigail's a brilliant little artist.'

I'd seen a display of Abi's work in the Memorial Hall once. Her talent was pretty exceptional.

'I know. But I need to let everyone know about it as soon as possible, or they'll be making other plans for the weekend.'

'How about Facebook?'

'That's a thought.'

'Ask everyone to spread the word. Then on Monday you could pop into school and pick up the posters yourself.'

'Do you think it will go alright? I mean, I have asked all the mums at school to bake, and some are coming along to serve teas and stuff.'

'It'll be fine. You do know we're having a Grand Auction in aid of the pool as well?'

'Tom's mum told me. It's after the play, isn't it?'

'Yep.'

'Just make sure you leave your jewellery at home this time. We don't want any more thefts, thank you very much.'

I blushed hotly. Guilt, let thy name be mud.

'You know we've caught him, don't you?' I said.

'What?'

'Has Sean not told you?'

'I haven't seen him, not since ...'

'But Toni, we've got him. We've got the burglar.'

'You are joking. Who is it, then?'

'Well, they've not exactly got him yet, but they nearly have. It's the chap who does the lighting for the Players. Steve Yates. And one of his cronies, Warren Craig.'

I went into the full story of the house next door to Mum's, my kidnapping, and the subsequent arrest of all three men.

'Oh my God, April. Are you alright?'

'I'm fine.'

'So, he must have been watching my house.'

'Toni, don't. Don't get upset. It's done. It's over with.'

She sighed. 'I know.'

'Have you got your burglar alarm yet?'

'They're coming next week. And it's not soon enough.'

'Well then, you'll be all safe and secure. It's a wonderful feeling.'

'So why did he do it? I mean, what made him do it? And poor Lady Barnstaple. At least we're still alive.' Her voice cracked with emotion.

'Toni, don't.'

'Sorry.'

'Look, it's late. Go to bed, read a good book, and get some sleep.'

'So, are we arranging a coffee some time soon?'

'We are. And listen, I'll be popping into the salon on Friday, touting for freebies. You up for it?

21

I always feel sorry for the manager of the Spar in our village. Well, for everyone who works there. They insist on having the air conditioning at the lowest temperature possible, so even in the middle of a heatwave the place is icy cold. No wonder most of them work part-time. And I bet their wages go a good way to buying thermals, too, the vests and the long johns.

Summer. It hadn't been a good one, but the mini heatwave we were having that week was pretty amazing. So, Friday morning, dressed in skimpy top and cropped jeans, I began scouring the village for goodies.

Spar was the first place I called into. It opens at seven, way before any of the other shops. There was a long queue, people chatting, buying their morning paper, paying for petrol. I stood there shivering, waiting in line, waiting my turn.

But Jeff, the manager, was lovely when I asked for a contribution.

'I'll check it out, but I can't see a problem with letting you have a few boxes of chocolates. Big ones, mind.'

He was a large chap, and the black padded gilet covering his torso didn't help much. But his smile was genuine, his blue eyes full of benevolence.

I smiled. 'Thanks, Jeff. That's really kind of you.'

'No problem. All for a good cause.'

I called in at the Ashbourne next. The receptionist, a tall young thing with long blonde hair, welcomed me with open arms. Until I gave her the reason for my visit.

'Well, I don't really know about that. I mean, I'll have to check with the manager.'

I smiled. 'Of course. Naturally.'

As I waited for her to return, I took in the ambience of the place, something I hadn't been able to do the previous time, when Sean and I had interviewed Lady Barnstaple's daughter. The long sofas and tall armchairs were now occupied by diners waiting to be called into the restaurant. I could smell fresh coffee, bacon and eggs, bread toasting, butter melting. My mouth watered. A group of businessmen in dark suits chatted awkwardly amongst themselves whilst reading the papers. A young couple in the opposite corner were obviously meeting clandestinely, nervously, holding hands but unintentionally checking the door every few minutes.

When he arrived, the hotel manager was charming.

'Good morning. I'm Malcolm, the manager here. I understand from Cristabelle you're having a Grand Auction.'

'We are, yes.'

'I did actually hear something about it. And your name is?'

'I'm April. April Stanislavski.'

Balding with a slight paunch, his grin was slightly off-key, my romance books obviously not good enough for him.

'Ah, the writer. Okay, tell you what – you come through to my little office and we'll discuss plans.'

Bemused, I followed him, the trail of fresh coffee filtering through to my very pores.

He must have sensed it. 'I've asked Cristabelle to bring coffee through. That's alright, isn't it?'

I returned his smile willingly. 'That would be lovely, thank you.'

'Good. Right. Here we are, then.'

Pushing open a sturdy door, he indicated the captain's chair directly in front of me.

'Thank you,' I said, still surprised at the fuss being made.

He inched round the small rectangular desk to sit down. Just at that moment Cristabelle arrived with coffee. A silver cafetière, two cups and saucers, a sugar bowl and milk jug, all set beautifully onto a silver tray.

'Thank you,' I smiled. 'This looks lovely.'

'All part of the service.' He clicked at the keyboard in front of him. 'Now then, let me see.'

I waited patiently as he searched online, picking at the keys with two fat index fingers, his shoulders moving rhythmically in time.

'Now then. We usually have rooms available the second and third weeks of November. Once summer has ended, but Christmas hasn't yet begun.' He looked up. 'What do you think?'

I had actually begun to think he was a bit confused, that he thought I was here to book a room.

'This is for the Grand Auction, isn't it?' I asked.

'Yes,' he replied. 'Of course.'

'I – I think we only really wanted a bottle of whisky or something,' I stammered.

He looked at me carefully. 'Here, let me pour the coffee. Milk? Sugar?'

'Milk, please. No sugar.'

He passed me a cup and I sipped. It was truly delicious, rounded and smooth.

'Thank you, it's very nice. What is it?'

'Organic. From Peru. Toffee, fruit and cocoa.'

'Mm, very nice.'

'Thank you. So, what I'm offering is a one-night stay for two, with dinner and breakfast thrown in. But it would have to be one of those two weekends.'

I put down my cup. 'This really is extremely generous of you. Are you sure that's okay?'

'April – may I call you April?'

'Of course.'

'April, if we can't do a little something like this for our local community, then we shouldn't really be in business, should we? Besides, it's good publicity, don't you think?'

'I – I really don't know what to say. Except yes, thank you very much. That's brilliant.'

'It's a deal, then. Shall we make it the second weekend? Then we know where we are.'

'Thank you. The WI will be so pleased.'

'Good. I'm glad we've got it sorted. Now, drink up your coffee while I make the arrangements.'

The next place on my list was Toni's. Her shop is on Station Road, just around the corner from the Ashbourne and along the road from the Flying Toad.

Station Road is so-called because it leads to the railway station, one of the great advantages of

Millerstone. It makes life so much less complicated for people, both young and old. I mean, Mum wouldn't have had the problems she had if she'd had access to a railway connection. And youngsters don't feel that urgent need to pass their driving test once they're seventeen. So the folks of Millerstone are indeed very lucky people.

Toni was busy cutting hair as I walked in. I think it was Mrs Wilson under the scissors (I often see her tottering about), although I couldn't be sure. People look so different when their hair is wet.

'Hi, April. Cup of tea?' called Toni as I closed the door behind me.

Mandy, Toni's assistant, her auburn hair scraped into a large bun, was busy with the kettle.

'No, thanks. I've just had coffee at the Ashbourne.'

'Ooh. Posh.' She smiled.

'I only popped in to sort out stuff for the Grand Auction.'

'Oh, of course. Yes, I'd forgotten.'

'They were really good about it. A one-night stay for two, with dinner and breakfast thrown in.'

'Crikey. Can you believe that?'

'Fantastic, isn't it?' I nodded.

'That'll get the punters bidding.'

'You sure you don't want a cuppa?' asked Mandy, pulling at the seat of her dungarees in her typical tomboy fashion.

'No. Really. Thanks, Mandy.'

'We have chocolate lollies if you want one. It's our Friday treat,' said Toni.

'I thought you were on a diet?'

She stopped snipping. 'Have you ever had one of the chocolate lollies from Spar?'

I shook my head. 'No?'

'You should. Honestly, it takes as many calories to break into the wrapping as you get by eating it.'

I laughed. 'No, I'm fine, thanks.'

'We'll eat them this afternoon, then. It can be pudding. So, you're touting for goodies, are you?'

'It doesn't have to be something expensive. A free cut and blowdry will do.'

'Well, it's good for business, I suppose. Free advertising.'

'That's what the chap at the Ashbourne said.'

'So, what do you think? A cut and blowdry, then?'

'Why not? It's as good as anything.' Sitting at one of the chairs, I fiddled with my hair before the huge illuminated mirror. Cathy had done a good job.

'Okay.' Toni waved her scissors through the air. 'A cut and blowdry, and throw in a couple of shampoo and conditioner sets too. Or a GHD styler. Or is that going a bit far?'

I felt guilty all over again. How could I ever have suspected her, my friend?

'Something like that would get plenty of bids, that's for sure,' I said.

'Okay, then. A cut and blowdry and a GHD styler. Two separate lots of bidding, though.'

'Thanks, Toni, that's really good of you. You're sure that's okay?'

'We're trying to make money for the pool, aren't we?'

I made my way home after calling at the veg shop (they volunteered a basket of fruit), the pharmacy (a box of smellies), the Deli (a build-it yourself chocolate cabin), the craft shop (gorgeous soft black teddy bear), the pool café (lunch for two), the post office (box of birthday cards) and various other establishments, all of whom were more than willing to help. Such generosity from such a small village.

*

The Flying Toad was very quiet. Even George was subdued as he handed me my Guinness. I counted three pound coins into his hand.

'You okay, George?' I asked.

'Fine, thanks, April. You?'

'I'm fine. It's just, you seem rather quiet, that's all.'

'Car's on the blink,' he murmured.

'Oh, no. Won't it mend?'

'I dunno, do I? I'm taking it in Monday morning.'

'What's wrong with it?'

'Engine, I think.'

'Oh. Sorry about that.'

'Not your fault. It's just old, that's all. I took it in last week, saw young Toby there. He's got himself engaged, you know. Wedding's in December.'

I smiled. 'Well, that is good news. A Christmas wedding. That'll be nice.'

'Up at the old Parish church, I think.'

'Lovely.'

'They're living with her parents apparently, until they've saved a deposit. There's plenty of room at their old place. And cash. Shouldn't take 'em long to buy their own.'

Was it my little conversation that had got Toby thinking, I wondered? Did he have a conscience after all? And was he finally growing up, taking responsibility?

I picked up my Guinness. 'Thanks, George. I hope the car's not too expensive.'

The rehearsal actually went very well. Alfie made us all laugh, directing one minute, dashing forward to perform his butler's role the next, pirouetting as he returned to being director.

'April,' he said at one point. 'I need you to flirt, my darling. Flirt as if there were no tomorrow.'

'Who with?' I asked, confused.

'With Sir William Tompkinson, of course. After all, you did have an affair with his brother. You weren't just his secretary.'

'Okay. Right. That should be fun.' I grinned.

He stared at me doubtfully. 'You have read through the script, haven't you, my dear?'

'Only very quickly.' I felt myself blushing. 'I've been concentrating on learning my lines.'

He frowned. 'Oh April, how are you supposed to get the nuances right if you don't know the ins and outs of the thing?'

I felt dreadful. 'Sorry, Alfie. I have been really busy.'

'I know, my darling, and I quite understand. But the show must go on, you know.'

He was right, and I felt truly repentant. 'I know. I will try.'

'Promise me you'll sit down this weekend and read it through?'

I nodded. 'I promise. Sorry, Alfie.'

'It's not that long a play, and I know you'll enjoy it really. But you need to know where Miss Forsythe is coming from. She was secretary to Sir Hugh Tompkinson, they had an affair, and this may have led to his going missing, or even to his death. After all, a woman scorned? So did he fake a suicide and move abroad to escape the mess his life was in? Did Miss Forsythe discover his affair with another woman and threaten to tell his wife, so he paid her off, and then ran off? Or did his wife discover his affair with Miss Forsythe and kill him, hiding the body?'

I had to admit, it *was* beginning to sound interesting. I hadn't thought I'd been given much of a part, but this was really gripping, something I could get my teeth into.

'Okay, Alfie. I will read it. Promise.'

'Good girl. I knew you hadn't read it. You're a better actress than that.'

'Sorry. I've had a lot on my plate, what with one thing and another.'

'That's okay. I'll help you get to grips as much as I can. Just ask if you need any help. After all, that's what I'm here for.'

It was just as the evening was ending that Alfie made the announcement.

'Rumours do abound, so as you are probably all well aware by now, Steve Yates has been taken into custody.'

There was a low murmur across the room. It was obvious some of us knew, but some didn't. Percy Wainstone, sitting at the far end of the table, raised his hand.

'If you're looking for a replacement, Alfie, my son would be interested. He's just left school and needs to get his teeth into something.'

Alfie smiled. 'That would be wonderful, Percy. But he'll have to hit the ground running.'

'That's okay. He can come over next week, if you like.'

'They're saying Steve Yates could be the burglar,' murmured Billie. 'And just think, he's been right here, in the middle of all of us.'

'Doesn't bear thinking about,' replied Gemma, shaking her head sadly.

Alfie clapped his hands loudly. 'Come on, ladies, come on. He's not been charged yet, so let's not get carried away. We need to sleep soundly in our beds tonight.'

22

I left the house at five-forty the following morning. It was still dark as I reached Bamford's beautiful Derwent Dam, the home of the World War II Dambusters, but I could see the crimson glow of sunrise in the distance. Driving on, along Snake Pass towards Manchester Airport, I rubbed my eyes as I concentrated on the road ahead, my headlights picking out the mist rising from the moors on either side.

Manchester Airport was fairly quiet for an airport. People with sleepy eyes and yawning faces gazed into space as they queued ahead of me, waiting. A group of teenage girls at the front, underdressed and overexcited, giggled at the slightest thing and made eyes at any guy who passed. Thankfully, they sat to the rear of the plane, away from me, so my journey was quiet and uneventful.

The plane touched down at Brussels Charleroi Airport at ten fifteen, Belgium time. Tired, excited, I rushed through Customs with my overnight bag, eager to see Colin, to feel his warm arms around me.

He did not disappoint.

'How was the flight?' he asked, burying his face into my hair. 'Mm, you smell good.'

'Exactly one hour and twenty-five minutes,' I replied, happily laughing at my own joke.

But he didn't laugh. Instead, taking my bag from me, he folded a bouquet of deep red roses into my arms. They were heavy, expensive, beautiful.

'For you.'

'Thank you. They're beautiful.'

*

The apartment was lovely, with tall wooden windows looking out over the *Rue du Président* below. The interior was slightly clinical, and I think the owner had a penchant for Audrey Hepburn (her picture was everywhere), but it was clean and well looked-after, with red velour sofas, an en-suite bathroom, and a huge brass bed. A cleaner came in every weekday while Colin was at work, so he didn't have much to do, other than cook and eat.

I made coffee while Colin heated croissants and pains au chocolate. I was starving, and they smelled delicious, reminding me immediately of a particular French patisserie I once visited in Paris.

Colin placed his arms around me as I washed up afterwards. 'Fancy a wander?'

'Couldn't think of anything better. I love new places.'

'You sure about that? You don't fancy doing anything else?' he asked, twirling me round to kiss me.

I grinned. 'I'm sure.'

'Okay.'

The air outside was warm, but the earlier rain had made the pavements shiny, steamy. Tourists were leaving their hotels tentatively, umbrellas and raincoats at the ready. We sauntered along *Avenue Louise*, a wide street bustling with shoppers, cars, trams, and lovely old chestnut trees. I popped into *Versace* for a few minutes. Okay, it was half an hour, but I still left empty-handed. So we continued our walk until we reached the *Grand-Place*, a wonderful cobbled market square going back centuries.

The *Grand-Place* was beautiful, replete with history, although it had nearly been destroyed in 1695 by Louis XIV. So when it was rebuilt, piece by piece, the bourgeois of Brussels restored it to its former glory, a faithful reflection of the original, rather than rebuilding in a contemporary style. And it really was beautiful, with the *Hôtel de Ville* and its gorgeous bell-tower rising to the sky. Opposite was the King's House, or the *Maison du Roi*, a museum, and my favourite of the two.

There were a couple of stalls at the centre of the square, their red canvas roofs attracting tourists by the bucketful. One sold paintings of Brussels, the other roast chestnuts. The aroma was delicious, rich and smoky, mouth-watering. So, after a quick lunch, we bought a small bagful before wandering out of the *Grand-Place* onto the *Rue au Beurre.* Full of delicious chocolate shops, the scent of cocoa and vanilla pervading my senses like a soft cloak, I bought two boxes of handmade pralines to take home. The rather plump woman behind the counter allowed me to try a couple before buying, and even though they were expensive, they were worth every penny. I knew Mum and Josie would love them.

*

Back at the apartment, Colin insisted upon making tea – he'd bought the ingredients especially - while I read and listened to music. But I was tired after my early start and fell asleep almost instantly, waking up to the scent of roast garlic and lasagne.

The meal was delicious. With the curtains drawn and soft candles flickering around the room, we ate roast veg and blue cheese lasagne, followed by *gaufre de Bruxelles*, a Belgian waffle, with strawberries, fresh cream and hot chocolate sauce. We drank red wine and finished with decaf coffee.

'You sure know how to treat a girl,' I smiled, sitting back into the sofa and curling my legs beneath me.

Colin sat beside me. 'I'll do the washing up in the morning. How about an early night?'

'What?' I checked my watch. 'But it's only nine o'clock.'

He grinned, taking hold of my hand and kissing it. 'I know.'

He was such a romantic; how could I resist? Yet I still played hard to get.

'That means it's only eight o'clock at home.'

'I know. Disgusting, what?'

'Definitely.'

'But you fell asleep earlier. I saw you.'

'So?'

'So you must need an early night.' His lips were working their way up my arm, his soft green eyes melting into my very existence.

I laughed. 'You're incorrigible.'

'You are so right.'

*

We awoke the following day to sunshine and birdsong. Two hours later, we were walking through Brussels Park, a typical European park with trees and a fountain. It was next to the main road, so there wasn't the peace and tranquility I'd have liked, but I still enjoyed it, and saw some spectacularly amazing buildings as we approached the entrance.

'You've found your way around quickly,' I mused, pushing my hands inside my coat pockets as a chill wind ran through me.

'I'm good, aren't I?' he cajoled.

'You been here before?'

He shook his head. 'Never. Not before this week.'

There was a very slight hesitation there. I wondered whether to pursue it, or whether to stay shtum. I should have stayed shtum.

'So what – you've been here in your lunch hour?'

Pausing mid-stride, he turned, pulling my hands out of their pockets and holding them. 'I met up with Tasha, Monday evening. She'd just finished work and offered to take me on a tour of the sights.'

'I'll bet she did.' I pulled away, running off, my heart in my mouth.

He ran after me. 'No, April – it's not like that.'

I stopped to sit at a bench, the ground beneath my feet uneven and rough with pebbles. Catching up, his breath coming in short gasps, Colin sat beside me.

'We're just friends. We're divorced, for God's sake. Honestly. I wouldn't spoil all this - us - for her. She's history. Yes, I was once madly in love with her, but then I saw her for what she was. It really is over between us.'

I looked him in the eye. 'You swear that? She's not trying to get her hands on you again?'

'I swear. I love you, April.'

*

We ate lunch on the *Avenue Louise*. A small café with round tables outside, green gingham parasols and padded chairs. Very Parisian. But I didn't eat much. My stomach was still churning at the thought of Colin and Tasha walking through Brussels Park in the sunshine, hand in hand. Okay, they probably hadn't actually held hands. Yet. But who was to say it might not happen in the future? Who was to say she wouldn't stumble and fall, so he had to catch hold of her, her very touch reawakening that same old passion they'd had years before? Who was to say there might not still be something between them?

'You okay, April?' asked Colin. 'You're very quiet.'

Swallowing my tagliatelle, I smiled. 'I'm fine. I think my early start yesterday must be catching up with me. This pasta's delicious, but I'm not really that hungry. Sorry.'

He took hold of my hand. 'It's okay. I understand. Well, it's my turn to come to you next weekend, so we won't need to explore anywhere. We can spend the whole weekend in bed if you want to.'

His eyes sparkled. His smile was a white snowdrop in the sunshine after a long, hard winter. I felt restored again, secure, safe.

My appetite suddenly returning, I returned his smile with a *Miss Piggy* impersonation.

'Moi? A teensy weensy little thing like me? In bed the whole weekend? I think not. Mama would not approve …'

He laughed loudly. 'April, how did I live without you for so long?'

*

It was on our way back to Colin's apartment that we bumped into his neighbour from the upstairs apartment. Aged about seventy, he was staggering towards the stairs carrying his shopping in two old cotton bags. Colin offered to help and he allowed us to escort him to his apartment. A widower, he lived on his own, his lined face and shabby clothing revealing the hardships he'd endured since losing his wife. Colin told me his life story later, but he had no need; I could tell just from looking at the chap he wasn't finding life easy. Feeling an inexplicable empathy with him, I listened as he chatted on about the price of food, the cost of heating, and the bus fares he had to pay whenever he chose to escape the city. Then, suddenly, alarmingly, I realised why I felt so close to him. He reminded me of my dad. He had that same impish quality.

We carried the bags into the chap's kitchen, and departed amidst much thanking and many requests to return and drink wine with him.

Back at the apartment, Colin made tea, and we sat comfortably on the lovely red sofa.

'So, what do you think to old Florian, then?'

'He's very nice.' I sipped my tea thoughtfully. 'He reminds me a bit of my dad, actually.'

'Does he?'

'I suppose he's got that need about him. Kind of vulnerable, needs someone to take care of, to take care of him. You know what I mean?'

He nodded.

'And he looks as if he's done manual work, like Dad. He was a builder, as you know, but he was also one of the great romantics, always bringing roses home for Mum.'

'He sounds lovely.'

'He was. But he died very young. Fifty-five.'

'What from?'

'Heart attack. Just like that.' I snapped my fingers together. 'Awful.'

'Your mum seems alright, though.'

'Well, she's had her ups and downs, to be honest. I mean, she was still working at the time, and I think that got her through. And of course, we all kept an eye on her. But these last few years, since she retired, it's not been easy. Dad's death was such a shock – so sudden.'

I thought back to the day it happened, to the sudden announcement over the phone from their neighbour Nancy, to the last time I'd seen him, the last time I'd said goodbye, the last, final, hug before heading home to Jeremy. If only I'd known, I'd have hugged him, held him, for longer. I'd have told him how very much I loved him, how I worshipped him, how I would always remember him.

Too late now, I thought, sudden tears rolling down my face. Much too late.

And now Colin was hugging me, holding me.

'Sorry,' I moaned, wiping my face.

'Don't be. It's okay.'

'No, it's not okay.' I pulled back. 'It's not okay. It's bloody awful. It all happened such a long time ago – why does it still upset me so much?'

'Because you cared? Because you loved him?'

I pulled a tissue from my bag. 'But you'd think I'd have got used to the idea, wouldn't you?' Standing before the huge mirror on the lounge wall, a drawing of Audrey Hepburn etched into its surface, I wiped my eyes carefully.

'Well, if it's still upsetting you so much, imagine how it's affecting your mum,' replied Colin.

I paused, staring at my reflection guiltily. 'I know.'

Poor Mum. And all I could do was drag her along to the doctor's and practically accuse her of dementia. She must have been through hell since Dad died.

I turned. 'You're a really nice guy – you know that?'

'So *that's* why you fell for me. And I thought it was my body.'

23

Millerstone, Derbyshire

GOOD news does travel fast. Just a week later, the whole village was brimming, its collective sigh tangible, yet ethereal, its relief echoing across the valley.

The burglar, the man who'd killed Lady Barnstaple, had been caught. Finally. Everybody was smiling. Everyone was happy.

Just to add to the wonderful effect, we'd had wall-to-wall sunshine. Opening the windows of my office to the world, I'd written reams and reams and reams. Bartholomew Ashington was fast becoming an interesting character, a man of power and soul. I'd

339

found a piece on the original character in the library at Bakewell:

He also gave, for ever, the yearly sum of £0.40s., by deed, dated 3rd May, 1718, granted to the poor of Millerstone, for the use of a public school, a piece of land in the small hamlet off Coggers Lane, adjoining the highway, containing four perches; and he further directed, in 1725, his executors to lay out the sum of £200 in purchasing freehold land, to hold to them and their heirs, in trust, that the rents should be applied to charitable and pious uses – viz. he gave to the poor of Millerstone, for ever, the yearly sum of 40s., to be paid to the vicar and overseers for the time being, (this is now distributed with Harriett's charity); and he gave to the vicar for the time being the yearly sum of £3, to be paid on St. Thomas's day, the vicar to preach a charity sermon on that day; and he also gave to the schoolmaster of Millerstone for the time being, the yearly sum of £5, to be paid on St. Thomas's day, provided that his heirs should have the nomination of the said schoolmaster, who should also teach ten of the poorest boys in Millerstone. The sum of £200 was never laid out in land, but annual sums of £0.40s., £3, and £5, are considered as being charges on the Millerstone estate. The building, erected on the land granted in 1718, on the small hamlet off Coggers Lane, called the Edge Green school, consisted of a school-room and two small rooms at the end. It ceased to be used as a school in 1807. About the year

1804 a new school was built by subscription in the village of Millerstone; this kind benefactor died 1716 aged 66 ...

Interesting stuff, indeed, and I was having great fun with the storyline.

*

Saturday arrived, the day of the garden party. And, as might have been predicted, the weather changed and heavy rain poured mercilessly all Friday night, hammering against my windows and sliding down my new back door. Which, thankfully, was completely watertight.

But as morning crept on, the clouds disappeared and there was bright, warming sunshine again. After breakfast, I took a half hour walk before showering, dressing, and driving out to Mum's.

'Hi, April.' Mum was still wearing her *pinny,* as she calls it. 'I've only just finished icing the carrot cake. I found some cute little carrot decorations in the supermarket, so I hope it looks alright.'

'Sounds lovely, Mum.' I followed her into the kitchen, which was clean and tidy, apart from the mixing bowl and utensils she'd just used. I smiled at the carrot cake, which looked incredible. 'Wow, Mum. You should go into business.'

She smiled her lovely smile. 'Oh no, not at my age. It's worn me out doing this little lot.'

But the worktop was a sight to behold. Two Victoria sponge cakes, a tray of gingerbread, and her delicious carrot cake, reminiscent of my teenage years when she *needed to use things up* and would teach me and Jo how to bake.

'It's really good of you, Mum. Do you need to get changed or anything? It's just, I need to get off pretty soon because I'm helping set up.'

'No, it's alright, I'm coming later. But I'll be there for when it starts, don't worry. I just don't want to be hanging round all morning.'

Confused, I bent down to stroke Lottie, silently thankful that dogs can't speak, after my *shed* incident.

'But how will you get there, Mum?'

'Jim.'

'Jim?'

'Jim's bringing me.'

'Oh.' I hadn't anticipated this, at least not so soon.

'I know. I hope you don't mind.'

I was really happy for her. Picking up Lottie, I smiled.

'Oh, Mum, that's lovely news. Of course I don't mind. I'm glad you've got someone to share your life with. I'm really pleased for you.'

Tears filled her eyes. 'Your father was special, you know.'

'I know that, of course I do. But I don't think he'd mind you seeing someone else. It's been a long time.'

'I know.' Her tears flowed freely now.

'Mum, don't.'

Putting Lottie to the floor, I hugged Mum tight, and she sobbed and sobbed, all the pain and the heartache of seventeen years rising to the surface.

Finally, she raised her head, her face flushed, her hair a mess.

'Sorry, love.'

'Don't be. Don't be at all. It's wonderful that you and Dad were so much in love. I've been trying to find that my whole life and never really have. So don't be ashamed. Here, I'll go and grab a tissue.'

Rushing through to the sitting room, I looked around. It was tidy, just like the kitchen, and serene, as if the angst of the past few years had been put to bed. The result of Sofia's cleaning? Or Mum's peace of mind? I pulled a tissue from the box.

*

I drove to Toni's an hour later.

Toni called out as I ducked beneath the weeping willow. 'Isn't it beautiful now?'

'It's a good job. It would have been awful if the rain had continued.'

'You are not kidding.'

'Right, okay, I have rubber gloves, apron, and a few bottles of white. And I've brought Mum's cakes. And my books are in the car.'

'Wine?' she queried.

'For the raffle.'

'Thanks, April, you are good.'

'Now, where do you want me?'

'You can help with this, if you like.'

She was fastening white paper cloths onto the trestle tables she'd borrowed. The tables were bone dry.

'How come they're not wet?' I asked.

'Jayne helped me carry them into the kitchen last night. A total pain, we couldn't move.'

I picked up the tub of drawing pins and began pinning. The job was finished in no time, but the end result was a lawn, beaming with sunshine, and five trestle tables covered in white.

'Doesn't look very exciting, does it?' I volunteered.

But Toni had that sparkle in her eye. 'Aha! Just you wait.'

Disappearing through the kitchen door, she came out with a large cardboard box.

'Here we go.'

She pulled out a dozen Chinese lanterns in shades of pink and green, some empty wine bottles, some old wooden trays that looked like they'd been used for growing seeds, and a few pretty tablecloths.

'Just to jazz the place up a bit.'

'Empty wine bottles?'

'Your Jo's going to fill them with flowers. She asked me to get them.'

'Oh. Right.'

That made me feel so much better; Jo's really good at that sort of thing.

An hour later, the garden was buzzing. Jo had turned up with her three girls. Catherine, the buxom and always jolly and smiling, first year teacher from school was there, too, with some of her pupils' mums, and Diane Downing, and Yvette, the well-heeled horsey type from the WI.

But it always astounds me how a few flowers in well-chosen places can transform a room. Or even a garden. It looked amazing.

Pink roses, fully bloomed and beautifully rounded, literally spilled out of wooden seed trays. Blood red oriental poppies filled Toni's empty wine bottles. Chinese lanterns hung from the branches of the conifers, and Jo had placed baskets of blue Veronica at the entrance to the garden, to show people the way.

Catherine and her team of helpers busied themselves arranging a table with various papier-mâché ornaments, birthday cards, Christmas cards, and patchwork birds, all amazing, all made by the kids in their art classes.

345

And the WI cake stall was out of this world. Small triangles of sandwiches Toni had made that morning competed for space alongside pink sponge cake, chocolate cornflake cakes, gooey chocolate buns, Mum's cakes, and snow-white meringues filled with thick, fresh cream. Diane and Yvette had brought urns for tea and coffee, and small bottles of orange juice for the kids, and with these they created a second stall. There were also decorated jars of home-made jam and chutney, topped off with red and blue gingham. Toni had placed a couple of long benches there, against the fencing, so people could sit down.

The fourth table was full of Jo's home-grown bulbs. There were pots of hyacinths, tulips, daffodils and narcissi. She hadn't messed about making them look pretty, but they looked good and hardy, and she sold out within the first hour.

I carried two boxes of my books, all signed in purple pen, from the car, then drove it onto Jaggers Lane so there was space outside Toni's for people to park. The books I set onto one half of another table, in between two rose-filled seed trays. And very attractive it looked, too. Vicky made me a sign from card and felt pen. *My auntie's books - £8.99 – all signed and all for a good cause.* I just had to smile.

The other half of my table displayed the raffle prizes. I took a hundred and fifty pounds in raffle tickets alone. My six bottles of wine had been increased by the four that Toni donated; there was a set of toiletries from Mr Williams at the pharmacy, a box of *Thorntons* from the Spar shop, and a hardback copy of my latest novel, not yet published, courtesy of Sandy.

Well, Millerstone sure knew how to enjoy itself. The sun was out, the birds were singing, Toni's house was easy to get to, and easy to find. She'd lined up notices on the High Street, pointing the way. Everyone was there. Visitors and locals alike popped in, even if it was just for a cuppa.

The garden was gloriously full of people. Sunhats brimmed with colour, warm smiles traded places with each other, and children ran to and fro, their mums with purses at the ready. The scent of suntan lotion permeated the air, while the gentle waft of coffee ran past me as I stood behind my book stall.

Toni was slightly upset with the elderly ladies hobbling round, their walking sticks prodding dents into her wet lawn, and with the pushchairs that were churning up the grass. Jo had put down a stretch of plastic matting leading from the entrance, but she could only do so much after the horrendous night we'd had, and she promised to repair the rest. My wonderful sister.

Toni and Abigail rushed round continuously, in and out of the kitchen, making sandwiches, providing plastic spoons, kitchen roll, paper plates. I called out to Toni as she passed.

'Toni, you are locking the door, aren't you?'

She smiled. 'Why? It's okay - they've caught the burglar now.'

'Well, yes, I suppose so. But don't become blasé. You never know.'

She waved the kitchen roll at me. 'I'll lock it.'

Just at that moment, Mum poked her head around the weeping willow.

'Hi, April.'

'Hi, Mum.'

Her cheeks rosy with sunshine, her summer dress prettily floral, she came up to me, followed by Jim Allsop, carrying two huge boxes of chocolates. *Hotel Chocolat*, no less.

I grinned. 'You shouldn't have.'

'Oh no,' Mum said, shaking her head. 'They're not for you. We've brought them for the raffle.'

'Thanks, Mum.'

Jim's deep brown eyes crinkled. 'Now, where do you want them?'

At that very moment, however, Toby Wilkinson caught my eye. He'd sneaked up while I wasn't paying attention, and was standing in front of my stall, holding tightly onto his girlfriend's hand.

'Miss Stanivlaski, I just wanted to introduce you to Rachel.'

She was pretty. Tall with long, dark, mirror-shiny hair, and chocolate-brown eyes.

I held out my hand. 'Call me April, please. I'm very pleased to meet you.'

Smiling, she shook it. 'You too. Toby's told me all about you.'

'Has he?' I looked pointedly at Toby. 'I hear you're engaged.'

'Yes,' he replied. 'And we'd like you to come to the wedding. That's if you've got the time.'

'Well, thank you,' I stammered. 'That's very kind of you. I don't quite know what to say, to be honest.'

'It's just, you kind of, like, talked me into it,' he said.

'Did I?'

He blushed. 'You, like, made me see sense.'

'So I have you to thank for this.' Rachel put out her hand, showing me her ring, a huge diamond on a broad white gold band. It was stunning.

'It's beautiful.'

'We have a baby together,' she said. 'So I suppose it's the right thing to do, really.'

I shook my head at her. 'The baby shouldn't be the reason you're marrying. I hope you're both still very much in love?'

She blushed prettily. 'We are.'

'That's wonderful. And yes, I'd love to come to your wedding. Thank you.'

She hugged me quickly, succinctly, and I returned it, slightly embarrassed, but happy. I felt I'd made a difference.

It was as they moved away, towards the WI table, that I spotted Emilisa Meadows-Whitworth teetering across the lawn, her husband following on behind. Dressed in a bright red dress and jacket, she was making her way towards Diane Downing and the cakes.

I watched as she chatted to Diane, bought two slices of chocolate cake, and moved along to the tea table. She and her husband then sat down beside the fence, drinking tea together and murmuring quietly between mouthfuls of cake.

I'd only seen Neil Meadows-Whitworth once before. He'd never struck me as a kindly person, although who was I to say? I hardly knew him. But first impressions, you know? Tall and angular, he looked just like the lecturer he was. Stern-looking, with a long nose, ready to seek you out if you didn't behave. I thought about what Bob Prendergast had said, about his poor son, already a junkie, being disowned by him. I wondered how Emilisa felt about it. She was still his mother, after all. How could you abandon your own child like that?

But my thoughts were interrupted when Rebecca, carrying a mug of hot tea, nudged my elbow.

'Do you want some cake, Auntie April?' she asked, her blue eyes staring up at me. 'The chocolate cake is really yummy.'

I accepted the tea gratefully. 'Thanks, Rebecca. But I'm fine with just tea, thanks.'

'Okay.'

'Are you having a nice time?' I asked. 'Making lots of money?'

'Yep. We've been helping sell the stuff the kids have made in school. Have you seen them – the patchwork flying birds? They're really cool.'

'They're good, aren't they? One would look really good flying around your bedroom.'

She shook her head seriously. 'They don't really fly, Auntie April.'

'No. They don't. Have you managed to get one yourself?'

She shrugged. 'I didn't bring any money, so ...'

I fished a ten pound note from my jeans pocket. 'Here, go and buy three, one for each of you. If you bring them back here, I'll put them under the stall so they're safe.'

She accepted it gleefully. 'Thank you,' and she ran off.

My books trickled away slowly. People were more interested in food and drink. Well, it was a lovely afternoon, not quite the kind of day for standing around reading the blurb on a romantic paperback.

351

But they did sell eventually, and by four o'clock I had an empty stall and three hundred and ninety pounds in the coffers. I'd even sold the seed trays, complete with roses. And Sandy, my agent, had agreed that all the money from my books, and not merely the profit, should be donated to the swimming pool fund.

Toni announced the start of the raffle at three thirty. Mum won a box of chocolates and Jim a bottle of white.

*

The afternoon had been a tremendous success. We'd made just over twelve hundred pounds. Jo even managed to sell her baskets of Veronica at twenty pounds a shot.

I sighed with pleasure as Mum and Jim left to go back to her house. But I was anxious to get back to my own, and to Colin, newly arrived from Brussels, the job a great success, the apartment just off the Avenue Louise small but pricey, the ex-wife still around.

24

St Raphael, France

ONLY a week later, we were driving towards St Raphael on the Cote d'Azur. The flight to Nice had been uneventful, apart from the little incident of Mum's tea flask. But the chap at Manchester Airport, a portly type with a hairy nose, had been very understanding, allowing her to pour the tea away, keep the flask, and proceed into the Departure Lounge. Phew.

It all passed over Jo's head, however, so excited was she to be on holiday without having to think about entertaining the kids, making sure they'd not forgotten anything, constantly checking they'd still got their bags, and generally be in charge of five people and not just the one.

The car I'd hired was a red Volvo Cabriolet. I'd ordered it especially; I wanted Mum to feel spoilt, special. Loved. I'd not realised when I arranged it that she'd be meeting up with Jim Allsop. Now *he* was the person to make her feel special and loved. And was he doing that? Oh, yes. I'd been taking notice, ever since the garden party. She was blooming, blossoming. I'd not seen her laugh so much in years. I'd invited them round for tea one Saturday evening. It was just me, Colin, Mum and Jim. I'd cooked grilled aubergine with spicy chickpeas and walnut sauce, followed by a delicious chocolate marquise with layers of After Eights. Well, it was a special occasion. And Mum was glowing. At one point, Jim reached out to hold her hand across the table. So romantic. Six months ago, I'd never have thought it possible for my mum to look so happy. I just prayed he'd never let her down.

*

Our destination this evening was Le Palmier Rouge, a small block of apartments on Rue du Littoral. Although where you'd find a red palm tree in France, I have no idea. But that was the place; a one bedroomed apartment twenty metres from St Raphael beach. Awesome.

It was an ochre-coloured concrete building that I guess had been built around the 1960's. Not especially pretty. But the view was to die for. Blue sea. Blue sky. Well, it *was* the Côte d'Azur. Jo and I left Mum in the apartment while we lugged the suitcases upstairs, puffing and panting as we went. We were on the third floor, and there was no lift.

Remnants of Colin littered the place, his penchant for *Blur* evident in the form of an out-of-place poster in the bedroom, two *Blur* coffee mugs and a glossy *Blur* annual on the teak coffee table. He'd also pinned posters of *Madonna* to the bathroom ceiling, and there was an orange Space Hopper lounging in one corner. I did wonder how long he'd had the apartment; it was like a teenage boy's retreat. So okay, maybe that's what it was, the place he retired to when he wanted to chill, to pretend life wasn't taking over, that he wasn't getting old. I know the feeling.

I opened the lounge window so I could stare at the sea, the view now dimming as the lights of the evening began to fill the shoreline. Breathing in soft, warm air, I smiled. The sudden scent of *Gitanes* and roasting garlic drifted up from the apartment below, and I knew I was in France.

'Where's the kettle, then?' called Mum, pulling a huge box of teabags from her case. 'I can't seem to find it.'

'They don't really use them, Mum,' I said. 'We just need to boil water in the pan.'

'You're joking,' she exclaimed. 'What a waste of energy.'

'They don't really drink tea. Not much, anyway. And they use a cafetière for coffee – there'll be one around here somewhere.' I began searching the kitchen cupboards. 'It'll be one of those clunky things that looks like it's out of a nineteen fifties sci-fi movie,' I explained.

'Well, that's no good then, is it? I'd better put the pan on.'

'How about some food instead?' I asked, returning to close the window. 'I'm starving. And there's a great place Colin's recommended, just down the road.'

'Brilliant idea,' said Jo. 'I'll just put on something sexy.'

*

The restaurant was called Le Nogent. Jo and I rechristened it The Nosh-ent. We ate there nearly every night. Well, it was convenient, the food was delicious, and it meant we could stagger home afterwards.

That first night we ate greedily, hungrily, after all that travelling. Jo spent ages on the phone afterwards, talking to Joe and the kids, telling them all about the journey. They sounded as excited as she was, and we promised to bring them over some time.

The following day we awoke to glorious sunshine and no breakfast. So we ate out, again, before heading to the local shops for supplies. I rang Colin to say all was well with the apartment, that we loved it and were having a great time.

*

Then it was off to the beach. Oh, glorious beach. The sun on our backs, the warm air swimming across our bodies. The sea was warm, and Mum looked amazing in her new red swimsuit and black film-star sunhat with its huge brim. If anyone could pull off such a combination, my mum could. Jo, too, had outdone herself, in a purple bikini that suited her down to the ground, and she still had the figure for it, despite having had three kids.

That week we spent nearly every morning on the beach, lazing, reading, chatting, and drinking coffee from the local bar. The chap there was called Adrien. Very flirtatious he was, especially with Mum, who constantly blushed at all the attention.

'Mum,' said Jo, sipping her cappuccino delicately. 'What is it with you just lately? You can't seem to leave the men alone.'

'I know. I think it's those tablets the doctor gave me,' she replied. She touched my arm gently with the tip of her hand. 'Thank you, April. I feel so much better, and I think it shows, you know.'

I squeezed her hand. 'I only did what you'd have done for me. But I'm glad it's done the trick. You do look wonderful, Mum.'

Recalling the state she'd been in, what – only four months ago? – I had to swallow hard. It would have been so easy to have listened to her, to do as she wished, to have just let her go on as she was. How her life had changed since then.

*

The South of France is totally different to that of the Jura region. Thank goodness. Sun, sand, warm air that seemed to sparkle in the sunlight. And the women there fascinate me. You see, they're not always beautiful, but they act as if they are. Writing for a living makes me an avid people-watcher, and I'm convinced French women have gained their reputation of being the world's sexiest women merely through their innate confidence and sense of humour. It just shines through. No wonder men adore them. And the men, too. Most of them aren't that good-looking, either. Okay, so you get the occasional Louis Jordan lookalike, or a Yoann Gourcuff. On the whole, however, they're just normal guys. But they ooze charm, and I'm convinced that's what does it. Also, they take such care over how they dress. Very nice.

But I digress. Yet again.

Jo, Mum and I usually began the evening with a little shopping, the local market our favourite port of call - leather goods, oil paintings, clothing, jewellery. All with the fine aroma of French perfume, guitarists singing in the moonlight, couples staring into one another's eyes, warm sea air touching my fingertips and blowing my hair softly. Bliss.

On the Wednesday evening we drove out to Frejus, St Raphael's neighbour. An old Roman town, Frejus contains the ruins of the old Roman amphitheatre, still an amazing sight and still used for music concerts. But the area surrounding it was busy with traffic, so we didn't venture too near. Instead, we wandered along the side streets, nipping into the quaint little squares that seemed to appear out of nowhere, admiring the architecture, making new discoveries. Our cameras were never still, it was so beautiful.

Our third night, the Monday night, Jo had become slightly the worse for wear over tea, having had a *Pastis* aperitif, two thirds of a bottle of white, and a coffee, fifty per cent of which was *Cognac*.

'Come on, you two,' she insisted, staggering out of her seat. 'Let's walk along the beach. It looks beautiful.'

Picking up her handbag, Mum smiled. 'What a lovely idea. I've not had a moonlit walk on the beach in years, not since Bridlington with your dad.'

I looked across the road. The moon was full, the sea was calm, and the air as still as a mountain. I agreed it was a marvellous idea.

'Okay, Jo. Let's do it.'

But as we said goodbye to Gabriele, Le Nogent's lovely Italian waiter, I noticed Jo's shoes.

'Jo, you can't possibly walk on the beach. You've got heels on. You'll ruin them.'

Shrugging nonchalantly, she giggled. 'I've walked in heels on the beach lots of times. It'll be fine. Come on!'

I took time to remove my rather expensive gladiator sandals and, oh, was it worth it. The sand was so cool and delicious between my toes, I could have walked for miles. Instead, I paddled at the edge of the waves, trying my best to splash Jo as she dawdled behind.

'Come on, take your shoes off. Come and have a paddle,' I called.

In the end, she removed them, holding them by the heels as she, Mum and I all splashed one another in the moonlight, happy and relaxed and carefree.

But for some reason, the vision of Jo in her high heels haunted me all that night and all the next day.

*

It was only as we walked along that same beach the following night, the moon shining, the waves sighing, Mum in her bright green kaftan and flowery hat, that it came to me.

'That's it.'

'What's it?' asked Jo.

'Why did she squeeze down the side of the house, across that awful muddy soil, when there was a perfectly good path into the garden? And – and when Toni had put signs out, and when you'd put pots of blue veronica there, to show people the way?'

'What?' Jo paused in her tracks.

I turned to face her. 'You put flowerpots there. There are flagstones - nice, cute little flagstones to protect the lawn. You even put plastic out so as not to mess it up. She was wearing three inch heels. She literally tottered, teetered, into the garden. And yet she still came through the other way. The wrong way. The way the burglar came.'

Poor Jo was by now completely dumbstruck. 'Sorry, April ...'

Mum was walking on ahead, totally oblivious, completely absorbed.

'Emilisa,' I explained. 'It was her. I'm sure it was her.'

'What was? And who's Emilisa, anyway?'

'Emilisa Meadows-Whitworth. She lives in Millerstone, that great big house on the main road.

She's married to Professor Meadows-Whitworth at the uni. She ...' Then another thought struck me. 'She's in the Village Players.'

Jo was catching on. 'She knows you idiotically put your jewellery into handbags.'

'Yes. Yes, she does.'

'I hope you don't do it now.'

'I bet she went that way just to check on the light, to see what had happened to it, to see if her handiwork had been repaired, perfectionist that she is.'

Yet I felt a strange crawling down my neck. The feeling was one of elation, but at the same time I felt disturbed. Was I doing it again? Was I accusing someone who was completely innocent? Again? And anyway, hadn't they already arrested Steve Yates and his cronies?

I sighed heavily. 'Oh, I don't know, Jo. Just ignore me. Come on, let's catch up with Mum.'

'Okay. Before she finds someone else to chat up.' She laughed.

I texted Sean first thing the next morning.

I know this sounds weird, but re burglary could you please check out Emilisa Meadows-Whitworth? Background, financial dealings, family problems (mother, son). Anything, really. Just a hunch. Thanks.

His reply was short, abrupt. He still hadn't forgiven me. Not really.

Holiday not going well? No confessions yet, so will look into.

*

On the Friday, the last full day of our holiday, we drove along the coast to Ventimiglia, a town on the Italian border. We'd heard such good things about the market, so had decided to go there to buy gifts for everyone. But the traffic crossing the border was horrendous. It took us an hour to inch our way across. Once we'd shown our passports, however, the traffic eased off and within minutes we'd parked up. Paying the fee, we grabbed our bags and raced to the Ladies.

But this queue was enormous too, and we had to stand in line while this very small, very round, Italian chap with dyed, black hair handed out loo roll. One piece at a time. It was tracing paper too, the old-fashioned kind. So funny; we couldn't believe our eyes. Of course, by the time we'd reached the Ladies, Jo and I were in stitches.

'Calm down, you two,' coaxed Mum. 'It's not that funny. Here, I've got some tissues.'

But that was it. We'd reverted to our childhood selves, and the rest of the day was filled with laughter, silly taunts, and wonderful memories.

In the market, Jo and I bought the most gorgeous cashmere jumpers. So cheap, and the most gorgeous colours. Mine was soft caramel, Jo's mustard. Very

363

French, we thought. Mum bought a sweater for Jim in a kind of mottled green, and for herself a delicate silk shirt in crimson - so delicate I worried it wouldn't last through one wash. But it looked beautiful when she tried it on.

But the food stalls. Mouth-wateringly wonderful, the colours of the rainbow. Red tomatoes, yellow peppers, purple aubergines, green cucumbers, lettuces, cabbages, oranges, apricots and tangerines. Everything. And then there were the cheeses, fresh pastas, succulent breads infused with rosemary, cheese, garlic, or sundried tomato. You name it, they had it. And the cakes. Layer cakes, butter cakes, creamy meringues, gooey chocolate buns, and fresh fruit tarts – my favourite. Buns with swirls of cream, cherries, chocolate buttons, jelly buttons, all shapes and sizes.

'You know, if I lived here …' began Jo.

'Yes?' I said, thinking she'd say something about growing her own fruit and veg.

'I'd weigh at least two hundred pounds.'

We took lots of photos. The stallholders didn't mind; some of them even posed.

We explored further after lunch. There was a small boutique, a claustrophobic room smelling of lavender, crammed with children's clothing. Jo bought some very on-trend pink dungarees and a handful of tee-shirts for Rebecca and Daisy, and

Mum purchased a couple of very cute dresses for Teru. A pharmacy filled with high-end toiletries provided perfume for Vicky, and fragrance for Joe and Colin.

I couldn't wait to see Colin again. The holiday was wonderful, amazing, but I was missing him dreadfully.

25

Millerstone, Derbyshire

THREE more weeks of rehearsals, a weekend of putting out chairs and cushions, bringing in milk, tea, coffee, sugar and shortbread, setting the stage, checking the lighting and pressing the costumes, all led, eventually, to the final production of The Mystery of Sir Hugh Tompkinson.

It was the third Saturday of October, the day of the Grand Auction.

The week had gone extremely well. The plot was brilliant, the set amazing, and Laura had outdone herself with the costumes. Toni was there every night, of course, fussing round with hair and makeup. Miss Forsyth was supposed to be in her thirties, so hadn't quite caught onto the Flapper scene. So my long chiffon dress was just right, and I had to wear white gloves and shoes. My hair was pinned up, with a sparkly comb to one side, and I had mountains of bling on my neck and arms. Laura wanted me to look 'moneyed', as she put it.

Toni usually goes home once we're all ready, but she was still there at the end of the first night, the Wednesday. I knew her mum was babysitting, so assumed she was meeting up with Sean after the show. We were alone in the dressing room, Billie and the others still chatting to the punters in the canteen, and I was undressing, looking forward to home and my nice warm bed.

It was just after I'd removed my sparkly bracelet from the Oxfam shop that Toni confessed. I don't know why she decided to confess there and then. Or why she confessed at all. But she did.

She'd begun to remove the grips from my hair, allowing it to fall into wispy curls.

'April', she began.

I looked up at her reflection in the mirror. Despite all the excitement of the first night, she looked sad, tearful. I kind of sensed what was coming.

'Yes?'

'You know that night, the night after we were burgled?'

'Yes?'

Her hands falling to her sides, she suddenly burst into tears. I turned.

'I'm sorry,' she sobbed. 'I didn't do it. I didn't lie to them or anything.'

'Who? Who didn't you lie to?'

'The insurance company.'

I didn't get her to elaborate; I knew that would come in its own time. Instead, I stroked her head as if she were a child.

'Well, that's good then, isn't it? So why are you crying?'

'Because I *did* think about it. I thought about claiming for that necklace. It's worth a bit, you see, and I'd never get what it's worth if I sold it. And I just thought ...'

'You thought if you told them it was stolen along with everything else, you'd get its full worth.'

She nodded, shamefaced.

'Oh, Toni.' I sat her down, pulling a tissue from the box nearby. 'Here, sort yourself out. Sean will wonder what on earth's going on.'

Blowing her nose loudly, she checked herself in the mirror. 'God, what a state. But I'm sorry, April, I just had to tell you.'

'Don't apologise, Toni. It can't be easy, bringing up two kids on your own. I don't know how you do it sometimes.'

'I'm not usually that dishonest,' she sobbed. 'I just thought I'd take advantage, I suppose, get something positive from the sod who burgled me. And – and I've finished with Sean. I couldn't face telling him. Please don't tell him.'

I was shocked. I thought they made such a lovely couple. 'Oh, Toni. I'm so sorry.'

'No. Don't be. It's my own fault. I've been incredibly stupid.'

'Is that why you're still here, to tell me this?'

'I needed to. I can't lie any more, April, not to you.'

I stared at her, her mascara in clumps, her eyes and nose red to match her hair.

I hugged her. 'Come here, you silly. You've done nothing wrong. You only thought about it. And no, I promise not to tell Sean. But I am really sorry about the two of you.'

'It's okay. It wasn't really going anywhere, anyway. I mean, we never got as far as the bedroom or anything.'

'Well, he's a nice guy, probably likes to take things slowly. But never mind – if it wasn't meant to be ...'

'I know. But I'm really sorry about the necklace.'

I forgave her. Immediately. No questions asked.

*

The audiences that week were amazing, laughing in all the right places, applauding loudly when we deserved it. Also, despite my reservations, the after-show events had worked well. The cast, still in costume, mingled with the audience while the WI served tea, coffee and cake. The punters flooded into the canteen area, chatting away, many coming up to me, enthusing over the performances, trying their hand at guessing who the culprit was. A few did so, and I had to ask them not to divulge it just yet; not until everyone had seen the play.

But I can now reveal the name of the culprit. It was Miss Forsythe, the very reason Alfie had had a go at me for not reading the script. She was supposed to have been in Scotland at the time of Sir Hugh's disappearance. Brigadier Worthing, madly in love with her and wrapped around her little finger, had connections with the hotel in Aberdeen, so was able to get the manager to verify her story to the police. In point of fact, however, Miss Forsythe was in London at the time of the disappearance, meeting up with Sir Hugh and his lawyer. Sir Hugh, meanwhile, was thought by his wife to have been holidaying in Guernsey. She was to join him there after she'd settled her elder sister, recovering from the flu epidemic, into a residential hotel in Cornwall. But when she arrived, he wasn't there, the hotel had no record of him ever arriving, and he was never heard from again. The big question was, however – was he dead or alive? The answer, as we know, was never revealed. But the supposition gained from the script was that Miss Forsythe had discovered his dalliance with a certain actress he'd met in London, and had threatened to tell his wife. Having gained her written letter of confidentiality, he paid her handsomely from the bank account he'd set up in secret, and had run off with the actress. Never to be seen again.

So Miss Forsythe, my character, wasn't actually responsible for his disappearance. She was more an accomplice, but the amount of money received and the letter still held by Sir Hugh's solicitor meant she could never reveal her secret.

I quite liked her. Actually.

*

So the Grand Auction began on the Saturday. Jim Allsop, a natural orator, announced its opening and fired off the bidding.

'Ladies and gentlemen, I beg you all to dig deep into your pockets tonight. This auction is in aid of the Millerstone Swimming Pool. This excellent facility is one of the very few heated open-air swimming pools in the country, and we must never allow it to close.'

There was a loud cheer from the back of the hall.

'So, if you will please consult your listing catalogue, you will see our first lot is a November weekend at the Ashbourne Hotel. Five hundred years old, this hotel has an excellent reputation and has been kind enough to donate a one night stay for two, complete with breakfast and dinner. So we begin with a low figure of, what – fifty pounds? Who will be my first bidder, please?'

The hall was jam-packed, people standing along both sides and along the back. *Health and Safety* would have had a field day. Bob Prendergast and his wife placed a bid on a basket of fruit, but didn't win; it went for thirty pounds. I was sitting near the front of the hall with Colin, so waved to them, mouthing *bad luck,* and Bob waved back. Catherine, the teacher from school, placed a bid on a small pine chest of drawers. She won it for ninety pounds, which was probably the going rate, but it was more money for the cause. Mum won a lady chauffeur for a night, the idea being that she and Jim could go out for a meal and he wouldn't have to worry about having a glass of wine or two. Then Josie placed bid after bid on a wooden seat for the garden, and was gutted when she didn't win.

Just for the record, the weekend stay at the Ashbourne went for a cool two hundred and fifty pounds. Marvellous.

Mum and Josie caught up with us as Colin went off to help Jim, busy collecting money from successful bidders.

Josie nudged my arm. 'He's very good, Jim, isn't he? You've got a good'un there, Mum.'

Mum beamed with pleasure. 'Thank you, Jo. But he's used to it, isn't he, being on stage and all that? And he's a wonderful teacher. I'm learning how to drive, you know.'

I grinned. 'We all think he's lovely, Mum.'

'Yes, and you look really happy,' offered Josie.

'I am,' she replied, her face wreathed in smiles.

The huge body of people was making the hall hot and sticky, so I popped outside for some air. It was cool and damp. I breathed in deeply. I began to think about Sean and his investigations into Emilisa. Obviously, nothing had come of it, or I'd have heard. Cringing guiltily, I returned to the hall. Maybe my writer's imagination really was running wild. Maybe I needed to be much more careful before going round accusing people. But then, I'd been so sure, so absolutely sure. There was something about her, something not quite right, even though I couldn't put my finger onto it.

The bidding continued after the interval, by which time it was getting on for ten o'clock. Colin placed bids on a *Rab* fleece jacket, forest green, thick and warm, and he got it for five pounds less than the retail price. Then I won three hours of ironing, which cost me thirty pounds, and would give me time off to do something much more interesting.

But the pièce de résistance was not the play, nor was it the Grand Auction.

It was the arrival of DI Forbes and her team of uniformed police.

The Memorial Hall was nearly empty, the auction finished, payments made, and the punters on their way home. I was en route to the dressing room when DI Forbes, smiling grimly, asked where she could find Emilisa Meadows-Whitworth. I showed her the way to the kitchen, where I knew she and Yvette were tidying up.

I saw Emilisa's expression only briefly, but her shock as DI Forbes arrived was palpable. Her face was pale, her eyes searching rapidly for a means of escape, while her long fingers with their black talons rubbed at the jug she was drying, as if it would magically transport her to some far distant place.

The other cast members were getting changed, so there was only Colin, Yvette, myself, and Don Edmunds, the caretaker, to witness the arrest. And we were shocked. Utterly shocked.

I was particularly disturbed because, even though I'd had a feeling about her, I couldn't for the life of me see how she'd carried out all those burglaries. It was just Toni's garden, and the fact she'd walked through it the wrong way, in three inch heels, that had made me think of her at all.

Colin and I walked home to my new bathroom, the bath big enough for two, and soaked in strawberry bubbles up to our necks. But I was in shock. Dire, unadulterated shock. Like discovering the tiny crack in your bedroom ceiling is actually subsidence so bad the house needs rebuilding.

The big question was, after all this time, had we finally found our thief?

26

BONFIRE Night. It was only five o'clock, yet the sun had already set over Millerstone. It was a wonderfully radiant sunset, the night sky as clear as glass, the air cold and dry. Pulling on my blue duffle coat and scarf, I picked up my keys from the hall cabinet and rushed out to the car. Sean and I had been invited to attend a small gathering at Sheffield Police Station.

I took the main road out of the village, beneath Toad's Mouth Rock, across the moors and past the sign announcing the city of Sheffield. Driving on, I was able to look down upon the city itself. The view that night was spectacular. Sharp bursts of light from bonfire parties filled the sky, splashes of pink, blue and yellow, and a distant putt-putt-putt sound echoed across the moorland, fading as the fireworks fell to ground.

I parked up easily outside the police station, a huge red brick building. A girl in reception, a bright young thing, asked for ID before showing me the way to DI Forbes' office, a banal room with a large desk, and a few chairs.

She welcomed me in with a smile and a handshake. Sean was already there, alongside a couple of guys in jackets and jeans, all drinking coffee from brown plastic cups.

I smiled. 'Sorry I'm late. Busy day.'

'Don't worry, April, we've not been here long. Coffee?'

She poured me a cup from the machine in the corner, and I sat down, nodding to Sean. Our only contact since my email from St Raphael had been my phone call to him the morning after Emilisa's arrest, asking for information. All he'd known when I emailed him was that Emilisa had backed out of producing the play because she spent time visiting her mother in London.

He'd been a busy man since then, however. Emilisa's father was a prominent man in Italy, so it was easy to trace his history. Sean discovered that his wife, Emilisa's mother, had actually died of pneumonia ten years earlier, in Milan. Sean had also learned that Emilisa's son, Sebastiano, had been attending the Priory in London, an expensive rehabilitation hospital, intermittently for the past two years. This he'd learned through another reporter, whose daughter was the friend of one of Sebastiano's schoolfriends and had seen his posts on Facebook.

Sean had therefore deduced that Emilisa was in fact visiting her son in London, and may have been stealing in order to pay his hospital fees. Although he was under the impression she and her husband were fairly well off, so at the time it didn't make sense and he'd no idea why she'd been arrested. It was at this point in our telephone conversation that I'd revealed my chat with Bob Prendergast, that Professor Meadows-Whitworth had completely disowned his son, completely withdrawing any funding for hospital fees in the process. This revelation had, of course, made Sean's day. Although he was still very cool with me over my accusation of Toni, and even though I said how sorry I was over their split, and tried to end the call on a conciliatory note, it hadn't really happened.

'Hi, Sean,' I murmured now. 'Long time, no see.'

He smiled. 'How's things?'

'Fine.'

'Good. That's good.'

I smiled quietly, anxious to be getting on with business.

DI Forbes, dressed in a dark grey suit, placed herself behind the desk. Her pale blue eyes appraising us, she waited for the room to fall silent.

'Let's get on then, shall we? First of all, may I introduce you all?' She nodded to the guy sitting to the right of the door. A six-footer in a brown leather jacket, with a balding head and glasses.

'This is Detective Chief Inspector George Watkins.'

He nodded, smiling.

'And Detective Inspector Jack Taylor.'

A much younger man with dark unruly hair, he waved at us, his denim jacket faded and worn.

'And this of course is April Stanislavski,' she continued.

I smiled, feeling slightly embarrassed at the formal introduction.

'And Sean McGavin, Senior Crime Reporter for the Sheffield Star,' she said.

Sean smiled, too.

DCI Watkins spoke suddenly, his Sheffield accent deep and strong. 'May I just say well done, both of you, on such a great piece of detective work? We're ruddy pleased to have wrapped this one up, I can tell you. I mean, I know it has to go through the courts and all, but we've got the confession, and that's half the journey.'

DI Forbes waved her hand, as if to say *just let me explain*.

379

'April and Sean have found our culprit for us, but they have no idea of the true circumstances behind the confession.'

I leaned forward eagerly.

'I'd just like to know where you found your evidence,' Sean said.

'Obviously, everything discussed within these four walls is strictly confidential. Not a word must leak out – Sean,' she replied, pointedly.

He nodded. 'Of course, DI Forbes.'

'You shall have your story once the trial is over.'

'And I promise to keep quiet, too,' I volunteered.

'Thank you, April.'

'So, come on then,' urged Sean. 'Evidence?'

'A murder investigation in London,' she said, her eyes suddenly cold and dark.

An icy, excited shiver ran through me. 'London?'

'This drugs ring you smashed, April - Warren Craig and his cronies. He lied. Neil Kennedy, the guy we arrested in Hull, wasn't the big chief. It was Martino Caban, a Spanish businessman living down in London.'

'Crikey,' said Sean.

'Neil Kennedy spilled the beans, eventually. But when the Met went to arrest Mister Caban, they found him dead in his apartment. They also found solid twenty-four carat evidence that led to the arrest of Emilisa Meadows-Whitworth.'

'My God,' I murmured, sitting upright again.

'What the hell's she been up to?' asked Sean.

DI Forbes sat down, pulled a sheaf of notes from the manila folder on her desk, and read out loud. 'We have charged Mrs Meadows-Whitworth with one count of murder, one of manslaughter, one of blackmail, and numerous offences of burglary and theft.'

'Murder?' I repeated.

She checked her notes. 'Martino Caban was found dead on Monday. He'd been dead for twenty four hours. Murdered, hit on the head with a rather large implement.'

But I was bewildered. 'So what does this …?'

She placed a finger to her lips. 'All will be revealed.' She turned to Sean. 'You know we've been tracing Emilisa Meadows-Whitworth's movements from the time you alerted us to her possible involvement in the Millerstone thefts?'

He nodded, his expression stern, focused. 'Yes?'

'We discovered that, yes, she did travel to London to visit her son. And yes, he is a junkie, disowned by his father. Neil Meadows-Whitworth did in fact know his wife was visiting Sebastiano, but to save face he asked her to lie about it. He's a big chief at the university, didn't want people gossiping.'

'Poor kid,' I murmured. 'But what does this have to do with the death of this Spanish businessman?'

'What Neil Meadows-Whitworth didn't know was that his wife was paying for their son to have treatment at the Priory Hospital in North London. He thought she was visiting him at his flat. Thousands of pounds worth of treatment, she paid for. Her husband would never have paid for it, didn't want to know, so she had to find it from somewhere.'

'She is the thief then!' I exploded.

She smiled, a small, sad smile. 'Yes, Emilisa is the thief. But there is more. Unfortunately.'

My elation fell to the ground as I realised she was talking about the murder charge.

'Yes, Emilisa Meadows-Whitworth murdered Martino Caban. The reason? He was blackmailing her, and she couldn't fulfil his demands.'

'So why kill him? Why not just report it to the police?' asked Sean, incredulous.

DCI Watkins, who had until then been picking at his nails, replied.

'Because *she* was blackmailing someone. The thefts in Millerstone weren't enough to keep her precious son in rehab, unfortunately.'

I turned to him. 'Who? Who was she blackmailing?'

'A resident of Millerstone. Abercrombie Jones.'

'Abercrombie?' Sean and I said together.

DI Forbes nodded. 'Yes. I know. Had his own little burglary, didn't he?'

'We interviewed him. He and his wife are really nice people. So why was she blackmailing him?' asked Sean.

DCI Watkins took up the story. 'Mr Jones had a homosexual relationship in his teens and early twenties. Meadows-Whitworth knew all about it, his lover being a friend of hers. Apparently, he told her years ago, but she's only recently acted upon it because she was so desperate, because she thought the Jones's had plenty of money, and because she knew Mrs Jones was unaware of her husband's 'tendencies', shall we say?'

'*Don't* they have plenty of money?' asked Sean.

'They do. But they have three daughters at uni, all with expensive taste, and all expecting Daddy to pick up the tab when they marry into inevitably wealthy families. Also, his investments in Portugal haven't been doing that well, what with the euro and everything.'

I shook my head in despair. Poor Mrs Jones. Such a kind woman.

'So when Meadows-Whitworth became desperate, when she still needed money to pay for her son's fees, despite having robbed half of Millerstone, she decided to blackmail our Mr Jones,' he continued.

DI Forbes frowned. 'And it worked.'

I felt slightly sick. 'So, all this time, she's been the thief. She's been sneaking around our homes, our places of work, our …'

'But how did she steal the Jones's safe?' interrupted Sean, puzzled. 'She couldn't possibly have carried that from the house, all by herself?'

'A set-up,' replied DCI Watkins. 'Jones got Caban and his cronies to arrange the burglary so he could claim on the insurance. That's how Caban knew Jones was being blackmailed. All he had to do was find out the identity of the blackmailer, then blackmail her, too. Some people are *so* trustworthy.'

DI Taylor, very quiet until now, interrupted. 'But she made one tiny mistake. They all do in the end.'

'What?' asked Sean.

'She made the mistake of not checking Mr Caban's own safe, well-hidden in his very pricey apartment. So when the Met found it, they discovered documents leading us back to Mr Jones, his employer.'

Baffled, I shook my head. 'His employer?'

'Abercrombie Jones.'

'Sorry. I don't understand,' I murmured.

'Mr Jones owns property in both London and Portugal. Caban helped manage them.'

I was intrigued. 'So how did these documents lead you to Emilisa?'

'They were the remainder of the ones stolen from Jones's safe during the 'burglary'. Sales ledgers and so on. The Met rang us, Millerstone being our patch, and we questioned Jones, not realising the whole thing was fraudulent. We'd merely been asked to get a statement from him because he knew Caban. In the end, though, the whole lot came out. Marvellous, it was. He admitted to Emilisa blackmailing him, to staging the burglary, claiming from the insurance - the whole damned lot.'

'I knew there was something fishy. I wondered why they hadn't let the dogs run loose,' said Sean.

DI Forbes nodded. 'So of course we arrested Meadows-Whitworth. Meanwhile, the Met had found a hair in Caban's apartment. A long, dark hair. She was careless on that one occasion, thought she was too far away from home to be caught. We'd also interviewed Laura Pickering again, seamstress for the Village Players.'

'Wardrobe mistress,' I corrected.

'Wardrobe mistress - who now remembers seeing Meadows-Whitworth in the corridor just before the end of Act Two, the night of the dress rehearsal. The thing is, I suspect you're all so used to seeing her around that you wouldn't think anything of it. So when the police took a statement the first time, Mrs Pickering had either forgotten, or didn't think to mention it.'

'Or maybe, subconsciously, she thought someone like that wouldn't steal a bag,' I added.

'A very likely scenario, April.'

'So how come there was no DNA showing up around Millerstone?' I asked.

'I asked Meadows-Whitworth that one during the interview. She always fastened her hair back carefully, wore a headscarf, used loads of spray. Then at night, she'd wear a beanie. But when she visited Caban to give him the money - or so he thought - she didn't want to arouse his suspicions, so left her hair loose. She was very clever, you've got to admit.'

DI Taylor coughed in disgust. 'Too clever. Nearly got away with it.'

'So what about Abercrombie? What's happening to him?' I asked.

'He's being charged,' he replied. 'Perverting the course of justice, fraud against an insurance company, et cetera, et cetera. He's already moved out of the marital home.'

'It's all so sad,' I said.

But then I remembered my conversation with Mrs Jones at the house. She'd said Abercrombie had studied drama and politics at university, that he was a patron of the Village Players, took a keen interest in them. I wondered for a second if Emilisa's friend was Alfie, but then dismissed it.

Then I changed my mind.

'So who was Abercrombie's lover?'

'Now that *is* strictly confidential,' replied DI Forbes. 'We don't want any more blackmail, do we?'

I suddenly recalled Alfie's holiday to Turkey, of him having been there before with his 'well-off' boyfriend, fresh out of uni. And I remembered Mrs Jones talking about Abercrombie's uni days. It *was* Alfie. I knew it was Alfie.

'It's Alfie Brighouse, isn't it? He's already kind of told me, so there's no need to keep it a secret. Not anymore.'

DI Taylor shook his head in desperation. 'Okay. If you already know.'

I smiled. 'So what's going to happen to Emilisa's son, I wonder?'

'His father's taken him back, by all accounts,' he replied. 'He's pretty upset at what his wife's done, kind of blames himself.'

'Let's hope that's a lesson for us all,' murmured Sean.

'But you two,' insisted DI Forbes, 'have been absolutely amazing. Thank you so much. And as a reward, and this is not from the force, this is out of my own personal pocket, I have here two bottles of Perrier Jouet. Well done, both of you. Thank you so much for all you've done, it's very much appreciated. Now – off you go and celebrate.'

*

The scent of wood-smoke filled the air as we left the station. I imagined bonfires burning, autumn leaves and wood reducing slowly to ash, children munching on hot dogs, parkin and marshmallows. I sighed. That was the thing about not having kids; bonfire parties just aren't the same.

Suddenly melancholy, I turned to Sean. 'Okay. So what happens now?'

'Chinese?' he said.

I nodded. 'Okay.'

'Back to my place?'

'Your place?' I asked, astonished.

'It's an old Victorian four-bed. I'm still doing it up, so it's in a bit of a mess ...'

'The problem is I'll have to drive home afterwards, so I won't be able to drink this.' I held up my reward proudly.

'Yes, you can. I'll order you a taxi. My treat – okay?'

27

THE ivory-white elephant caught my eye as I looked up. Half awake, very sleepy, I had the faint impression someone had moved my rug. Then I wondered about the colour. It seemed more eggshell than blue. Maybe it was the light.

The light. It was coming from the wrong side of the room. The curtains were on the wrong side of the room.

'What?'

I sat up quickly, my heart racing, pulse pounding, and stared. At the blue quilt, at the flattened pillow, at the tall Victorian ceiling with its ornate cornice.

The scent of toasting bread suddenly filled the room, making me hungry.

And then I remembered.

The End

An April Stanislavski Murder Mystery

MURDER
ON HER DOORSTEP

ALEXANDRA JORDAN

CHAPTER 1

She finds it sticking out of a bedside drawer. Putting aside her duster, she pulls at it. It's a crumpled page of A4, torn from a refill pad. Not a proper letter at all …

CHAPTER 2

Chatsworth, Derbyshire

IT all began with a lovely afternoon walk through the Derbyshire countryside. A November chill clawed at the air as I wrapped my soft cashmere around my neck and stepped away from the car.

The sky in the distance was a deep watermelon pink. Long fingers of orange stretched down to earth like flames. It was a beautiful sunset. At only four o'clock.

Dash, my excitable King Charles spaniel, tugged impatiently at his lead. But I stood my ground, admiring that beautiful sky, the rolling hills, and Chatsworth House in the distance. Gold leaf on the window frames and roof finials reflected the afternoon sun, shining pure and bright like new-bought wedding rings.

Up high and to the left of the House stands the Hunting Tower; to the right the Cascade. Completed in 1701, it's an amazing feature, a manmade waterfall specially designed to entertain the masses, and I love it.

Heading towards the Cascade, we turned right to walk along the bank of the river, the Derwent. A scent of rotting leaves filled the air as I pushed my walking boots through long, clinging grass and smiled at the breeze skimming my face.

Just over half an hour later I stopped, hot and breathless and panting even more than Dash, with his lolling tongue and his happy shining eyes. We were quite alone beside the river and it was now completely dark, the only source of light the waxing moon. Pulling out my torch I tugged on Dash's lead and headed back to the car, back to Edensor, the delightful village owned by the Chatsworth Estate, with its cobalt-blue doors and windows. My Mini convertible was parked on the kerb opposite, just outside the estate's offices.

To avoid walking along the main road, I climbed the grassy bank to Edensor and paused beside a hefty oak tree to catch my breath. The 217 bus drove by, and a couple of small cars, otherwise all was silent. Hungry now and ready for home, I pulled on Dash's lead. But he resisted. He was sniffing greedily at the ground.

'Come on, Dash,' I said, pulling him away.

But he barked at me in a way I'd never seen before. A single, low bark. Sharp. Fearful. Then he backed slowly away.

My heart was pounding.

There was something there.

TO ENJOY THIS BOOK:

https://www.amazon.co.uk/dp/B08CPLDDY3/

Acknowledgements

A great big *Thank you* to all the people who have encouraged and supported me

To the lovely people who trusted me enough to buy my very first novel

To my wonderful family and all my friends, without whom ...

I do hope you've enjoyed *One Tiny Mistake*.

If you have - the best way to thank an author for writing a book you've enjoyed is to leave an honest review.

Click here: https://www.amazon.co.uk/One-Tiny-Mistake-Stanislavski-Mystery/product-reviews/B088GJHHM6/ to post your review of *One Tiny Mistake*.

Thank you so much for taking the time to let other readers know what you thought of my book.

Alexandra Jordan is the author of the Benjamin Bradstock Tales: *Snowflakes and Apple Blossom, Seasalt and Midnight Brandy,* and *Stardust and Vanilla Spice.* She has also written *One Tiny Mistake* and *Murder on Her Doorstep, April Stanislavski Murder Mysteries.*

Snowflakes and Apple Blossom was shortlisted for the Writers' Village International Novel Award 2014. *Seasalt and Midnight Brandy* has been serialised on BBC Radio.

Alex practises yoga, walks, reads, eats chocolate, and treads the boards of the amateur stage. She lives in the Peak District with her husband and twin boys. Find her on Facebook, Twitter@Alexjord18, and

Instagram. Please visit
https://alexjordan1.wixsite.com/author to leave an
email address for updates on Alexandra's new
publications. Thank you.

Printed in Poland
by Amazon Fulfillment
Poland Sp. z o.o., Wrocław

64389604R00240